OCCUPYING
Love

OCCUPYING *Love*

MARILYN CHAPMAN

AMELIA PRESS

OCCUPYING LOVE

First published in Great Britain in 2016
Second edition 2021

ISBN: 978-0-9929749-2-3

Amelia Press, Great Britain

Typeset by Chapter One Book Production

Printed and bound in Great Britain

TO MY DAUGHTERS

Amy and Chloe

IN MEMORY OF

David Richard Brown

The Guernsey boy who never came home

CONTENTS

THE PUBLIC ARE NOTIFIED THAT NO RESISTANCE
WHATEVER IS TO BE OFFERED TO THOSE IN MILITARY
OCCUPATION OF THE ISLAND.
THE PUBLIC ARE ASKED TO BE CALM, TO CARRY ON
WITH THEIR LIVES AND WORK IN THE USUAL WAY AND TO
OBEY THE ORDERS OF THE GERMAN KOMMANDANT.

CONTROLLING COMMITTEE OF
THE STATES OF GUERNSEY

JUNE 1940

CHAPTER 1

Guernsey, June 1940

The shock of that day never left her; it invaded her dreams and shadowed her waking moments. She could see herself now, carrying an old brown suitcase down the ship's gangplank, her chocolate-coloured hair tousled by the fresh Guernsey breeze. In the year since she'd left the island nothing had changed. Fishing boats rocked from side to side, slapping waves against the harbour walls, yacht sails shimmered in the early evening sun, fine wisps of cloud skittering across the sky like pockets of hand-stitched lace.

Up ahead, the old tomato lorries wound their way like a wooden snake towards the cargo ships bound for England. Her papa had grown tomatoes in the greenhouses behind their home for as long as she could remember. Nowadays he didn't need the income, but the twelve-pound fruit baskets – or 'chips' as the locals called them – were his pride and joy. Feeling exhilarated at the thought of seeing her parents again, Lydia headed for the bus terminus, stopping to tie her shoelace by the harbour wall.

It started as a low rumble, like a vast swarm of bees in flight, growing steadily louder till it turned into a roar. Startled, she shaded her eyes from the sun and stared up into the sky. Three planes came into view, bright lights shining from their wings. A wave of raw fear rose up from her stomach. Someone shouted,

'*Enemy aircraft*', and her limbs froze. Lydia dropped to the ground, her face hitting the dirt as she landed. Bullets ricocheted over her head as she cowered in terror while the bombs plunged with sickening accuracy on to the harbour.

A piercing scream brought Lydia back to reality – it came from her own lips. All around her people were crying or standing motionless in shock. Blood dripped on to the pavements while air raid sirens, woken from their reverie, shrieked in protest. Coughing, she gasped for air, dense now with smoke, and tried to roll over.

'You okay, miss?' A policeman loomed overhead.

She fingered a cut on her face. 'I think so. What happened?'

'The Jerries have bombed the tomato lorries. Must 'uve mistaken them for tanks.' He gripped her arm. 'Can you get up?'

Nodding, she let him pull her off the ground.

'I'd get out of here, if I were you. Fast as you can. It's not safe.'

'But Papa, what about Papa?' A vision of her father lying dead in the rubble flashed in front of her eyes. 'He'll be in one of those lorries—'

'If he's out there now, miss, there's nothing you can do for him. You'd best find shelter in case the Jerries come again.'

Her suitcase long forgotten, Lydia headed for the dockside where a lone mother sat in the debris, cradling her daughter in the shelter of the harbour wall. The child was silent, but the woman sobbed as smoke rose into the sky like a giant funeral pyre.

Lydia stumbled on, ignoring the shouts of well-meaning people, '*Come shelter with us, miss*' – the roar of fire engines and the sickening smell of burnt flesh. Where was her father?

A familiar face appeared through the smoke. 'Tom – *Tommy!*' She'd known his family for years. 'Have you seen Papa?' She gestured towards the smouldering lorries.

'The Jerries got their target, all right, but there's plenty of folk sheltered under the pier. No one can get through.' Tommy Tostevin scratched his head. 'What on earth are *you* doing here?'

'It doesn't matter now. I'm here and that's the end of it. What can I do?'

'Go home, my girl. Go to your mother. It's going to be a long night.'

Lydia nodded, too numb to cry. She stumbled on down the Esplanade towards the Weighbridge, the familiar granite tower now oozing smoke. Next to it stood a burnt-out car with just one headlight clearly visible among the wreckage. Staring up at the Weighbridge's clock face, she saw that the hands had stuck at two minutes to seven.

Just then an ambulance came to a halt, its rear doors opened towards St Julian's Avenue. With a burst of adrenalin, she headed towards it and jumped inside.

'You injured, miss?' The white-coated doctor looked up as she landed beside him.

'No, I'm fine. It's just that I know a bit about, well, medicine, and I wondered if I could help?'

'There's lots of injured people down there. It's not a pretty sight. We could do with another pair of hands, though.' He glanced at her. 'Are you sure you're up to it?'

She nodded. 'Just tell me what you want me to do.'

'Patch up your face first.' He handed her a box of dressings. 'Then follow me.'

They edged their way back to the burning lorries, the roar of engines filling the air again: the enemy planes had returned. Lydia ducked and covered her head with the palms of her hands, her heart pounding louder than the shells that shook the ground.

She shut her eyes but the sight of blood mingling in the gutter with the juice of crushed tomatoes would stay with her forever.

Four hours earlier

Lydia ducked as the seagull swooped down on to the deck, its broad wings clipping her face. Losing her balance, she threw herself forwards and clung to the ship's rail. For a moment she was a child again running barefoot over the sand, picking her way through the rock pools with her best friend Maggie, their skin the colour of liquid gold.

'Steady on.' The stranger grabbed her arm, pulling her back to safety. 'Are you all right, miss?'

'I think so.' She swallowed hard, licking blood from her lip. 'I wanted to see Guernsey appear on the horizon – it's my favourite bit of the journey. I hope that seagull's not a bad omen.'

'Here, take this.' The man pulled out a large white handkerchief and handed it to her, recognition softening his features. 'Blow me, if it isn't Lydia Le Page. I haven't seen you since Amherst School.'

'Arthur Le Moigne! I thought I recognised you. Always keen to help, as I remember.' She pressed the folded cotton square to her face. 'I see nothing's changed.'

'So, what brings you back here *now*? I heard you were in England swotting for some fancy diploma?'

'I came to see my parents.' She shielded her eyes from the sun. 'They're terrified of an invasion, so I think they should leave the island. Is it true the Germans are coming?'

Arthur nodded his head, strands of brownish blond hair straying over his brow.

'It's true enough. I've been working over in England where my wife's from, but I'm here to finish off some business while I've still got a chance. Most of the school kids have been evacuated already. You're all best out of it.'

She frowned. 'So how long do think the war will last?'

'It's hard to say. Some reckon it'll be all over by Christmas, but

I wouldn't bet on it, now the Jerries have overrun France. Hitler's a madman, if you ask me, and there's no knowing what he'll do next.' As if sensing her fear, he changed the subject. 'You were a bit of a brainbox at school, as I recall. What'll you be doing when all this is over?'

'I want to be a pharmacist. That's the plan, anyway.'

'A pharmacist? Surely you don't need posh exams to work in Boots the Chemists?' He grinned. 'Studying's a waste of time for the ladies if you ask me.'

'Well, I'm not asking you, Arthur Le Moigne. And I'm not doing all this studying just so I can sell toiletries.' Her words chided but her eyes were smiling; to be honest she was glad of the company. The two years she'd spent at Leicester College of Art and Technology had opened her eyes to so many things. She'd missed home, naturally, but when she first stepped on to English soil something had stirred inside her, something she still couldn't quite understand.

'Do you smoke?' Arthur's voice interrupted her thoughts.

Lydia shook her head.

'Good. It's a nasty habit.' Pulling out a packet of Craven A, he grabbed the last cigarette and scribbled an address on the back of the pack. 'Keep this with you. And if you ever need help – I mean really need it – get in touch.'

She smiled back at him. 'Thanks, Arthur.'

'Don't mention it. Oh, and Lydia. Don't take any risks. The phoney war is over. Believe me – this is the real thing.'

Later that night

'Mama – it's me – let me in.' Emily Le Page threw open the door, howling with a mixture of fear and delight.

'Lydia, my poor child, you look dreadful.' She enveloped her daughter in a hug. 'What on earth has happened? What are you doing here?'

'They said the Germans were planning to invade. I needed to know you were all right.' Lydia's eyes scanned the room. 'Where's Papa? Has he ... has he gone to the docks?'

'No, not tonight. He wasn't feeling well. He heard the commotion and went out to check on the greenhouses.'

'Thank God for that. I thought he'd been killed.'

'Killed? Dear Lord, why on earth would you think that?'

'Because the Germans have bombed the harbour, Mama. They've blown up the tomato lorries.'

Her mother's face paled to the colour of candlewax. '*Cae afaire d faire*! I heard the air raid sirens and the noise.' She faltered. 'But how do you know?'

'I watched it happen. The tomato lorries were burning with the drivers still inside. I thought Papa had—'

'Well he hasn't. But *you* could have been dead on the dock. Whatever were you thinking of coming home now?' She wrung her hands together.

'I would've helped with the injured, Mama. I really wanted to. Then more bombs fell and a doctor found me and bundled me into a van. There were a few of us sobbing and shaking, some far worse off than me. I still don't know the driver's name.'

'Oh, Lydia, my poor dear girl. Come along now, sit down and I'll make you a cup of hot tea.'

'Tell me first – what's wrong with Papa?'

'He's been having pains in his chest. I made him see Doctor Wren tonight. He didn't want to, mind. Reckoned the tomatoes were far more important.' Her face suddenly crumpled with fear. 'Please, Lord, save us all.'

'What is it? Mama, what's wrong?'

'He sent young Freddie Le Saint instead.'

'Who did?'

'Your papa. He asked young Freddie to drive the lorry.' She stood up and buttoned her cardigan, fingers moving mechanically over the fine grey wool. 'Wait here, Lydia. I must find Freddie's mother.'

Lydia ran to the back door and threw herself at her father.

'Papa – PAPA! Thank God you're safe. I thought you were dead.'

'I'm all right, my girl, but what about you? What the dickens are you doin' here, eh?' He prised her out of his arms, his eyes glistening with tears.

'I came to make sure you were okay. It's almost the end of summer term and there wasn't much left for me to do, and so I thought that—' She was gabbling now, unsure of what to say, how to tell him what had happened. 'Then I got off the boat and then the bombs came and—'

'Shush now, never mind the Jerries – it'd take more than a few bombs to frighten your old papa. By rights you shouldn't be—' He glanced round the room. 'Where's your mother?'

'She's gone to find Mrs Le Saint – she's worried about Freddie. It's the docks, Papa – they've bombed the docks.'

Realisation swamped the old man's face. His eyes turned towards her, but his mind was already elsewhere.

'I must go down to the harbour and find the lad. I sent him there and it's up to me to bring him back.'

'Wait, Papa.' Lydia clutched at his arm. 'Wait until we hear something. You'll never find him on your own.'

He pulled his arm free. 'I must go, my girl, don't you see?'

'Please?' Panic strangled her voice. Some of the lorries had taken a direct hit. She'd seen them pulling out the bodies…

'I should be there by rights, not him. I should never have listened to your mother. I must go, and that's the end of it.'

'What about your heart?'

'Never mind my heart. There's a war on.' He grabbed his cap and disappeared through the door.

CHAPTER 2

'Don't smile at them, they're the enemy.'

'I wasn't smiling.' Maggie pulled a face. 'I just nodded, that's all. I'm trying to be civil. Besides – what am I supposed to do?'

The two friends were walking down the Grange on their way to town, passing German soldiers on bikes or on foot at almost every turn. With her shapely figure and glossy brown hair, Lydia stood out against her friend's chubby build and plain features.

'Ignore them, Maggie, that's what. They'll be stealing our homes and our jobs next.'

'I'm sorry, but I can't help feeling happy, despite the stupid Occupation. It's so good to have you back again.'

The two girls had been friends since before they could walk. At the age of nine they'd scratched their arms with a penknife till they drew blood, vowing solemnly that nothing and no one would ever pull them apart.

'It's good to see you, too,' Lydia said, linking arms, 'but we're prisoners here now, don't forget. We need to be careful.'

'Do you mind very much not being able to go back to England?'

'Of course not,' Lydia lied. Just days after the Germans had landed she already felt trapped. 'There are far worse places I could be. Like the prisoner of war camps in France. Most people there have done nothing wrong. Anyway, the war won't last forever. I'm sure Professor Williams will take me back when it's all over.'

'Pa says the Jerries will be gone by Christmas.' Maggie had always been an optimist.

'I hope your papa's right, but I'm not so sure.'

'Oh, Lydia, you're far too serious for your own good. Just look at the soldiers – they're tall and muscular – not a bit like our lads. Which reminds me, Charlie Vaudin asked me out *again* last week. I don't like him, not in that way, but I'm running out of excuses. What can I say to put him off?'

'Oh, Maggie! How could you be so heartless?'

'Don't sound so horrified. I've turned him down before.'

Lydia pulled a face. 'You know very well that's not what I meant. Now come on. We'll be late for the shop.'

Ever since she could remember, Maggie's father had run a thriving luggage shop in the Pollet, the town's main shopping street. Trade had dried up the minute the enemy arrived, so he planned to set up a barter counter where people could swap what they no longer wanted for something they needed: handbags for shoes, stockings for warm socks, with a small percentage going into his own pocket.

'Are you sure you don't mind helping out?' Maggie frowned. She'd worked in the shop since she left school and envied her friend for 'escaping' to the mainland.

'Why ever should I?'

'Because you're brainy, not like me. And shop work is beneath you.'

Lydia burst out laughing. 'Beneath me? The only thing beneath me these days is the bed I sleep on. Besides which, I like the idea of a barter shop. I could swap my silver pen for a dress seeing as I lost all my things at the harbour. Now if you can take your eyes off those soldiers for a minute, I'll race you the last half-mile.'

By lunchtime the two girls had worked up an appetite. Lydia looked up.

'I'll go and get something for us to eat. Do you need anything from the shops?'

'Get some tins to put by, will you?' Maggie called from the back of the shop. 'You never know when we might need them.'

Lydia set off for Le Riche's store. People were already stockpiling essentials and it was anyone's guess how long the supplies would last.

'Halt!' The soldier's eyes wandered leisurely over Lydia's body.

'What do you want?' How dare he look at her like that?

'You have the dark eyes, the dark hair? I think you are perhaps a Jew, *Fräulein?*'

Lydia shook her head. 'I was brought up in the Church of England, I'll have you know. I'm a Guernsey girl, born and bred.'

'*Ein – Missverständnis*. How you say – a misunderstanding? We Germans like the blonde hair and blue eyes, do we not?' His sneer revealed a set of crooked teeth. 'Why have you come here today?'

'I've come to buy some food.' She nodded towards Le Riche's store.

'You people eat many tomatoes. You have no need of more food.'

'Like you, we also get hungry.' Lydia held his gaze. 'May I go now?'

'Off with you.' The soldier lifted his rifle, pointed it at her face, then gestured angrily down the street.

'*Jewish bitch.*'

The words echoed in her head as she walked away.

Emily Le Page stared at the headline on the *Guernsey Star*. She always read it from cover to cover and tonight was no exception.

'German Officer Saves Guernsey Child from Fire! "Heroic Rescue," says Kommandant.'

Heroic rescue? It didn't make sense. Could this really be the enemy? Murder, rape, bombs and torture were the legacy of the Nazis in Europe and here they were trying to make friends. Already the wretched Germans had spoilt her beloved island. Cars forced to drive on the right-hand side of the road, barbed-wire littering the coast – whatever would they do next? She cast her eyes round the drawing room with its carved oak furniture and sweeping bay windows. An unspeakable tragedy had brought them to this house, yet she had known more happiness within these walls than she'd ever thought possible.

Built of pink granite on a cliff overlooking Saints Bay, Sea Breeze was visible on a clear day many miles from shore. Behind the house stood a small orchard of apple, pear and plum trees, and beyond that lay the greenhouses where her husband spent his days.

Their life had not always been easy. Emily's father was a farm labourer and her mother took in washing so that Emily and her sister May, five years her junior, had warm clothes and food in their bellies.

At twenty-eight, Emily married Jack, a greenhouse worker who lived round the corner in Tower Lane. Always the dreamer, May travelled to England where she met and fell in love with a wealthy Austrian banker. They married in Marylebone, London, two years later and set up home in Surrey.

Picking up the picture frame from the mantelpiece, Emily gazed fondly at her sister's smiling face. Two weeks after the photograph was taken the couple were killed in an accident.

'You still miss her, don't you, Mama?' Lydia's voice cut into her thoughts.

Emily's face lit up at the sight of her daughter. 'You're here now – that's all that matters. How's Maggie?'

'As cheerful as ever. I caught her eyeing up the German soldiers in town, but she means no harm.'

'Mmm.' The older woman frowned. 'Wants to watch herself that one, she's too friendly for her own good. Now, my love, I have a job for you. Take some biscuits to old Mrs Tostevin at Torteval while they're fresh from the oven. If she's not in, just leave them by the plant pot at the front door.'

Lydia had always loved Torteval. An isolated parish on the southwest of the island, it stood high above sea level with grandiose cliffs guarding the foam-capped waves.

As a child she would cycle to Portelet Bay taking with her a picnic of Guernsey biscuits, fresh fruit and *gâche mêlée* – a heavenly mix of apples and cinnamon that only her mother knew how to make properly. With the wind in her hair she would find her favourite spot, a circular trench cut into the turf with a central stone raised up like a table, known locally as the Fairy Ring. There she imagined fairies dancing in the moonlight, mixing magic potions and mending broken hearts. Lydia wasn't sure back then how a heart could be broken, but since Mama said one would mend in time, she knew it must be a job for the fairies.

Today she could see Hanois Lighthouse, a signal of hope on the island's most treacherous coast. As she walked down the narrow lane, Torteval Church appeared through the trees, its rounded steeple raised to the sky, like the pointed hat of the Lady of Shalott. Gazing at the familiar sight she stumbled in the undergrowth and, with one loud yelp, fell heavily to the ground. Clutching her wounded ankle, she cursed out loud.

'Damn and blast the Germans. I hope they rot in hell.'

'Are you okay, miss?' The man appeared out of nowhere.

Lydia looked up, her face flushed with embarrassment.

'I'm fine, thanks. I just tripped on some barbed wire. The wretched Germans leave it everywhere these days.'

'You don't look fine from where I'm standing. That's a nasty wound on your ankle.' He leaned over and pulled her gently to her feet. 'Come with me – your foot needs bathing.'

Taking her arm gently in his he led her, still protesting, to the church gates. As she walked through the carved oak door and into the nave, the sound of silence took her breath away. In front of them, the centre aisle, exquisitely tiled in intricate patterns, led to the altar rail.

'Shouldn't we ask permission?' she ventured in a whisper. 'To be, you know, here in the church.'

Throwing his head back, the man roared with laughter. 'I should have introduced myself sooner. I'm Martin Martell, Rector of Torteval Church. And you are?'

'Lydia Le Page.' Her face reddened again. This man looked nothing like a clergyman. At six foot tall he towered above her, his mop of dark hair strangely dishevelled, his handsome grin revealing a row of white teeth.

'I'm not an imposter, if that's what you're thinking, Miss Le Page. I don't always wear my dog collar as it can put people off.' His face turned serious now. 'Come into the vestry. We need to dress that ankle before it becomes infected.'

The rector sat her down in a battered leather chair, returning minutes later with a bowl of water, cotton wool and a towel. 'Right, this should do the trick.'

'I really don't want to be any trouble.'

'It's no trouble.' He winked. 'You'll just have to take my word for that.'

A frisson of excitement ran down Lydia's spine as he took her bare foot in his hand. Despite his strength, this man's manner was gentle, and she found herself relaxing in his company. Soon they were deep in discussion about the enemy.

'How could they loot all the empty houses?' Lydia frowned. 'Those poor souls will have nothing left when they get home.'

'It's too late to help them now. We must concentrate on those left behind.' He ran his hands through his hair. 'Pardon me for saying so but I hate this blasted war.'

'I do too, but what can we do to stop it? We're just so powerless here.'

'Hitler got his troops on to British soil – that's what this is all about. Churchill has abandoned Guernsey so now we have to free ourselves.'

'Do you really think that's possible?'

'It's up to us to make it possible. The British must never be allowed to forget that the Germans are here.' He stood up. 'And now, enough of the rhetoric. I'm taking the car to town now, so let me drop you home on the way.'

She felt an unfamiliar pang of regret at the thought of leaving him.

'Town will be fine, thanks. Besides, I've taken up too much of your time already.'

When they arrived at the Esplanade he stopped the car, got out and opened the passenger door. Only then did she realise she'd lost Mrs Tostevin's biscuits.

CHAPTER 3

'So you've met the handsome new rector, you lucky girl.' Maggie's eyes twinkled. 'What did you think of him?'

'He's good-looking, I'll give you that. I gather you haven't been introduced?'

'I've had the odd glimpse since he replaced old man Ozanne, but believe me, tongues are wagging. Some folks say he's a double agent put here by the Jerries, and that he daubed "V for Victory" on the prison walls. Isn't it exciting?'

'Exciting he may be,' Lydia kept her voice casual, 'but he's not really my type.'

'Oh, but you would say that, wouldn't you? You mean you fancy him!'

'I mean nothing of the sort, Maggie. He's a rector, not a movie star – don't you think of anything but the opposite sex?'

'Not very often, to be frank. I think of food, of course, seeing as there's never enough to go round, and going out after the curfew, and being able to buy whatever I like in the shops. What else is there to occupy my mind?'

'You could help with the Sunday school at Torteval. The lady who leads it has gone to England.'

'Me? Help with the Sunday school? You do make me laugh. There's hardly any kids left on the island and those who are here wouldn't gain much from me. Or much that would do them any good. I think all that book-learning's gone to your brain. You need to relax a bit more.' Maggie winked. 'There's a picture on at the Regal tonight. Do you want to come with me?'

Lydia pulled a face. 'It's German, with English subtitles. Are you still sure you want to go?'

'You never know who you might meet.'

'Oh, Maggie – you really are a hopeless case.'

'Requisitioned? What do you mean, requisitioned?' Jack Le Page's face was the colour of dead violets.

'I mean,' Emily said, her voice choking, 'the Kommandant is stealing our home.' She stared at the letter in front of her, stamped at the top with a black swastika. 'He's going to live here. We have to get out.'

'But that's ridiculous – they can't do this.' He turned to his daughter. 'Can they, Liddy?'

'I don't know, Papa.' Anger hardened her voice. 'It seems they can do what they like.'

Her mother let out a loud wail. 'Where will we go? Can we take our things?' Clutching her forehead, she closed her eyes, swaying back and forth on her feet.

'Let me worry about that.' Lydia's mind was racing. It was bad enough being thrown out, but the Kommandant and his cronies sleeping in their beds? The thought made her want to vomit. She led her mother gently to her chair. 'I'll call Doctor Wren — he'll know what to do. Then I'll make us a hot cup of tea.'

When the doctor arrived, Jack showed him straight through to the bedroom.

'My wife's had a bit of a shock. The Jerries are taking our home for the boss to live in.'

'I see.' The doctor shook his head. 'Kindly leave us together.'

Lydia jumped as her father appeared at the door. She'd been

clattering about in the kitchen, trying her best to keep busy. 'Is everything okay, Papa?'

'The doc's with your mother now. The Jerries were sniffing around here last week. Reckoned they were looking for weapons, but I knew they were up to something.'

'Why didn't you tell me?'

'I didn't want to worry you.' His eyes flickered. 'I'm not sure how your mother will cope. She's lived in this house since you were knee-high to a grasshopper.'

'It won't be for long, Papa, I promise. We've lots of friends who'll help out. I'll speak to Flo Brouard this afternoon. She's been like a sister to Mama. I'm sure she'll let you stay with her.'

'And what about you, my girl?'

'I'll go to Maggie's. I'll be safe there.' Her voice was hollow.

'Blasted war.' Jack wiped his eyes with the back of his hand. 'My poor Liddy, I wish you hadn't got involved.'

'I'll be fine. Maggie's my best friend. You just look after Mama.'

'Anyone home?' The doctor coughed as he entered the kitchen. He had known the Le Pages since before they were married and looked after the family ever since. 'I've given your wife a sedative to help her sleep. You're quite right, she is in shock, but she'll come round soon enough.' He shook his head. 'It's a terrible thing that's happening to us all.'

'It is that.' Jack's voice cracked. 'Thank you, doctor. I'll see you out.'

'Good night. And try not to worry.'

Lydia avoided her father's eyes. 'I'll go and make sure Mama's comfortable. She'll be better when she's had a rest.'

'You do that.' He grasped her arm. 'Blasted Germans – look what they've done to your mother already. Pity the man who tries to harm a hair on *your* head.'

Lydia kissed her father's cheek. 'Believe me, Papa, I can look after myself.'

Martin paced up and down his study like a caged lion. He couldn't stop thinking about Lydia: her green eyes full of mystery, the mass of dark curls, the way her cheeks flushed when she realised her mistake. So why had he agreed to let her call on him? When young Tom from Torteval Farm had arrived with the note earlier, he'd been too startled to refuse.

He glanced at his watch. She'd be here in half an hour and he was acting like a lovelorn schoolboy. He'd be courteous, of course, offer her some tea, enquire about her health and that would be the last time he'd see her. Whatever he was feeling he couldn't allow it to go on.

Martin paled as a vision of Janet's face appeared in front of him. He could never change the past, but at least he could control the future.

Sunlight broke through the clouds as Lydia arrived at Torteval. Leaving a tin of fresh Guernsey biscuits outside Mrs Tostevin's cottage she headed straight for the rectory. Though she'd never tell a soul, the Reverend Martin Martell had given her hope, venting the rage she'd felt every day since the first bomb fell.

To her disbelief, most islanders had accepted their fate and got on with their lives as best they could; but not this man. She had no idea why he was so angry with the enemy but she needed to avenge her parents' humiliation and right now he was her only hope.

'Do sit down, Miss Le Page.'

The low table was set with an engraved silver teapot, matching hot water jug and a mismatched assortment of bone china in various shades of blue and yellow.

'Please call me Lydia, and you really shouldn't have gone to all this trouble. I've brought a jar of homemade loganberry jam to thank you for rescuing me the other day.'

She took it out of her bag and placed it self-consciously on the table. The rector had clearly made an effort, despite the lack of a woman's touch.

'That's very generous, but anyone would have done the same. I trust your ankle has healed.'

'Yes, thanks, just a scar. I think I got off lightly.'

'So, remind me.' He sat down on the chair opposite her. 'What were you doing before the war?'

'I was studying pharmacy in England.' Surely he couldn't have forgotten already? 'I'd just finished my first year when all this happened.'

'Yes, of course. Let's hope you'll be back soon.'

The polite exchange continued until Lydia could stand it no longer. 'The thing is, Reverend,' she persisted, determined to say her piece.

'The name's Martin.' He lifted the teapot and poured steaming liquid into the two cups. 'Is something troubling you?'

Lydia took off her gloves and gulped the hot tea till it burnt the back of her throat. 'The fact is Otto Kruger – the Kommandant – has requisitioned our home for himself.'

'Your home?' He let out a low groan. 'I heard the owners were thrown out, but I'd no idea you were related. How are your parents?'

'My folks have taken it very badly. They seem to think it's their fault. They weren't always well off, you see. Mama's younger sister and her husband died in a motor accident in 1919.' She knew she was babbling.

'And they left you the house?'

'Not exactly. It was bought with our inheritance.'

'I'm glad you've told me.' Martin shook his head. 'You don't deserve this. I'll do everything I can to help.'

'It's not your help we need, though the offer is much appreciated. I just want to get my own back on the enemy. They've no idea I've come back to the island and that's how I want it to stay. All this anger is a waste of energy, and I can't just sit round doing nothing.'

'Now what makes you think I want to thwart the enemy, Lydia?' His grey eyes twinkled.

'You're the first person I've met since the Occupation who seems ready to put up a fight.'

'Some of the islanders think I'm a plant – you know – that I'm here to spy for the enemy.' He leaned forward in his chair. 'You could be getting yourself into serious trouble.'

'You're no more a plant than I am,' she retorted, sounding far more confident than she felt. 'I think you like to shock, that's all.'

'I'm sorry to say that the role of assistant spymaster has already been filled,' he winked, 'but if you're looking to volunteer I can find you plenty to do. Washing up, cooking and cleaning for a start. As you can see, I don't have a housekeeper.'

Lydia was determined not to rise to the bait.

'I'm not sure that housework will avenge any wrongdoings on behalf of the enemy, Reverend Martell, but I'll do anything if it helps.'

'The name's Martin.' His face softened. 'More tea?'

'No, thank you. I must be getting back.' She stood up.

'You could help at the school now and then, I suppose. Keep an eye on the pupils when the headmaster is on business. Most of the children were evacuated with the teachers so these days it's down to me.'

'I'd love to, if you think I'm up to it.' Her spirits lifted.

'You'd have to be vetted, of course, then we'll see how we go from there.'

She gave a mock salute. 'When can I start?'

Maggie threw her arms round her friend.

'Ma's got the attic room ready for you. I'm sorry you've lost your home – it must be a terrible shock.'

Lydia swallowed hard, bile scorching the back of her throat.

'Don't worry – I intend to get my own back, however long it takes.'

'Just be careful, that's all. When do you have to leave?'

'We've been given the rest of the week to pack. That's more than some folk, from what I hear. My parents are still in shock.'

'Where will they go?'

'Flo Brouard's taking them in, thank goodness. She's got lots of space in that bungalow since Alf died, and she could do with the company.'

Tears welled into Maggie's eyes. 'It's such a lovely house, Sea Breeze. No wonder the Jerries want to get their hands on it.'

Lydia put her arm round her friend. 'I bet that's not the only reason. The place would make an ideal observation post.'

'Oh, Lydia, don't let anyone hear you talk about the Jerries like that. If you ask me, it's safer to keep in with them.'

'Keep in with them? They don't even know I'm here in Guernsey and that's how it's going to stay. I intend to keep as far away from them as possible.'

Maggie forced a smile. 'If you say so. Anyway, what about your Ma and Pa – do they need any help with the packing?'

'That's kind of you, but they're leaving most of the furniture behind. Besides, Mrs Ruaux promised to help. She moved out of her cottage last week with her three boys and took all their stuff in a wheelbarrow, so she knows how it feels.' Lydia bit her lip.

Privately she wondered if her parents would survive the ordeal. While Papa was acting like nothing had happened, Mama had taken to her bed and refused to move. God help them all.

*

Emily Le Page let out a scream. 'Don't make me go – please don't make me go.'

Her husband bowed his head. 'It'll be worse if we stay, my love – much worse. They've asked us politely so far, but if they have to force us out we may end up in one of those bloney German holiday camps. We've just got to make the best of it.'

'But this is our home, it's where we belong.' She was crying now, violent sobs that shook her body.

Lydia cradled her mother in her arms, rocking her gently back and forth till the tears subsided.

Grabbing her mackintosh, Jack wrapped it gently round his wife's shoulders. 'Come on, my love. It's time to go.'

Emily didn't move. 'I haven't blacked the grate. I can't leave without blacking the grate.'

'We'll do it together then, shall we?' Patiently, he put down his bag.

Emily pulled out a large checked handkerchief and noisily blew her nose. 'You're a good man, Jack Le Page. You're as stubborn as a mule, but your heart's in the right place.'

'Come on then, old girl.' He wiped his eyes with the back of his sleeve. 'Let's get cracking. Then we can hold our heads up and get on out of here.'

She lifted her chin. 'You're right. Let's go while we still can. They can blacken their own bloney grate.'

The procession moved slowly down the lane, the elderly couple with their eyes cast to the ground, their precious belongings spilling out of the handcarts behind them.

'Well, I'm blowed if it's not the Le Pages from Sea Breeze,' Connie Gaudion whispered as she scrubbed the stone steps of her cottage. 'They look just like nomads.'

'Don't gloat,' a voice cut in from the open window next door. 'It could be your turn next.'

'I don't reckon the Kommandant would want my humble abode,' Connie grinned. 'It's not posh enough for the likes of him.'

'Be grateful, then,' the other woman sighed. 'They're good people, Emily and Jack. They don't deserve this.'

'A bit above their station, from what I've heard. Just look at that rocking chair – it must've cost a fortune. So where are they off to?'

'Flo Brouard's taking them in. I bet she could do with a bob or two. It's an ill wind that blows no good, I say.'

Tutting loudly, her neighbour slammed the window shut.

Lydia grabbed the brass knocker and banged on the door. Flo Brouard lived in St Martins in a black and white painted bungalow with a large greenhouse and vinery at the back. A wide gravelled path led up to the front porch where two porcelain dogs with floppy brown ears stood to attention like sentries.

The old woman's face broke into a warm grin as she opened the door. Generously built with rosy cheeks and a dimple in her chin, Flo had been widowed some five years since, and had no children of her own.

'Come in, my love, your mother's busy in the parlour. Never stops, not for a minute, that one.'

She led Lydia down the long hall and into a cosy room where a coal fire burned in the blackened grate. At either side of the hearth, glass-fronted cupboards were filled with an assortment of pottery and jugs in brightly painted colours.

Emily was peeling potatoes in an old enamel bowl in her lap. Dropping the knife and bowl, she rushed into her daughter's arms.

'Lydia – it's you! I'm making some broth for supper. Will you join us? I'm sure Flo wouldn't mind.'

'Mind?' Flo clattered around the scullery, opening and

shutting drawers. 'It's time we had some young blood round here. Now where did I put my spectacles?'

'How are you, Mama?' Lydia asked as soon as Flo had left the room.

'I'm managing well enough, thank you, my love. You'd be amazed what I've had given. Clothes, food, even an old warming pan. Some folks round here remember me and May when we hadn't got two pennies to rub together—' Her eyes filled with tears.

'And Papa?'

'He misses his greenhouses. From what I've heard the Jerries are letting them go to rack and ruin. He's cleared out Flo's, mind, and reckons he can have good strong plants growing next spring – that's if we're—' her voice faltered, 'you know – still here. How are the Galliennes?'

'They're fine, though I hardly see much of them. Edna keeps busy with the WVS and Reg spends most of his time at the bowling club. He can't do much, what with his lumbago, but I think the company keeps him out of mischief.'

Emily smiled. 'Well, I'm glad you and Maggie have got each other. Like the old days, I shouldn't wonder. Now then, I hope you're making the best of a bad job and keeping up with your studying.'

'Of course,' Lydia replied, a shade too quickly. 'I'm going to help out at Torteval School. Just for an hour or so when they need a hand.'

The door opened and Flo Brouard bustled back into the room.

'That's better. I can see now. Torteval, did you say? Is that where they've got that new young rector?'

Lydia nodded. Why did the thought of him make her insides churn?

'His name's Martin – Martin Martell. Some say he has radical views, but he just wants to see the back of the Jerries.'

'I hope he's not too outspoken for his own good. A dead rector is not much good to anyone. And now, let's get that broth on the boil. You will stay for supper, my dear?'

'That's very kind of you, Mrs Brouard, but I've promised to visit Freddie Le Saint in hospital.'

'Ah yes, young Freddie. How is the dear boy? Terrible business with his leg.'

Lydia glanced sideways at her mother. 'He's still poorly but his hip's finally responding to treatment. They're hopeful he'll make a full recovery.'

'*Mon Dieu.*' Flo clasped her hands in front of her. 'And so say all of us.'

The boy at the back of the classroom looked younger than the rest. His hand shot into the air as the headmaster opened the door.

'Can we go out to play now, sir?'

Timothy Vaudin shot him a tolerant smile.

'Not just yet, Ernest. I want you all to meet Miss Le Page.' He gestured to Lydia who was standing behind him. 'She's come to help with your lessons. She will start by demonstrating how to make firewood from the twigs you collected on your way to school.'

'Can't we just steal it from the Jerries?' This came from a tall lad of about ten who looked like he might be the class ringleader. 'My pa says they nicked everything from us in the first place.' The room erupted into nervous giggles.

'We have to teach mixed age groups, I'm afraid,' Mr Vaudin explained under his breath. 'Just do the best you can.' Out loud he added, 'I'll leave you with Miss Le Page. Make sure you behave now, boys and girls.'

As the door closed behind him a paper dart landed at Lydia's feet.

'Which one of you is wealthy?' she asked, her eyes scanning the room. No one moved.

'I'll have to guess, then, won't I?' She pointed to the suspected ringleader. 'Your name is?'

'Reggie Begin, miss.' His face folded into a smirk.

'Ah, Reggie. Maybe you're the one with money to spare seeing as paper is so precious these days. Perhaps you'd come to the front and show us your skills in origami?'

'Ori what, miss?'

'Paper folding, Reggie. I take it you're the culprit?'

The lad shuffled his way to the front.

'You're not a *proper* teacher, are you, miss? You've just come to help the rector.'

'Perhaps you'd like to take over, then, seeing as you're so knowledgeable?' She sat down and looked at her watch. 'You've got exactly one hour on how to make firewood, starting from now.'

CHAPTER 4

Martin was sitting on his own in the middle of the nave as Lydia approached. Her heart lifted at the sight of him.

'Good morning, Miss Le Page. I hear you did an excellent job at the school.'

'It was quite a challenge, I must say. I just hope I've been of some help.'

'Of that there's no doubt. The headmaster is singing your praises. He seems to think you'd make an excellent teacher.'

'That's not quite how the class saw things!' She smiled at the memory.

'So – to what to I owe this pleasure?'

He was standing so close now that her courage almost failed her. 'Folks say you turn a blind eye to "V for Victory" signs when you see them. Is it true?'

'It might be. What do you think?'

'I hope so. I'd like to believe I've found a kindred spirit.'

'You mean you'd break the law, too?'

She avoided his eyes. 'So you've heard the gossip?'

'Lonely bachelor of this parish.' His eyes twinkled. 'Is that what you mean?'

'You know it's not.'

'Okay – do you think I look like a spy?'

'No, but you don't look like a man of the cloth, either. Besides, I've no idea what a spy looks like.'

He ran his hand through his hair. 'Nor have I, thank goodness. There's no mystery about me, Lydia. I'm just trying to protect us all from the enemy.'

'Damn the enemy!' Anger spurred her on. 'I'd do anything to get my revenge.'

He was looking at her intently now, as if reading her thoughts.

'Be careful. I care what happens to you.'

She nodded, her heart thudding. 'Does that mean…?'

He lifted her arm and planted a kiss on the back of her hand.

'It means we're friends and I hope we always will be. And now it's time you went home.'

'Lydia – come quick – it's *him* at the door.' Maggie's voice echoed up the stairs.

'Who's him?' Lydia stepped out down on to the landing.

'You know, the rector. Are you expecting him?'

'Martin? Of course I'm not. It's your house. If I'd known he was coming I'd have told you so. Go on, then, open it.'

'But he hasn't rung the doorbell.'

'Oh, Maggie, you do make me laugh.' Lydia made her way to the front door and undid the catch. 'Martin! What a surprise.' Her heart flipped over. 'What are you doing here?'

'I was over this way so I've brought you some freshly baked *gâche mêlée*. Old Mrs Belben made it for me, bless her, but I couldn't possibly eat it all.' He grinned. 'It's a bit short on the apples, but I can still recommend it.'

Maggie's inquisitive face appeared over Lydia's shoulder. 'You must be the Reverend Martell? Pleased to meet you. Do come in.'

'And you must be Maggie.' He stepped into the vestibule. 'Are your parents at home?'

'I'm afraid not. They play bowls down at Delancey Park on Saturdays, but they'll be sorry they missed you.'

'As I said, this isn't an official visit. I've come bearing gifts.' Martin handed her the brown paper bag.

'Oooh, my favourite.' Maggie peered at the contents then tugged at his arm. 'Come through to the parlour and join us for a cup of tea.'

'That sounds more like an order than an invitation.' Lydia nodded at Martin. 'I don't see how you can refuse.'

'So how did you come to join the Church?' asked Maggie, cutting the apple cake into three chunks. 'You don't look a bit how I imagined.'

'And how's that?' A smile played on Martin's lips.

'Well you know, old, grey-haired, boring, that sort of thing.'

'Maggie, please—' Lydia almost choked on her tea.

'Leave her be,' Martin said affably. 'She's only saying what she thinks.'

'You could have been a politician,' Maggie continued dreamily, 'making a speech in the Commons, having your say.'

'That's very kind of you, but I think they'd have thrown me out of the House of Commons by now for insubordination.'

'You sound just like Lydia, Reverend. She always uses one big word when two little ones would do.'

'There are several little words I'd like to say to Mr Churchill for leaving us in this mess, but I'm not sure it would be right in front of ladies.' He turned to Lydia. 'What do you think?'

'It's us against them, as far as I'm concerned,' she said. 'If the British won't help, then we'll fight the Hun on our own.'

'Any more for anyone?' Maggie picked up the teapot while finishing the last few crumbs. 'I'll never let the Jerries starve *me*.'

'You should've seen the way he looked at you.' Maggie closed the door behind Martin. 'I think the man's smitten.'

Lydia blushed, despite herself.

'I've told you before, you're just a hopeless romantic. He was just being kind, that's all.'

'He's a bit out of his parish then, from what I can tell, unless the Jerries have moved the boundaries.'

'Or unless he's checking up on me.'

'Now why would he want to do that?' Maggie looked genuinely puzzled.

'I don't know – it's just a feeling. There's something about him I don't quite understand.'

'He's good-looking and he's taken a fancy to you – what is there to understand?'

'I feel powerless sometimes, like I shouldn't be stuck here in Guernsey – and I think Martin does, too.'

'We could be here for years, Lydia, so you might as well make the best of it.'

'I do hope you're wrong.'

'About the war, or Martin Martell?'

Lydia burst out laughing. 'About both.'

Martin walked back through the town. He'd come miles out of his way to discover where Lydia lived, though she'd probably seen through his ruse. At least Maggie hadn't minded; she clearly took life as it came, war or no war. Besides, he must check every detail if he was to continue with his plan.

Over the weeks, he'd enquired about Lydia around the island, discreetly of course, and the response was always positive. Some folks had been jealous when the family came into money, though the wealth didn't seem to have spoiled them. Jack Le Page had kept his daughter grounded – he was a tomato grower at heart and always would be – and Lydia clearly worshipped him. The affection, it seemed, was mutual, and Martin was beginning to understand why.

'Morning, rector. You're a bit off the beaten track today, aren't you?'

Martin doffed his hat. 'The same could be said for you, er, Mrs Romerill, isn't it?'

'It is indeed. I'm collecting some sewing– it gets me out and about and keeps the wolf from the door. Not that there's much to spend my money on these days.' Her smile was rueful. 'I'd best get on, so I'll bid you good day.'

Martin watched the old woman as she made her way up the road, a battered wicker basket under her arm. *Janet loved haute couture. She would have made a brilliant designer. If it wasn't for him she would still be here now.*

Lydia knocked on the rectory door, hopping from one foot to the other.

At long last Martin appeared.

'Oh, it's you again. Sorry about the wait. The servants have packed their bags and gone to the south of France. Most inconsiderate of them, don't you think?' He kept his face straight, but his eyes danced with amusement. 'How can I help?'

She shot him a nervous smile. 'Can I come in?'

'Be my guest.' He gestured her through the dimly lit vestibule, his arm lightly brushing hers. Once in the drawing room she saw he'd tidied meticulously for her first visit. Today the shelves at either side of the hearth were crammed with books, some laid flat on top of others where he'd run out of space, while endless papers, pens and what looked like a plan of the island were scattered all over the floor.

'Excuse the mess.' He waved his arms around. 'I have other things on my mind besides church work these days.'

'That's the point. I don't know what it is you're doing but whatever it is I want to help.'

He studied her face for a moment. Opening the bottom drawer of his desk, he took out a sheet of tomato-packing paper covered in black type and handed it to her. At the top of the page was the word GINA, enclosed in a large V.

'What's this?' she asked.

'See for yourself. It's the latest news from the Allies.'

Lydia eyes widened. 'Good news from Britain and France. Where did you get it?'

'Now *I* can't even tell *you* that.' He lowered his voice. 'But the man responsible risks his life every day listening to the wireless.'

'So not everyone has handed in their sets to the Germans?' Requisitioning of wireless sets had been an enormous blow to the islanders.

'Around eight thousand have already been taken, from what I hear, but some people have buried them or are making their own crystal sets. They're the fortunate ones.'

Fortunate until they're found out, she thought. *Then their lives won't be worth living.*

Out loud she said, 'How often does the news-sheet come out?'

'Every day, except Sunday. We take the BBC's nine p.m. news bulletin and a summary of the eight o'clock news on the morning of publication.'

'We?'

'Let's just say there are a few of us. It has to be distributed carefully, of course. I just help out. We can't afford for it to get into enemy hands.'

Lydia's lips tightened. 'Why are you risking your life to do this.'

'You've seen the *Guernsey Press.*' Martin frowned. 'German propaganda day after day, with gaps where the censor's been. People were losing hope. I had to do something.'

'So where do I come in?'

'You could take copies of the news-sheet on your parish visits. It's risky, but then everything's a risk nowadays.'

A frisson of excitement shot through her.

'I'd be proud to help and won't let you down, I promise.'

He looked up, his grey eyes full of concern.

'Just be sure you never tell anyone what you're doing. And now, Lydia, come and sit down by me.'

An hour later they had discussed everything from the scarcity of food to the Germans' latest ban on cars and motorcycles.

'I've enjoyed our chat.' She stood up. 'But there's something I'd like to know, if it's not too forward?'

'Fire away.'

'At the risk of sounding like Maggie – why *did* you choose the Church for a living?'

'The Church is old-fashioned, out of date and in need of radical change.' Martin guided her to the front door. 'Does that answer your question?'

'At least you're honest. And by the way, who's GINA?'

'It stands for Guernsey Independent News Association.' Martin grinned. 'She's not my girlfriend, if that's what you're thinking.'

She could still feel the warmth of his hand on her skin as she hurried away.

CHAPTER 5

Lydia studied the crystal mosaic on the parlour window. 'Jack Frost's here, Maggie. At least *he's* not afraid of the Germans.'

'He's the only one round here who's not. I can't believe it's nearly Christmas. The Jerries have put the damper on that, too.'

'I'll be at Torteval on Christmas morning. Martin thinks faith will pull us through.'

'Fat chance.' Maggie pulled a face. 'What do *you* think?'

Lydia shook her head. She knew she was falling in love with Martin and the thought scared her. He clearly didn't feel the same. Martin was a loner. He was outspoken one day, considerate the next and had a tendency to disapprove of anyone who didn't agree with his views.

'I still think he fancies you.' Maggie interrupted her thoughts. 'So what *will* you do to help?'

'I've asked everyone I can think of to come and join us on Christmas Day. If we sing loud enough it'll drown the sound of the enemy.'

'What's the point? *"It'll be Christmas in my house when the Jerries go home, and not before,"* old Mrs Belben says. And I reckon we all agree with her.'

'In that case Christmas could be a long time coming. We have to do something now.'

'You don't give up, do you?' Maggie grinned. 'You'll be

dressing up as Father Christmas next and riding through the streets on a sleigh.'

'What a good idea! To hell with the Germans. We're British and proud of it. I think we should have a carol service.'

'A carol service? That's hardly what I'd call resistance.'

'It's passive resistance in my book – anyway, why not? Church is the only place people can get together these days.' Lydia felt the anger rising inside her. 'Look at our newspapers. They're full of German news. Our cinemas are showing German films and our money – even that's in marks! "Away in a Manger", I say, sung at the top of our voices.'

'I'll second that. But right now, I'm off to meet a friend.'

'Anyone I know?' Maggie wasn't usually secretive.

'Just someone from school.'

'I'll walk you to the end of the road, then I'm off on my parish visits.'

'Parish visits?' Maggie raised her eyes. 'Anything to please the rector. Good heavens. You'll be taking holy orders next.'

The clang of the shop bell brought the old woman from the back room. Peering through the half-moons perched on the end of her nose, the woman smiled.

'Lydia Le Page! How are you, my love? We're all out of rations today, I'm afraid.'

'I'm fine, thank you, Mrs Mauger. Don't worry, I'm here for the Reverend Martell. He's sent me to pick up his eggs.' She placed her wicker basket on the counter.

A flicker of understanding crossed Connie Mauger's face.

'Ah yes, four large eggs coming up.'

Grabbing the basket, she turned round, pulled the news-sheet from under the lining and slipped it into her apron pocket.

'I'll wrap them in newspaper to stop them breaking. We can't have them damaged now, can we?'

'Thanks – that's kind of you.' Lydia handed over the ration book.

'Next time we might have a bit of gammon.' The shopkeeper gestured at the silent bacon slicer. 'I heard you were doing your bit at the church. The rector must be glad of the help.'

Lydia's pulse quickened. She hadn't expected small talk. 'Oh – er – actually I'm filling in at the school now, seeing as most of the teachers have gone to England.'

Mrs Mauger shook her head. 'It's a poor do, sending our youngsters away like that. They must be quite homesick, don't you think?'

Lydia was about to reply when the shop bell burst into life.

'*Guten Tag.*' The young soldier, barely out of his teens, doffed his cap and bowed towards them.

'Good morning to you. I've not much food today, I'm afraid.' Mrs Mauger's smile was set. 'Folk are buying in for Christmas now.'

'I do not need the food.' The soldier shook his head. 'Only matches.'

Lydia made for the door. 'I'll be off then. Good day to you both.' Once outside, her skin broke into a cold sweat. Connie Mauger must have seen the soldier coming and kept her chatting to calm her nerves. She walked slowly down the lane, her pulse racing. As soon as the shop was out of sight, she broke into a sprint and ran for her life.

Later that day Lydia arrived home exhausted. Since her first drop at the grocery store she'd kept her conversation to the minimum, appreciating the need for a quick exit. She'd visited the Emergency Hospital, the Guernsey Purchasing Commission, several shops in the arcade and finally the Priaulx Library, leaving the news-sheet in a pre-arranged position where it could be accessed easily. The library was the worst as the place was full of soldiers. Though she'd tried to appear nonchalant, the fear of a hand gripping her shoulder had rendered her immobile. Breathing deeply, she hummed a carol under her breath and gazed intently at the shelves until the fear ebbed away.

When she got home, Lydia climbed on to her bed and pulled the counterpane tightly round her shoulders, like she did as a child when the nightmares came and water slammed into her nose and mouth until it smothered her face. If the truth were told she was both scared of the enemy and scared of appearing weak, especially in front of Martin. At least they were friends and for that she should be grateful. Anything more was out of the question.

'Will you have a glass of Flo's sherry, my love?'

'What for?' Emily frowned at her husband.

'It's Christmas Day – we always have sherry on Christmas Day.'

'I will celebrate the birth of Christ, as I always do, Jack Le Page.' Emily pursed her lips. 'But as for sherry, not one drop will pass my lips until the Germans leave our island. I don't care how long it takes.'

'You should have gone to church with Flo,' he sighed. 'It's no good sitting here moping.'

'I'm not moping. As a matter of fact, I'm just making my stand against the enemy.' Emily's eyes filled with tears.

She watched as Jack sat down in his armchair by the fire, though it wasn't exactly *his* chair – he'd left that at Sea Breeze. This one had belonged to old Alf Brouard. Today a fire burned brightly in the grate, for the first time in weeks. It had been worth Flo sacrificing that old wooden stool in the attic to keep them warm.

A loud bang interrupted Emily's thoughts.

'Quick, Jack. There's someone at the door.'

Good King Wenceslas looked out
On the Feast of Stephen
When the snow lay round about
Deep and crisp and even.'

Jack pulled open the door.

'Liddy! Reverend Martell! What a surprise. I thought you were carol singers.'

'We are.' Flo's cheeks were the colour of ripe apples. 'We've been singing our hearts out all morning. Don't just stand there – welcome us in. It is Christmas Day, after all.'

'I never expected to see the rector, not on Christmas Day.' Emily beamed as if God himself had come calling. 'This is a great honour.'

'You have to thank Mrs Brouard for that.' Martin smiled at their hostess. 'She didn't like the thought of you missing church, so she kindly invited us round.'

Emily straightened the collar of her pin-tucked blouse. She'd have worn a dress if she'd realised they were having company. Watching Lydia chatting happily to the rector she felt a stab of envy. Her daughter had a poise that she, Emily, had never possessed. Lydia wore her clothes with ease – a simple scarf at her neck, a flower in her lapel and she looked like a mannequin.

'Some sherry, Emily?' Flo's voice broke into her thoughts.

She held out her glass. 'Just a little one, maybe?'

'How about you, Rector?'

'Yes please, Mrs Brouard. I've not tasted sherry since before the war.'

Flo beamed. 'My late husband kept it for a rainy day.' She glanced out at the winter sun. 'And though it might not actually *be* raining, I think he'd agree the time was right enough.'

The rector raised his glass. 'Here's to peace. May God bless you all.'

CHAPTER 6

'Mrs Le Quesne?'

'Yes – what can I do for you?' The grey-haired woman stood at the door, arms folded, an apron covering her thin frame.

'It's Lydia – remember? I've come from Torteval church. And I've brought you this.' She held out a pot of black butter, an ancient island delicacy made of apples and liquorice. 'I thought it might cheer you up.'

A faint smile appeared on the other woman's face.

'Come in, my dear. That's so kind. I shouldn't have left you standing on the doorstep. It's just that since—' Her voice broke. 'Since the little ones have gone I've not been out much. There doesn't seem any point.'

Hilda Le Quesne's daughter had died of TB several years ago. Since then she'd dedicated her life to bringing up her grand-children: Anne, eleven, and seven-year-old Wendy.

'It must be hard managing without them.' Lydia's eyes scanned the photographs that covered the walls. 'But I'm sure they're in good hands.'

'I had a Red Cross letter last week,' Hilda nodded. 'They're somewhere called Lytham St Annes in Lancashire. They're close to the beach and not far from the country and they've seen sheep – they'd never seen sheep as they've not been off the island before – and ridden on the railway. Isn't that wonderful?'

'Yes, it is. They'll have so much to tell you when they get home.'

'But will they – will they ever come home? I should have gone with them. Why didn't I go? There's nothing to keep me here.' She covered her head with her hands.

'The children left for the best of reasons,' Lydia said without conviction. 'You did it out of love. They're safe from the Germans, safe from the bombs, safe from—'

'But they don't have a mother, do they? I'm all they've got.' Hilda was crying now. 'It's been almost a year. I'd no idea it was going to be so long.'

Lydia shifted in her seat. 'They're young. It's an adventure for them, they've no idea that the world is at war.'

'We were told it would only be for a few months,' the old woman's voice rose into a high-pitched wail. 'They've taken my children – *they've taken my babies.*'

Lydia stretched out her hand. 'Please—'

'I'm sorry, my dear, I shouldn't behave this way. It's kind of you to call, but I'm not really up to visitors right now.'

'Of course.' Lydia stood up. She'd intended to leave a copy of the news-sheet but she changed her mind. It would only remind the poor woman of her loss. 'I'll let myself out, but if you need anything – anything at all – you know where we are. Oh – and the children will be fine, I promise.' Her eyes stung as she walked away.

That night Lydia had the dream, the one that had haunted her since childhood. She was lying on her back as the waves enveloped her, water streaming relentlessly into her lungs.

'Stop, please stop,' she shouted. 'I'm drowning, I'm drowning—' but the words grew fainter till they could no longer be heard.

*

They were sitting in the vestry, each immersed in their own thoughts: Martin scribbling notes for Sunday's sermon while Lydia cleaned the brass. She glanced at him from under her lashes. He seemed comfortable in her presence, and she was thankful for that. Anything else was just wishful thinking. Her heart pumped twice as fast when she saw him and being in such close proximity felt like agony. Sometimes she caught him staring as if he was trying to understand what was going on inside her head. How could he? She didn't understand it herself.

'I called on Hilda Le Quesne the other day,' she broke the silence at last. 'The poor woman's missing her grandchildren desperately.'

Martin looked up, his forehead creasing into a frown.

'I meant to talk to you about Hilda. More bad news, I'm afraid. Her nephew, Charlie Coutanchez, has been arrested.'

'Arrested?' The candlestick slipped from Lydia's hand and crashed to the floor. 'Why? What for?'

'For stealing German property.'

'But he's a policeman, isn't he? How can they arrest a policeman?'

'They can arrest who they like. Don't forget, Hitler makes the rules.'

'And what's poor Charlie supposed to have taken?'

'He confiscated some food one of the waiters had stolen from the Grand Hotel, then took it home for himself. Or that's the story, anyway.'

'Do you believe it?'

'It's hard to say. Hunger has no logic.'

Lydia shivered. 'Neither do the Jerries. So what will happen to him?'

'A German internment camp, I shouldn't wonder. Depends on the outcome of the trial.'

Retrieving the candlestick, Lydia rubbed it furiously, tears stinging her eyes.

'Let *me* tell Hilda. Poor Charlie hasn't got a bad bone in his body. When he was a boy, he helped Papa in the greenhouses and his face always had a smile on it. Besides, he's all the poor woman's got now.'

Martin rummaged in his pocket and handed her a handkerchief.

'Don't let anyone else see your tears. You've a heart of gold, Lydia, and I admire you for that. Just be careful, that's all. Feelings can get you into trouble.'

'What do you mean?' She lifted her eyes to meet his, hoping for some sort of recognition, but his mind was already elsewhere.

Twenty minutes later Lydia slipped unnoticed from the vestry. She'd arranged to meet her father in town and didn't want to be late.

She was out of breath when she arrived at Candie Gardens, one of the few public places still open to the islanders. Papa was sitting on a bench contentedly smoking his pipe, and his face lit up when he saw her.

'Hello, my love. Do you miss your old pa as much as he misses you?'

'No, even more.' Lydia bent down and scooped up a handful of wild flowers. 'You brought me here to play ball when I was little, do you remember? Mama didn't approve of ball games, but you said you needed your constitutional, so she let me come too.'

'Those were the days.' The old man stood up and tapped the bowl of his pipe on the bench. 'She was strict back then, your mama, but she always meant well.'

'Oh, Papa, I feel like a child again—' Lydia's words were lost on the wind as she ran ahead of him.

Jack followed behind her, pretending to limp.

'Come back, Liddy. I'm not as young as I used to be. My arthritis is playing up.'

'You're barely sixty,' Lydia grinned, rejoining her father. 'And as for arthritis – don't make me laugh, you're fit as a fiddle.'

'Apart from the old ticker,' Jack frowned, 'but the doc's sorting that for me. Now come on, tell me, how's that man of yours?'

A knot formed in her stomach. 'What man?'

'You know very well what man. The Reverend Martell. If you ask me you're sweet on him.'

'Well, I'm not asking you.' She crinkled her nose. 'I help occasionally with the school, go on parish visits, but nothing more.'

'Yes, yes, I know all that. But your eyes shine at the mention of him and that so-called church work seems to take up a fair bit of time these days.'

Lydia opened her mouth to object. She'd thought about Martin constantly since she'd started to help with the news-sheet.

'I'm very fond of him, Papa, though perhaps not in the way you mean. He struggles with his conscience every day, encouraging people to accept their lot while privately despising everything about the enemy. He wants the church to move forward, but I sometimes think he should lead by example.'

'So what do you suggest?'

'He lives in that big house on his own, for a start. He could take in families who've lost their homes to the Jerries. People need *help* now, as much as religion.' She hated lying but she needed to cover her tracks.

'Try telling him, Liddy, that's the only way.' Her father's eyes narrowed. 'How does he feel about you?'

'I think he sees me as a friend. Besides, neither of us has time for romance. He's struggling with the diktats of the *Kommandantur* and, as for me, I'll be back studying in Leicester soon.'

Jack took hold of his daughter's hands and held them in his.

'I hope you're right. But watch out for love, my girl. It can hit you when you least expect it. Come on – I'll race you to the gate.'

The following Sunday Lydia woke early. She dressed quickly in a sweater and tweed skirt, pulled on her mama's leather brogues and set off for Pleinmont Point. The wind lifted her hair as she watched the early morning sun tease its way through the hedgerows. Higher and higher she went, breathing fresh air till her head spun and her heart thudded. Reaching the top, she gazed out over the Channel towards the Atlantic, the vast expanse bringing back memories of childhood. On summer days Papa would bring her to this spot, weaving stories of mermaids and seahorses who frolicked in the waves. At lunchtime they ate fresh homemade bread, spread with butter the colour of sunshine, and drank cups of water laced with fresh lemon. Later as they walked home, Papa would give her Parma violets – tiny lilac-coloured sweets that tasted of summer – winking as he pressed them into her hand. Mama disapproved of sweets; bad for your teeth they were, she said, so these became their shared secret.

A sudden squall brought Lydia back to the present, as overhead clouds blotted out the sun. Funny how this was the only place she really felt safe. She had come here to try to make sense of her feelings for Martin. With his dark shaggy hair and unorthodox views, he seemed able at will to incense and inspire her, to lift her spirits one minute then bring them crashing down the next. Now, at last, she knew why she loved him. He reminded her of her own dear Papa. Both had a conscience. Both would break the rules to make the world a fairer place.

Lydia let out a sigh. Guernsey had been abandoned by the War Office, its people left to 'get on with it'. Food stocks were running low and folks were hungry and dispirited. Standing where she'd once stood as a child, she felt a sudden sense of purpose. If Martin needed her help, whatever the reason, she would give it gladly.

'I've brought you some daffodils, Mama.' Lydia sat down at the kitchen table. 'I picked them at Pleinmont. Do you remember when you used to pin them in my hair? I thought it made me look like a princess.'

'Those days are gone, my girl.' The older woman gave a weary nod. 'Daffodils are no use to me any more. I need food.'

Lydia loved her mother dearly, but the two of them had never really been close. Emily Le Page had steered her daughter through the trials and triumphs of childhood, like an actress perfecting her part, yet in many ways they were still strangers. Her love for her mother was returned, of that she had no doubt, but never demonstrably so. It seemed as if Mama had buried her emotions long ago, determined never to let them surface again.

Watching her now peeling potatoes at the kitchen sink, Lydia felt a wave of tenderness. 'I'm going to make us some Guernsey bean jar, Mama.' She delved into her bag and pulled out a handful of haricot beans.

'Where did you get those?'

'I bumped into Rob Falla. He *found* them on his way home.'

Emily frowned. 'But we need pigs' trotters. We can't make bean jar without them.'

'Oh, Mama – poor Reg was crying.' Lydia grinned. 'One of his pigs had died. He'd told the Jerries it must be buried quickly as it had picked up a rare disease.'

'Buried?' Her mother paled. 'And did he?'

'Of course not. The poor old pig will be roast pork soon.'

'You're so good to us, my girl.' A smile softened her lined face. 'I just wish with all my heart this war would end.'

'It will, soon enough.' Lydia nodded. 'Where's Papa, by the way?'

'He's helping the church this afternoon.'

'Papa – at the church? What's he doing there?'

'The menfolk have gathered carrageen moss from the beach for the women to make into puddings.'

'Pigs and puddings.' Lydia laughed. At least we won't go hungry tonight.'

'Am I disturbing you?' Lydia opened the vestry door and stood, half hidden, in the shadows.

Martin turned towards her, dark circles under his eyes.

'No, I'm just reading. But what are *you* doing here?' He glanced at his watch. 'It's almost midnight. You should be at home in bed.'

'I'm sick of the curfew.' She shivered. 'I couldn't sleep.'

'Wait here and I'll go and find you a blanket.' He stood up, tossing the newspaper on to the floor. 'Why the hell do the Jerries have to censor every story? Whatever happened to the freedom of the press?'

'I suppose it's gone with the rest of our freedom.' Lydia cringed at the thought of the soldier who'd raised his gun at her. 'We're always looking over our shoulders now.'

As Martin pulled the door behind him, something caught her eye, a photograph no bigger than a cigarette packet, wedged behind the skirting board. She reached over and pulled it free, her curiosity aroused. A pretty girl in her early twenties was smiling at the camera, shading her eyes from the sun. She was wearing a straw hat over corn-coloured hair, with a ribbon tied round her chin. Lydia studied the image carefully. Whoever could it be?

Bursting back into the room, Martin snatched the print from her grasp.

'Where the hell did you get that?'

'I found it on the floor here, I'm sorry, I didn't mean to—' she stammered.

'Didn't mean to pry? Is that what you were going to say? It's a bit late for that now. And if you must know, it's Janet. My former fiancée.'

Lydia's face burned. 'I didn't realise you were engaged.'

'I'm not, not now, anyway.' His eyes avoided hers. 'She saved herself from an unhappy marriage.'

Lydia gave an involuntary shiver. 'I'm very sorry.'

'Don't be. It happened a long time ago. Is there anything else you'd like to know?'

'Well, yes, there is now you mention it.' She was desperate to change the subject. 'You can tell me what's *really* going on at the church. It's not just an underground newspaper you're running, is it?'

'There's nothing to tell.' He yawned. 'I lead the church, oversee the school and do my best to thwart the enemy. If you're looking for anything deeper, I assure you I'm not your man.'

'Deeper? What makes you think I'm interested in *you*?' Anger boiled up inside her. 'Just who do you think you are, anyway?'

'I could ask you the same thing, Lydia le Page. You've abandoned your studies, volunteered your services and now you're acting as if I owe you a living.'

'I came here because I wanted to help.' The anger hardened her voice. 'Is that so difficult to believe?'

'No.' He rubbed his face then ran his hands through his hair. 'Please go home and forget we ever met. Believe me, it's for the best.'

'Best for *you*, more likely.' She spat the words from her mouth. 'Goodnight, *Reverend* Martell. We'll speak again, no doubt, when you finally find your manners.'

CHAPTER 7

Martin covered his face with his hands. Why had Lydia come here so late at night? And why did he feel so drawn to her when all his instincts told him to leave her alone? Damn him for being so harsh. Now he had made a fool of himself, he could never tell her the truth.

His thoughts strayed back to the night he first met Janet; a bohemian party on the edge of Windsor Park where wine flowed and the talk was of literature and love.

She had come up behind him, slightly the worse for wear, and covered his eyes with her hands shouting, 'Guess who?' Remembering her startled expression when she realised her mistake, his mouth broke into a wry smile.

On their first date he scarcely had a chance to get a word in edgeways. She had socially ambitious parents, two married sisters and a successful brother who wanted her to work in his law practice. Janet, meanwhile, had set her heart on fashion design.

They had great fun in the early days – he admired her strong will and her crazy sense of humour – but then the dark moods set in.

He closed his eyes and dropped his head in his hands, trying to dispel the memory. He'd been right to push Lydia away. He would only destroy her in the end.

*

The following Monday after school Lydia locked up and made straight for Maggie's shop.

Her friend's face lit up when she appeared at the door. 'What a nice surprise. Is there something you need?'

'Not really. I just needed a walk. How are you?'

'Oh, I'm all right. Still eyeing up the opposition.' Maggie winked. 'Don't look so disapproving – I'm only joking. How are you?'

'I'm fine. It's just the stupid rector. One minute we're getting on famously and the next he's pushing me away. I just don't know what he wants from me.'

'I could guess.'

'Oh, Maggie, how could you say such a thing? The man's infuriating.'

'I'll take your word for it. I still think you're sweet on him, mind.'

Lydia's cheeks flooded with colour. 'Don't be ridiculous. We're friends, that's all. Or we *were*.'

'*Friends, that's all,*' her friend mimicked. 'Okay – if that's what you want to believe.'

'Can't you see? He's bad-tempered, not to mention bigoted – and he thinks he can save us all.' She decided not to mention his fiancée.

'Well, until we're saved, I've got more important things to deal with.' Maggie held up a pair of sheer stockings. 'What do you think of these? Aren't they heavenly?'

'They're beautiful,' Lydia gasped, her troubles momentarily forgotten. 'Where did you get them?'

'Old Mrs Vibert brought them in today. I reckon she's had them since the last war. She swapped them for some bed socks.'

Lydia giggled. 'You do make me laugh. Don't you ever take anything seriously?'

'Of course not – what's the point? There's enough people round here feeling miserable.' The stockings slid through her fingers. 'Every cloud has a silver lining.'

'So come on, then, where's my silver lining?'

'He's at the church. Waiting for you now, I shouldn't wonder. See you tonight, then. And don't forget what I said.'

Lydia's heart took a dive as Martin's face appeared at the classroom door.

'May I come in?' His eyes were bright.

'Please do,' was all she managed to say. How dare he interrupt her teaching after the way he'd treated her? She turned to the class. 'Stand up, boys and girls, and say good morning to the rector.'

'Good morning, rector,' they chanted, clearly glad of the distraction.

'Please sit down—' Martin gestured with his hands, 'and carry on with what you were doing.'

'We were just learning some German. It's obligatory now.' Lydia avoided his eyes. 'Would you like to join us?'

'I'd be honoured, Miss Le Page. I might even say a few words myself. Erm – *verstehen Sie mich*?'

'Of course I understand you,' Lydia hissed. Couldn't he see she was angry? Turning to the class she said, 'Right, children – *eins, zwei, drei, vier, fünf* – one, two, three, four, five. Now copy the numbers off the board, please.'

'One, two, three, four, five, once I caught a fish alive,' a voice rang out defiantly from the back of the room.

'Thank you, Alfie.' Her eyes didn't move from the blackboard. 'You will copy the numbers – in German – fifty times over, in the back of your exercise book. I shall expect your work on my desk first thing tomorrow morning. And, if you have indeed caught a fish, I suggest you share it with the rest of us.'

'Yes, miss.'

As the children began writing, Lydia turned to Martin.

'To what do I owe this honour, Reverend Martell?'

'I came to see the headmaster so thought I'd say hello.' He ran his hands through his hair. 'I didn't know you spoke German.'

'I learned it at school, and then at college. Why do you ask?'

'Does this mean you understand what the enemy are saying?' He was whispering now.

'Mostly. It's not difficult.'

'I just didn't think... Well look, anyway, I need to apologise about the other day. I clearly made a mistake.'

Her hands flew to her cheeks. To think she'd felt attracted to him.

'There's no need to apologise. You're entitled to your opinions. Besides, your past life is none of my business.'

'I behaved very badly. I'm sorry. You touched on a nerve, I'm afraid, but that really is no excuse.'

'Thank you, Reverend, for your concern, but I have quite forgotten about it.' She kept her voice terse. 'And now, if you will excuse me, I must get on with my lessons.'

'Of course.' He turned to the class. 'Goodbye, boys and girls.'

'Goodbye, Reverend Martell,' they replied in unison.

To her dismay, Lydia blushed from her neck to the roots of her hair as he left the room.

Emily studied the newspaper, her brown tortoiseshell glasses perched on the end of her nose. Parsnips, water, carrageen moss; how she hated these wretched war recipes. Sighing, she picked up the potato peelings and covered them with boiling water. She'd promised Flo she'd make broth for dinner so she'd better get on with it.

Just then Jack appeared through the doorway, interrupting her thoughts.

'You'll let the heat out,' she tutted, jumping up and banging the door shut behind him.

'Not much bloney heat to let out these days.' He sucked on his empty pipe. 'Have you heard from Liddy?'

'Why do you ask?'

'I've not seen her for days.'

Emily stirred the contents of the saucepan, without looking up. 'She's busy with her school work, I shouldn't wonder, and there's church too. If you ask me, she does too much.'

'She's always got time for her dear old pa, though, hasn't she? Maybe she's poorly?'

'You've never grown up, Jack Le Page, that's your problem. You treat her like a child when she's quite old enough to look after herself. And don't smoke your pipe in the kitchen.'

'I'm not smoking it,' he sighed. 'I'm out of tobacco. I'm just chewing on the bloney thing. What's the harm in that?'

'It's a dirty habit, that's what, especially when there's food around.' Emily lifted the lid on the watery soup. 'If you can call this food.'

'Let's have a sing-song one evening.' Jack ignored his wife's long face. 'I've heard Bert Falla's got a crystal set. It's all hush-hush, mind, but I could ask him to bring it over. If we're lucky we might get some news from England.'

'Just be careful, that's all. The last poor soul found with a wire-less set was locked up and sent to France.'

'We've got to have hope, my girl,' he shook his head, 'even if it does mean taking risks. I'll go and have a word with Flo and see what she thinks.'

Emily busied herself with the washing up. She hadn't meant to be sharp with Jack, but she wished he wouldn't fuss so much over Lydia. One thing was certain – having their daughter back had made him feel young again. He smiled more than usual and yesterday she'd heard him humming a nursery rhyme as if the years had rolled away.

If it troubled Emily that Lydia had always been closer to Jack, she shrugged off her concerns. They were so alike, father and daughter, always worrying about others, always trying to put wrongs to right. She knew Jack gave away most of the food he grew, and she respected him for it. Before the Occupation, apart from a weekly delivery to the Channel Islands Hotel, he would take the tomatoes to hospitals, nursing homes and schools, leaving the 'extras' outside their home, for passers-by. A farrier by trade, Jack had been invalided out of the Great War by a fragment of metal that almost pierced his heart. Though he never spoke of it, the operation to remove the metal had been such a success it made medical history.

Emily sighed. She loved her husband, and always would, but their differences had grown with the passing years. Some folk said it was *she* who had changed, what with all that money and the big house on the hill. 'Above her station, she is,' they'd whisper when they thought she was out of earshot.

But then they didn't know the truth. Sometimes in the night, when the wind howled over the cliffs at Saints Bay, the fear would rise up into her throat and threaten to choke her. They had buried their secret, she and Jack, but the Lord would make them face up to it in the end.

Lydia brushed her hair till it shone, dabbing the rim of the empty perfume bottle behind her ears. Though its contents were long gone the lingering scent still lifted her spirits. Her parents were having a sing-song tonight with a few friends and she was looking forward to a lively evening. She took one last look in the mirror. The burnt orange silk dress had seen better days but it showed off her hazel eyes, which thankfully had not quite lost their sparkle.

Since the day Martin had come into her classroom Lydia had tried her hardest to avoid him. She'd been to church as usual, disappearing discreetly before the end of the service, and kept up her parish visits without seeking his advice. She was hurt, bitter even, at the way he'd spoken about his fiancée, but that only made her more determined to stand her ground. The love she felt for him would never dim but right at this moment he had lost her respect.

By the time she got to Flo Brouard's the party was in full swing. Her mama greeted her with a hug. 'You're just in time for the broadcast. I still think it's a bit of a risk but Jim and Flo are all for it.'

'Ssshh – it's the news next.' This came from Bert Falla , who was clutching his crystal set like a mother with her new born son. The room fell instantly silent.

'The House of Commons has been informed today that the German battleship Bismarck *has been sunk with more than 2,000 crew on board. The* Bismarck *had been a specific target of the Royal Navy and the Royal Air Force following the loss of the British battle cruiser* HMS Hood.*'*

'No wonder the Jerries don't want us to hear it,' someone gasped. 'We're winning the war… *We're winning the war!'*

Everyone hugged, shouted and cheered as Bert hurriedly replaced the set in its box. 'I'll put this back in my saddlebag,' he said, a triumphant smile stretching from ear to ear.

'Come on, let's sing.' Flo's voice rang out 'All together now, one, two three… *Keep the home fires burning, while your heart is yearning, though the boys are far away they dream of home—'*

Lydia thought fleetingly of Martin. Here they were in Flo Brouard's parlour, cocking a snook at the enemy, while he, doubtless, was alone with his thoughts. She had no sympathy. He didn't know what he was missing. Jumping to her feet she joined in the chorus at the top of her voice.

'*Turn the dark clouds inside out, till the boys come home.*'

'So how are you, Liddy, my girl? Jack's face softened. 'Exhausted, I bet, after all that singing. Come and sit next to me.'

'I'm fine.' Lydia dropped down beside her father on the sofa. 'I enjoy teaching and it keeps me out of trouble.'

'I should bloney well hope so.' He winked over the top of his pipe. 'And how's the Reverend Martell?'

'Martin? Oh, he's immersed in the lives of the parishioners. We don't get much time to talk these days.'

Jack patted her hand. 'There's always time to talk, if you ask me. Otherwise, what's the point of it all? These blasted Jerries think they've got us under the thumb, but we know different. The Allies are fighting back – we will win this war, Liddy, just see if we don't.'

'Of course we will, Papa.'

'That's what I like to hear.' He winked. 'Now – don't tell your mother but I've saved you my last piece of bread.'

The following morning Emily woke at sunrise. Glancing at the empty pillow beside her, she padded downstairs to the kitchen where Jack was already hard at work.

'What're you doing up so early?' she asked.

'Mincing up cabbage for dinner,' Jack smiled. 'That was a good night, eh, my love? The best we've had in ages.'

She nodded. 'A bit risky, though, Bert Falla bringing his wireless here.'

'There's plenty of folk with crystal sets under the floorboards. Jerry can't send us all away now, can he?'

'I hope not,' she sighed. 'So what did you make of our Lydia?'

'I reckon she's all right. She's made of strong stuff, that one, so I wouldn't worry yourself too much.'

'You were the one who was worrying, Jack Le Page, don't forget.' Emily fetched the flour from the pantry. 'I asked her about the rector but she wasn't for telling me anything. A pity. They'd make a lovely couple. I suppose I'd got up my hopes.'

'Well, you'd better just get 'em down again. Liddy's no time for all that nonsense, if you ask me.'

'And you know best, don't you, Jack Le Page? You always know what's best for Lydia.'

The genial smile disappeared. 'No more, please, Emily. That subject, as you well know, is closed.'

Emily pursed her lips. He could keep quiet for as long as he liked. But one day they'd both have to face the consequences of what they had done.

CHAPTER 8

Jack marched into the drawing room, muddy boots forgotten.
'I saw him, the rotten, no good—'

'Saw who?' Emily looked up, startled.

'The blighter who kicked us out.'

'The Kommandant?'

'Nah – his lackey – the big bullish chap. He was In the post office in Smith Street, acting like he owned the place.'

'You didn't speak to him, did you?' She was frightened now.

'I couldn't help myself. I felt like I wanted to kill him with my bare hands. Ordering everyone about, he was, telling them what to do, if you please. He yelled at me to get out so I stuck my tongue, swore at him and scarpered.'

Emily covered her face with her hands, but Jack hadn't finished. 'There's none of our people serving behind the counter now. They're all Jerries – did you know that? Who do they think they are, eh? Coming over here with their bombs and guns. Robbing folks of their jobs and their homes.' He threw his cap on the floor.

'It doesn't matter about Sea Breeze, really, if that's what you're thinking.' Awkwardly, Emily held out her arms. 'It broke my heart at the start. But we've got Lydia back, that's all that matters, isn't it?' She hesitated. 'And we've got each other.'

Jack leaned on her shoulder, his face purple. 'I'm sorry, my love. You're right, I know. It's just an old man getting carried away.' He slumped down into the chair, resting his head in his hands. 'This blasted war. It'll get the better of me one day.'

'Never.' She grabbed the kettle from the hob. 'Come on, Jack Le Page, I've just picked up our rations. Let's toast our health with a cup of *real* tea.'

Emily poured steaming liquid into two china cups, adding a drop of milk to each. What on earth had got into her husband? In all these years she'd never seen him so angry. From being a young lad, he'd been happy to work in the greenhouses, never complaining or saying a cross word to anyone. When they'd come into money he'd carried on the same way – only now the greenhouses were his instead of somebody else's. Stubborn he could be sometimes, even downright awkward, but never angry.

Putting these thoughts aside she asked, 'How's that greenhouse of Flo's doing?'

'I've got the vines back healthy, right enough.' Jack's face softened. 'They were old Alf Brouard's pride and joy. The place'll be full of geraniums soon, just like Sea Breeze. Little Liddy used to love the geraniums.'

Emily smiled. When Lydia was small he'd taught her how to grow beans and peas, raspberries and loganberries in her own vegetable patch. She learned to value the things money couldn't buy, like sunshine, flowers, the smell of sweet peas and a rainbow at the end of the day. Yes, Lydia knew Jack better than anyone. She would know what to do.

Later that afternoon Emily arrived at the door of Torteval School.

'Mama!' Lydia's face lit up. 'What are you doing here? Would you like some homework, too?'

'Bah – you get cheekier every time I see you. I've come to walk you home, seeing as the sun's out.'

'Give me one minute and I'll be right with you.'

Lydia s reappeared with a handful of books in one hand and a key in the other. Pushing the key through the ancient lock she turned it till she heard a loud clunk.

'So, how's the Reverend Martell these days?' asked Emily, as they set off down the road. 'Still causing a bit of a stir, from what I hear.'

'What do you mean, Mama?'

'Well, you know – he's outspoken, with a bit of a puzzling past – some folks can't fathom him at all.'

'No, I don't know, Mama. Why do you have to listen to gossip? And what's wrong with wanting to modernise the church, anyway?'

'Nothing, if you've got the church's welfare at heart. But I've heard he stands in the pulpit challenging the old stalwarts in their Sunday best hats. We can't all be young and handsome, can we?'

Lydia suppressed a smile. 'And we can't all be fuddy-duddies either, Mama. This is 1941, don't forget, and if it wasn't for the war we'd be much more progressive.'

'You've changed since you went to England, Lydia. I hardly know you these days. I wish you could be a bit more like Maggie.'

'Oh, Mama. Maggie's my best friend, and always will be, but you gave me a good education, a chance to do something with my life. You don't begrudge me that, surely?'

Emily shook her head. 'We always wanted the best for you, your papa and I, but you're still a Guernsey girl, and don't forget it.'

'I won't, I promise. Now, what are you really here for? Is something worrying you?'

'How do you know?' Emily pursed her lips.

'You've got that look on your face. The one that spells trouble.'

'It's Papa. He's not right, I tell you. Not right at all.'

Lydia stopped walking. 'Is it his heart?'

'His head, more like. He swore at that German officer – the one who threw us out of our home. Says he'll swing for him, no less. I've never seen him so angry in all my life.'

'Oh, that's just talk. Maybe it's his way of protecting you. Of proving that he cares?'

'He's a funny way of showing it.' Emily blinked back a tear. 'Nothing's the same anymore. We've lost our home, most of our possessions, and now we live in fear of our lives.'

Lydia clutched her mother's arm. 'We're safe as long as we stick to the rules. And that means no yelling at the enemy. Now take this hankie. I'll have a word with Papa, I promise.'

'Would you?' Emily blew her nose. 'I know he'll listen to you.'

Lydia rose at dawn the next day and set off for the fish market. She'd heard they might have mackerel today, and mackerel was Mama's favourite fish. Walking in the sunshine along the Esplanade she felt a tiny surge of hope. Herm Island rose up in front of her, like the face of a trusted friend, and the clear sky above seemed to herald the start of summer. She stopped to gaze at the shoreline, watching the pebbles as they journeyed back and forth on the tide.

As she shaded her eyes, Lydia's mind slipped back to a summer's day at L'Ancresse Bay when she was barely eight years old. The beach had been crowded then; children played in the rock pools and splashed in the sea, families sat side by side with sandwiches and flasks of tea stretched out on the sand, old men in deckchairs, their eyes closed, faces tilted towards the sun.

'Look, Papa – they've got ice cream here,' she'd shouted. The shiny new ice-cream van was a few yards away behind the stone wall. Her father pressed a penny into her hand and watched as she walked up the slipway. Then she saw it – a pure white seagull, its head trapped in a gorse bush, its wings flapping wildly as it tried to escape.

She ran to the rescue, excited at first, and then worried what would happen to the stranded bird if she couldn't do anything to save it. Stretching her arms out, she tripped and fell into the sand dune, landing on her back with a thud. She watched, helpless, as the seagull cut loose and soared away above her head. Her eyes scanned her makeshift prison for a way out but all she could see was sand. The sounds of the beach had disappeared, and the wind whipped her hair from her face. Slowly she opened the palm of her hand, but the penny was no longer there.

It was then that Lydia started to cry. What if she couldn't get out of the hole? How could she explain the lost penny? And how long would it be before Papa came to find her? They would be late for tea and Mama would be mad and, oh, how she hated it when Mama was mad. It was several minutes before Papa's worried face appeared, the longest minutes of her short life. To this day she could still hear him murmuring into her ear as he carried her back to safety, and the thud of her own heartbeat as she clung to him for all she was worth.

The screech of a car hooter brought Lydia back to the present. A German jeep careered along the Esplanade in front of her, almost knocking her off her feet. Dusting herself down, she stepped back on to the pavement, lifted her chin skyward and hurried on towards town.

Lydia had always loved the fish market; the noise, the smell, the rows of stalls laden with food. She could picture the lobsters with their huge claws waving out of the cooking pot and the crabs edging sideways along the granite slab, their fate also sealed. Today as she approached the market hall, its blue roof tiles rounded like fish scales, the stalls were almost empty, save a few at the far end where women and children clustered around.

'Mrs Le Quesne! How are you?'

The old woman at the back of the queue looked paler than usual, but she smiled wanly when she saw Lydia.

'Not too bad, my dear. It's a long time since I've come into town, but I heard there might be some fish today. I always was partial to a bit of mackerel, but I'd be glad of anything.'

Fishing – once Guernsey's pride and joy – was now a dying trade. Every boat that took to sea carried a German soldier to prevent islanders from trying to escape to England. As if that wasn't enough, around three quarters of the catch had, by law, to be handed back to the occupying forces.

'I'm sure we'll get some mackerel today,' Lydia reassured her. 'Tell me, have you heard from the children?'

Hilda Le Quesne's face lit up. 'I got a Red Cross message last week.' She pulled it out of her bag and began to read. '"*Wendy fine. Can now ride bicycle. Anne doing well at school. Both girls growing fast and making new friends. Sending all their love to Grandmama*".'

'That's wonderful news.' Twenty-five words were the maximum allowed, and even these were censored. But at least they brought comfort, Lydia thought, steeling herself for the next question. 'And how's your nephew?'

'Charlie's gone away.' Hilda stared at the floor. 'I think he's in France now. I don't understand this war work but he had no choice, so I know it must be important.'

Lydia stifled a groan. War work! So that's what the police had said. No wonder they wanted to give her the news themselves.

It made sense, she supposed. If Charlie was in an internment camp, he at least had a chance of survival. And this way it saved the old woman from more heartbreak.

'I'm sure you're right,' she managed at last.

'You won't mention it to a soul, will you, my dear? I've been sworn to secrecy.'

'Your secret's safe with me. Now come on, Mrs Le Quesne, if we keep our places there should be enough fish for both of us.'

Lydia carried the mackerel back along the Esplanade, clutching the precious package to her chest as if it were made of gold. Her parents deserved a treat and she couldn't wait to see the look on their faces when they unwrapped the parcel. Since that dreadful day at the post office, Papa had looked pale and drawn, barely making an effort to speak to his family let alone anyone else. He seemed older and slower somehow as if some unseen burden was weighing him down. He'd loved and protected Lydia all her life and she dearly wished she could give him something back. She shivered as a gust of wind blew off the sea. It was almost a year now since the Occupation began. *Please God, let it be over soon.*

Emily and Jack were resting in the parlour when Lydia arrived at the back door.

'Can I smell mackerel?' Her mother raised her head.

'You can, Mama – I've got enough for all of us. You'll not sleep hungry tonight.'

Her mother's eyes filled with tears.

'You're a good girl, do you know that?'

Lydia smiled broadly. 'Stay there, both of you, and keep your feet up for a change while I get the fish on the stove.'

Emily scanned the newspaper as her daughter vanished into the kitchen.

'Have you seen this here about the Jews in Jersey?'

'What about them?' Jack tapped his pipe on the heel of his shoe.

'They're rounding them up. Hitler's orders.'

'Rounding them up? That's crazy. What harm can the poor souls do?'

'Their shops are being taken over by *Gentile administrators*.' She tripped over the unfamiliar words. 'They're putting up signs reading: "Jewish Undertaking".'

Jack shook his head. 'How the devil do they know who's Jewish?'

She read it out loud, her voice cracking as she did so.

'"Anyone with grandparents who belonged to the Jewish religion is deemed to be of the Jewish faith and must present for registration at the island's Aliens Office." *Mon Dieu* – that must be terrifying.'

'Well, I for one don't care about their bloney old rules. I've bought my tobacco from Joe Jacobs for years and if I have my way I'll do it again. It's nothing to do with us.'

'You're right, Jack.' A prickle of fear ran down Emily's spine. She reached over and patted his hand. 'Nothing to do with us at all.'

CHAPTER 9

Lydia was heading back home when she caught sight of her father at the top of Smith Street.

'Papa!' She waved her arms in the air. 'Papa – it's me.'

Smiling broadly, she started up the road towards him. How she wished they could meet more often. Just then a German car appeared in front of her, blocking her view.

She heard an engine revving and someone shouting, 'Watch out!'

A piercing scream filled the air followed by a loud bang.

'Papa – Papaaaa… Are you all right?'

Someone grabbed her by the shoulders and dragged her back down the street. 'Let me see him, *let me see him,*' she screeched, struggling to get free.

The soldier's eyes were full of hatred.

'Too late for him to have help now.'

Lydia stood in the police station, her eyes raw with tears.

'My father – Jack Le Page – I need to know how he is.'

The constable nodded. 'And you are?'

'Lydia Le Page.'

'I believe you witnessed the accident?'

'It wasn't an accident. The German officer drove right into him. I saw it with my own eyes. Have you any news?'

The policeman shuffled awkwardly on the spot.

'Your father died of his injuries before he got to the hospital. There was nothing anyone could do.'

'Died?' Lydia recoiled in shock. 'You must be mistaken. He was on his way to see me. He'd been making a bicycle tyre out of hosepipe – he's good at that and there's such a demand these days what with the war on and no other means of transport—'

'Sit down, please, miss – can I get you a drink of water?'

'Mama, where's Mama?' Lydia's voice rose to a shriek.

'She's on her way to the hospital now, miss. Would you like me to take you there, too?'

Lydia nodded dumbly as her world began to unravel around her. The tears came slowly at first, trickling down to her lips until the bitter taste of salt filled her senses. She heard a scream, distant, removed, as if it belonged in another world. Then came the sobs, deep and rhythmic, right from the centre of her soul.

She remembered little of her journey to the hospital. Outside, the trees waved in the breeze as they'd always done, the gardens were full of flowers – blue, red, yellow and scarlet fluttering in the warm breeze – but inside, her world was colourless, withered and empty. The policeman helped her out of the vehicle and accompanied her to the matron's office. He cast her a pitying smile and then disappeared.

Matron led the way through the long corridor, her starched white cap rising and falling with each step. Stopping outside a pair of scuffed wooden doors she pushed firmly with both hands.

Emily Le Page stood upright by her husband's body, her face motionless, her eyes devoid of tears. Seeing her daughter, she ran forward and held out her arms.

'Mama, tell me he isn't gone.' Lydia clung to her mother, silent sobs shaking her frame.

'He's gone to a better place, my girl. He loved you more than you'll ever know, and I loved him.'

'Did you, Mama?' Lydia looked up. 'Did you ever tell him?'

'I didn't need to. We had no secrets. He knew everything, my Jack.'

'Oh, Papa—' Lydia inched towards her father's bed and stroked his lifeless hand. 'Why did it have to be you?'

'God takes the good ones,' Emily whispered. 'That's how it's always been.'

'God didn't take Papa.' Lydia shivered. 'The Germans did. And the Germans will pay – I promise.'

The polished oak coffin rose on the arms of the pallbearers, their eyes cast to the ground. Inching its way down the aisle, the procession came to rest at the foot of the altar.

'Oh, Papa,' Lydia whispered. 'We had so much more to—' the words died in her throat as the organ above them burst into life. Instinctively the mourners rose from their seats as the notes dipped and soared like the wings of a giant eagle; happy, joyful notes that lifted her broken heart.

Lydia began to sing, softly at first then stronger, louder, till her words rang out – a lone voice among the mourners.

'Land of Hope and Glory—'

First one, then another joined in until the walls of the ancient church echoed with song. She turned to the congregation, every one of them linking arms against the enemy. Beside her Emily Le Page stood upright, Jack's blue checked handkerchief clutched in her right hand.

"'I am the Resurrection and the Life, saith the Lord: he that believeth in me, though he were dead, yet shall he live, and whosoever lived and believeth in me shall never die.'" Martin's grey eyes locked on the prayer book in front of him.

As the congregation sat down, he lifted his head, the frown leaving his face.

'The day I met Jack Le Page he was in his greenhouse, tending to the first crop of the season. Looking me in the eye, he held out a young green tomato, his face full of pride, because he'd nurtured the plant from a tiny seed. Jack was a family man who, like the seed, never forgot his roots. He dedicated his life to his wife and daughter who stand here today side by side, as a testament to his love. Jack died on June the eighteenth 1941, aged sixty-one, defending his homeland and everything it stood for. We are here today to celebrate his life, his courage and his dedication to all he held dear. Jack Le Page – we salute you.'

Lydia looked round the church. They were clapping their hands, every single one of them: man, woman and child, applauding her beloved father.

Clutching her mother's arm, she whispered, 'It wasn't just you and me, Mama. They all loved him, too.'

Lydia stood in the Foulon Cemetery, her mind lost in time. Fine rain clung to her face, camouflaging the tears.

'Earth to earth, ashes to ashes, dust to dust.' Struggling with grief, she bowed her head as the coffin was lowered into the ground. Her strong, stubborn, courageous father, her best friend in the whole world, had gone.

'Will you come back to the house, Reverend Martell?' Emily looked straight at the rector. 'To Mrs Brouard's? I know Jack would have wanted you to. Tell him, Lydia, tell him it was your papa's wish.'

Lydia nodded politely. 'Of course, you are very welcome.'

'I wouldn't want to intrude, ladies.' Martin's eyes flitted nervously from one to the other.

'Just do as she asks, please,' Lydia whispered. 'That's all that matters now.'

Back at the bungalow, Flo had done them proud. The parlour

table was laden with food: a bain-marie full of tomato soup, home-made relish, tinned ham that she'd kept from before the war, a large pot of black butter and, in the centre, a bowl of fresh ripe strawberries.

'I'm so sorry for your loss, my dear.' Flo's eyes shone with tears as she hugged Lydia. 'You're a good girl, God bless you. You don't deserve this.'

Lydia picked up a strawberry and placed it on her tongue. It tasted of rosehips, cool spring water and honey warmed by the sun.

'Papa didn't deserve this,' she lifted her chin in defiance. 'He should still be at home, working in the garden he loved.'

'Ah, *ma chérie*, Sea Breeze.' The old woman's eyes filled with tears.

Lydia's mouth creased into a wistful smile. 'If I'd had my way we'd still be there now, laughing and singing, away from the worries of the world.'

As a young child, Lydia loved to play with Papa in the gardens surrounding their home. She had wanted to stay there forever, but one wet September day Mama dressed her in a stiff white blouse and plaid skirt and her father walked her to school. She closed her eyes as her mind travelled back through the years.

'Papa – is any man in the whole world better than you?' Looking up, five-year-old Lydia had lost her footing and slipped into a puddle.

'Why do you ask?' Jack Le Page picked up his daughter, tucked her under his arm and carried her across the playground.

'Because I don't want to leave you. I don't want to go to school. Can't we go back and play hide and seek – just like we always used to?'

'Bless you, my girl. Your mama and me, we love you very much and that's why we're sending you here today. You were born on Christmas Eve, my love, really and truly a gift from God.' Jack wiped his eye, depositing his daughter outside the vast wooden door. 'There now, you can walk into school without slipping.'

'Don't leave me, Papa, please.'

'I'll be waiting for you at home time. Now run along inside.' Turning to wave, he walked down the lane and disappeared.

Lydia opened her eyes, glancing round at the mourners, their conversation stilted, their faces without expression. This time Papa wasn't coming back.

'Can I come in?' Martin stood outside the classroom running his hands through his hair. 'I need to talk to you.'

'Of course.' Lydia's heart jolted. 'The children have gone now. I'm just doing some preparation for tomorrow.'

He followed her into the room. 'Look, Lydia—'

'Just say it, Martin. There's been too much misunderstanding between us already.'

'Right, then I will. Can we just forget our differences? I know you're still in mourning, but I've really missed having you around. Whatever I said to you I bitterly regret. You're the last person in the world I want to hurt – especially now.'

He looked so vulnerable standing there, his stiff white collar dipped at a crazy angle, his dark eyebrows knitted together.

'If you're sure that's what you want.' She pretended to straighten a sheaf of papers. 'It meant a lot, you conducting the funeral service. Papa liked you. I know he did because he told me so. Sometimes I think you reminded him of himself when he was young.'

'Hot-headed, you mean?'

'Let's just say you follow your own heart.'

'And do you, Lydia?'

'I'm trying to.' A nervous smile tugged at the corners of her mouth.

'In future—' he patted her shoulder clumsily, 'I'll try not to make it more difficult.'

'Thank you, Martin. I'd appreciate that very much.'

Walking towards the door, Martin swivelled his head round to face her again.

'Meet me on Saturday morning, nine o'clock at the top of the old quarter.'

She nodded in assent, but he had already closed the door.

Lydia rose before dawn. She put on the clothes she'd chosen with care the night before, and then brushed her hair and pinned it to one side with a tortoiseshell comb. Glancing in the mirror, she pinched her cheeks to add some colour and set off for town. Her heart lifted at the prospect of seeing Martin again. She'd missed him these last few weeks – his sense of humour, the way he crumpled his eyes when something troubled him or smiled when he thought she wasn't looking. She never wanted to fall out with him in the first place and now, maybe, they could be friends again, even if nothing more.

Lydia saw him instantly, his forehead creased into a frown, his eyes gazing out over the old harbour.

'Martin.' She ran the last few yards without stopping for breath.

'Lydia – thank you for coming. I'm so glad you're here. I have something important to tell you.' He held her gaze. 'I should have told you sooner, but I needed to be sure.'

'What is it?' Her stomach flipped over.

'You were right to question me about the church. There *is* more to my work than the news-sheet. GINA's an important part of it, yes, but there's something else, too—'

'What do you mean, something else?'

'As you know, I run a prayer group every week at the rectory and sometimes at other people's homes.' He glanced nervously around. 'To gather, shall we say, information about the enemy. Church is the only place allowed to hold public meetings these days, so the Jerries leave us alone.'

'I see.' She swallowed hard. 'But why are you telling me this now?'

'Because I want you to join us.'

'Join you? What could *I* do to help?'

'You believe in the cause.' He studied his hands. 'And I hope you believe in me.'

'You know I do, Martin.'

'I want you to think hard before you give me your answer. There are so few of us and so many of them. It could cost you—'

'My life? Is that what you mean?'

'Let's just say it could cost you a great deal. Do you understand?'

'I understand. But there's one thing I need to know. How did you get involved in the—' She hesitated.

'Resistance? You can say the word, Lydia.'

'All right – the Resistance.' She held his gaze.

'You'd have to know about my past to understand that.'

'So, tell me, when you're ready to, that is.' She mustn't let her feelings get in the way. 'Then I'll give you my answer.'

CHAPTER 10

Two weeks had passed with still no word from Martin. The silence made Lydia uneasy. Did he lead the Resistance? What other explanation was there? She stood at the scullery sink absentmindedly stripping leaves from the sweet peas she'd picked that morning. Thrusting the flowers into a glass bowl, she carried them through to the drawing room and set them down at the side of the hearth where miniature copper milk cans were lined up like soldiers ready for battle. It was high summer and streaks of sun shone through the chintz curtains, adding a warm glow to the room. Lydia stared at her reflection in the mantel mirror and pulled a face; her skin was pale, her hair hanging limply round her face. Since her father had died she had lost interest in many things, including her appearance. She knew Mama was suffering, too, but the older woman remained out of reach.

After the funeral Lydia had offered to stay on at Flo's bungalow but Mama insisted it wasn't necessary.

'There's two of us widows together now,' she said simply, 'and we can keep one another company.'

Lydia tried to understand. She and her mother were both grieving, both trying to come to terms with their own loss. Sometimes they were like two strangers forced to sit in the same compartment on a train, exchanging newspapers, passing the time of day, all in an atmosphere of polite indifference. Maybe this was Mama's way of coping. Lydia had read somewhere that grief could make people do strange things. She wished she could speak to Martin, for he was used to dealing with grief. It seemed so long since they'd spoken. Besides, it was time he told her about his past.

She was standing by the Weighbridge staring across the harbour when a voice interrupted her thoughts.

'How are you today, Lydia?'

'Martin! You made me jump.' She swivelled round. 'It's ages since I've seen you.

'I've been busy, that's all. Sorry if I startled you. Come, walk with me.'

They walked in silence down the Esplanade till they approached the Val des Terres, the sound of their footsteps echoing between them. As they started up the steep incline he finally spoke.

'I promised to tell you about my past, so here goes. I was only young when I went to theological college. I thought I could make a difference, you know by bringing the Church of England into the twentieth century. It was around that time I met Janet and I realised that she supported me in my beliefs. She was lively and intelligent and seemed to want to change the world, too. After I was ordained at St Phillips Church, St Helier – we got engaged, but unfortunately the relationship broke down. The reasons were very complicated. Her personality had changed, and she became moody and withdrawn. I wanted her to see a doctor but she wouldn't. I said it might be best to postpone the marriage till she was feeling better.' Martin stopped suddenly and put his head in his hands. 'She threatened to sue me for breach of promise.'

Lydia drew a deep breath. 'Go on.'

'A week later I was summoned to the mainland by my bishop and asked to "repent my sins". I refused. They decided not to de-frock me as the publicity would give them a bad name. I was banished to a teaching role in Africa. They brought me back to the Channel Islands just before the war started, but I have lived with my shame ever since.'

Lydia stood motionless, watching the evening sun as it shimmered through the trees.

'I'm sorry, Martin,' she said, at last. 'It can't have been easy for either of you.'

'It's the past. It's of no significance now. I've one goal in life and that's to destroy the enemy.'

'What happened to Janet?'

'She left me,' his voice wavered, 'and never came back. Is there anything else you need to know?'

'The prayer group,' Lydia smiled in defiance. 'When can I join?'

Emily clutched the wooden tongs, tugging at the wet cotton sheets till her arms ached. It was barely sunrise when she woke these days; she found little solace in sleep. Leaning over the old copper she closed her eyes, breathing the steam into the back of her throat. She picked up the blue dolly bag and turned it round and round in her hand, as if it possessed some magic power. If only she could turn back the clock.

A loud bang at the front of the house interrupted Emily's thoughts. Running down the hallway, she pulled open the door.

'Mrs Le Page?'

'Yes. What is it?'

'My name is Constable Mahon. I'm very sorry to trouble you at this difficult time. I've come to explain what happened on the day your husband, er—' He bit his lip. 'May I come in?'

She stepped backwards and gestured him through with a cursory flick of the hand.

'What is there to explain, constable?'

'The German officer – Oberleutnant Weiss – was outside the

post office in Smith Street on the day in question, arresting an islander for offences against the Third Reich. When Mr Le Page saw this, it seems he spat in the officer's face—'

'Spat in his face?' Emily bristled. 'Not my Jack. He would never do that. You must be mistaken.'

'There's no mistake, I'm afraid.'

The policeman stared at his notebook. 'It appears that the officer was still angry when he got into his car.' He coughed; a nervous rattle that hung in the air between them. 'Your husband's death was an unfortunate accident.'

'It wasn't an accident, constable, it was murder.' The words came out in a shriek. 'Nothing you say will make me think otherwise. Now if you'd kindly take your leave, I have my washing to do.'

Emily closed the door then slumped forward as her knees buckled beneath her. Then the world turned black.

'Lydia! It's good to see you.' Martin's face broke into a smile. 'Come through to the drawing room – there're some people I want you to meet.'

She watched, mesmerized, as his hands moved to the rhythm of his speech. It seemed as if an invisible thread was pulling her to him, squeezing the air from her lungs. She took in every detail: too-long hair falling in thick waves over his forehead, the grey eyes smiling from a face etched with worry, the way he leaned towards her when he spoke. If he thought his confession would push her away, he was very much mistaken.

'Thanks,' she said at last. 'It's good to be here, too.'

'I want you to meet Lydia,' Martin's voice carried across the room. 'She's joining the prayer group, so please make her feel welcome.'

She gazed at the sea of blank faces, twenty of them at least, feeling like a child on her first day at school.

'Hello, everyone.'

'How do we know she can be trusted, Reverend?' The man at the back of the room was rolling a cigarette, a fuzzy grey beard disguising his face.

'I trust her as much as I trust you, Frank, or believe me she wouldn't be here.'

'Can I ask what Miss Le Page will be doing in the prayer group?' This came from a woman of about forty-five who Lydia recognised from one of the shops on Smith Street. 'We could do with some help with refreshments. Oh – and does she know the rules?'

'She will memorise the rules tonight, like the rest of us, then she'll destroy the paper they're written on.' Martin glanced round the room. 'Does anyone else have any questions?'

'Yes, I do.' Frank lifted his hand again. 'Isn't she old Le Page's daughter? The one that ran off to England to do some learning? Bit young for the job, isn't she? Rum stuff if you ask me.'

Martin thumped the table in front of him.

'I'm *not* asking you, I'm afraid. She's still in mourning for her father, so show some respect. Anyone who objects can leave now. Is that clear?'

A hush fell on the room. Lydia cast her eyes over each one; some unfamiliar, some she remembered from childhood. Young men stood side by side with middle-aged women, looking ridiculously like judges at the annual flower show as they balanced cups and saucers in their hands. So this was the Guernsey Resistance. She'd no idea what had brought these people together or why a sense of duty had touched them all. She just wished they would be more welcoming. Heaven help her when she had to face the enemy.

Half an hour later the tension began to ease as a buzz of conversation filled the room.

'Hello, Lydia, I'm Betty.' The smiling woman with hand outstretched couldn't be more than thirty. 'I just wanted to say welcome.'

'Thanks, Betty,' Lydia smiled. 'I must say, it didn't feel very welcoming earlier.'

'Take no notice of the old fogeys. They're jealous of your youth, that's all. You're the youngest here, so be proud of it.' She reached into her bag. 'Here – take this and guard it with your life.'

The envelope contained a single page of tissue paper – the sort Martin used for the news-sheet. At the top was written the single word 'PRAYER' with a list of what looked like instructions underneath.

'Prayer?' Lydia hesitated.

'Please Remember All Your Enemy Rules, is what *that* stands for.' Betty's face creased into a grin. 'The title was my idea, but the words are Martin's. Following the rules will keep you out of danger. Can you memorise them now rather than waiting until this evening.' She winked. 'Mum's the word.'

Lydia rubbed her eyes and peered round the darkened room. Her neck ached and her right arm hung from her side like a dead weight. Arriving back at Maggie's from the prayer meeting earlier, her head was still buzzing with the rules she'd sworn to follow. With the house cloaked in silence she must have fallen asleep on the sofa.

She stood up and yawned, rubbing her arm till it burst back into life. Then she remembered the dream. She was floundering in the waves on a dark winter's day at Vazon Bay, freezing water numbing her senses. A crowd had begun to appear in the distance and soon the entire prayer group stood motionless, watching her from the shore. Why didn't they do something? Why didn't they help her? She waved her arm frantically to attract their attention, but the current pulled her inexorably towards the seabed.

Lydia shuddered. She had joined the Guernsey Resistance to avenge Papa's death. It was too late to change her mind now.

CHAPTER 11

'You didn't half give me a fright, Em.' Flo's face was the colour of snowdrops. '*Mon Dieu*! I thought you'd died on the doorstep.'

Emily lay on the sofa, a cup of tea in her hand.

'Stop fussing, I'm fine. I was just taking a nap, that's all.'

'Taking a nap, my foot! There's beds for that sort of thing and well you know it. You fainted, Emily Le Page, and that's a fact. And if I hadn't let myself in through the back door, I reckon you'd be there still. Just wait till I tell your Lydia.'

'No, please, don't tell her. She'll only worry. The poor girl's got a lot on her mind just now.'

'Like what?'

'I'm not sure, if truth be told. She seems distant somehow. She's always at the church, out all hours, from what Maggie tells me, never mind the curfew.'

'Maybe it's the rector who's taking up her time?' A smile played on Flo's lips.

'Who knows? I wish it was that simple. I reckon she's up to something. She's got a mind of her own, that one. Not to worry. It'll all come out in the wash.'

'I'm sure it will. Now then, I've made some broth with left-over bones old Tom let me have from his farm. Will you have some?'

Emily did her best to look grateful. She was empty inside and the thought of food made her feel queasy. She wanted to tell Lydia what the constable had said, but how could she? The poor girl already blamed the Germans for her papa's death. If she thought they were spreading foul rumours about him, heaven only knew what she'd do.

'It's been a long day,' Emily replied at last. 'If you don't mind I think I'll just get to my bed.'

'Don't forget the prayer group's here at the rectory again tonight, Lydia.' Martin looked up from his desk. 'I thought it might make you feel more at ease.'

She eyed him suspiciously. 'I'm not frightened of the militants among you, if that's what you think.'

'Militants? Don't be ridiculous. These are humble people trying to protect themselves. They're naturally suspicious of everyone.'

'Not me, surely? I'm supposed to be on their side.'

'Of course you are,' Martin sighed. 'But most of them live in fear. Why should they trust you? Or anyone come to that? How do we know who is the enemy?'

'I'm sorry.' She sat down in front of him. 'It's just that they seemed so hostile. It's not what I expected.'

'Not hostile, just cautious, that's all. Don't expect anything, Lydia, then you won't be disappointed.'

'Aye, aye, captain.' She gave him a mock salute. 'Now, is there anything you need me to do?'

'Just check that everyone brings a prayer book. One with a stamp inside. We don't let them in without one.' He took a copy from his desk and handed it to her. 'Best to avoid gate crashers. We start by singing a hymn. It gets us into the spirit of things and puts the Jerries off the scent. After that – well, just watch and listen. You'll soon get the hang of it. I presume you speak Guernsey French?'

'She nodded. Mama spoke to me in patois as soon as I could talk. Why do you ask?'

'Because that's what we use when we meet each other in the street. Never English.'

She smiled. '*Chuna fra-ti*? Will that do?'

'That'll do perfectly!'

An hour later the room was more than half full. *They could almost be here for afternoon tea*, Lydia thought wryly, as she collected coats and organised seating. The younger ones – mostly men – moved easily among their peers, laughing at jokes and chatting about the food shortages.

'Hello, my dear.' The woman from the grocer's shop beamed at Lydia. 'How are you settling in?'

'Not too bad, Mrs Mellanby. I'm doing my best.'

'Call me Irene.' She raised her cup to her lips. 'Real coffee, mmm… A bit more than your best as far as I can see.'

'Oh – Martin, I mean the Reverend Martell, got that before the war.'

'The war? Oh, my dear girl, we don't mention the war.' Irene winked. 'Now I've just seen an old friend of mine over there. I'll let you get on.'

Just then Martin appeared at her elbow. 'How's it going?'

'Fine, I think. It seems different tonight. Everyone's much friendlier.'

She looked at her wristwatch. 'It's curfew in just over an hour. What time does the meeting start?'

'This is it, Lydia.' His eyes skimmed the room. 'We're having an *informal* meeting. Words are being exchanged and the business is being done.'

Understanding lit up her face. 'You must think I'm stupid.'

'Not at all. None of us is an expert, we're all still learning. Don't be so hard on yourself. Oh – and Lydia?'

'Yes, Martin?'

'Stay behind when everyone leaves, will you? There's someone I'd like you to meet.'

Lydia finished washing the pots and let herself into the study.

'Who is this mysterious—' She stopped mid-sentence. 'Arthur?'

'You've already met?' Martin frowned.

'We were at junior school together. I thought you'd gone back to England?'

'I'm sorry – I had to lie to you – it was too dangerous otherwise.'

'And your wife? Is she safe?'

'She is, thank God.' He lowered his eyes.

'So, you're a part of—'

'The prayer group, yes. I helped set it up.' He winked. 'Never could resist a good anthem.'

For the next ten minutes they continued the small talk until Lydia's curiosity got the better of her.

'So why are you here today, Arthur?'

His face grew serious. 'We need some information and Martin thinks you may be able to help.'

Lydia glanced at Martin, who was staring straight ahead, a blue vein pulsating just above his brow.

'I'll try, if I can. What is it you want?'

'Intelligence that's vital to our cause.' He paused. 'It would involve you, er, getting to know the Kommandant.'

A thin bolt of fear sliced its way through her.

'Getting to know him? In what way?'

'Gaining his confidence. Making him believe you're on his side. We've heard he has an eye for a pretty face.' Arthur didn't flinch. 'It's dangerous work, mind, so we'll understand if—'

'If I decline?' Frantically she turned to Martin. Why didn't he look at her? Why didn't he say something? Had he planned this all along? 'I'm not afraid of danger.' She lifted her chin in defiance.

'We've considered this carefully, believe me, and there's no one else who could carry it off.' Arthur was still talking but Lydia was no longer listening. 'We need Major Kruger to trust you. So, if you feel you can—'

'What exactly are you asking me to do?' She tried to pull her thoughts together.

'Whatever you think might be necessary.' His voice softened. 'There's no need to answer straight away.'

Her heart thumped so hard she felt her chest would burst. She'd been wrong about Martin, and crazy to think he had feelings for her. She stared at the papers strewn across his desk, the pile of dusty hymn books, the jar full of farthings that had probably been there for years.

'I'll do it,' she said, her eyes flashing with unleashed fury. 'Whatever it takes, I'll do it.'

Arthur smiled with relief, oblivious to the tension that hung in the air like a storm threatening.

'Thank you, Lydia. You'll be approached by a member of the group within seven days.' He handed her a piece of paper. 'This is your password. In the meantime, don't ever attempt to get in touch with me – even through Martin. Is that clear?'

'Perfectly.'

'And now, if there's nothing else, I'd better be off.'

After seeing Arthur to the door, Martin returned as if nothing had happened. Picking up a pile of papers, he sifted through them. 'I didn't realise you two had met.'

'It was a long time ago. He's just a—'

'The Kommandant is a means to an end. You understand that, don't you? Nothing more.'

Lydia nodded. Who was this stranger in front of her? She hardly recognised him at all.

'You look tired.' He was moving towards her now. 'It's time you went home.'

She took a deep breath. *A few more seconds and she would be out of the room.*

'Lydia – I—'

'There's no need to explain.' A tear welled up in her eye. 'Goodnight, Martin.'

'Mama, Mama—' Lydia burst through the front door of Flo's home, her voice hoarse with excitement. 'Good news at last.'

'Whatever is it, my girl?' Emily wiped her hands on her apron. 'Come and sit down.'

'It's Freddie Le Saint. The doctors say he's well enough to leave the convalescent home.'

'*Mon Dieu* – where did you hear this?'

'I was at the hospital this morning, delivering the parish magazine. I heard the nurses talking. Freddie's the last one with bomb injuries to be discharged. Isn't it wonderful?'

The old woman's eyes filled with tears that seeped down into the worn lines on her face.

'It's a real miracle. Has anyone told his mother?'

'Mrs Le Saint was there when he got the news. She cried so much they had to sedate her. They reckon Freddie will walk again, with a bit of a limp, that's all.'

'I must get down there and see the lad.' Emily took off her apron and patted the back of her hair with her hand.

'I'll take him some of my caraway seed cake – it's still warm from the oven.'

'Don't worry.' Lydia beamed. 'We'll beat Jerry in the end.'

*

Martin appeared at the classroom door, his face grey from lack of sleep. 'Sorry to disturb you at this hour.'

'It doesn't matter. I'm just preparing my lessons for the day.' She glanced round the empty room.

'I'm relieving you of your stand-in duties here, Lydia. I'm sorry.'

'But why?' She dropped the book she was holding and got up from the desk. 'Have I upset Mr Vaudin?'

'The headmaster's more than happy with your work, but it's, let's just say, too dangerous now.'

Lydia's stomach clenched. She'd been dreading this moment.

'Sit down, please.' He handed her a thick brown envelope. 'It's time to start your new role.'

So this was it. What did she expect? To wake up one morning and simply walk into the Kommandant's life? Hands shaking, she broke the wax seal and opened the envelope.

'Where did this come from?' She scanned the pages.

'That doesn't matter. It's a fictional résumé of your life to date, omitting the time you spent in England. We couldn't risk changing your name, but thankfully Le Page is common enough here. The Jerries must never know that you left the island, or be able to trace you back to Sea Breeze.'

'I understand.' *How could he let her be a part of this? Did he care nothing for her at all?*

Martin's face gave nothing away. 'I want you to study the contents and memorise every word. Leave the envelope here, go for a walk and then come back when you think you've digested it. Then repeat the exercise all over again. Meanwhile, don't stop, or talk to anyone.'

Lydia nodded, too scared to speak. Biting her lip till it bled, she sat down and started to read.

An hour later Lydia slipped out of the back door and wheeled her father's bicycle to the school gates. The road ahead was clear except for a black-coated policeman, the strap of his helmet lodged midway across his chin.

'Good mornin', miss,' he called genially. She raised her hand in greeting and took off down the lane. From now on she couldn't trust anyone.

CHAPTER 12

Lydia stepped gingerly into the dress – pale lilac crêpe de Chine with a fitted bodice and full skirt, the collar and cuffs trimmed with Victorian lace and tiny hand-stitched pearls.

'Oh, Lydia, it's a perfect fit.' Emily's eyes shone. 'Your Auntie May would have been so proud of you.'

'Why have you kept it for so long?'

'It reminds me of my sister, that's why. And one day I hoped it might fit you.'

Emily had gone prematurely grey when May died and still looked older than her years. Her face was free of make-up, except for a dab of *papier poudre*, and her steel-rimmed spectacles were perched on the end of her nose.

Lydia glanced at the photograph of the young sisters, arm in arm, smiling broadly at the camera.

'I know how much you still miss her. She was so pretty.'

'Not as pretty as you in that dress, my love.' Emily took out a handkerchief and dabbed the corner of her eye. 'Besides, you said yourself you'd nothing to wear for the dance.'

Lydia felt a stab of guilt. 'Well, yes, but—'

'No buts, my girl. There's bound to be some important folk there and it's ages since you had a night out. It's no more than you deserve.' She gestured to the worn leather trunk at the end of her bed. 'They're all in here, your Auntie May's clothes. She had them made specially to go touring and I've never touched them since.'

'Oh, Mama.' Lydia crouched down and reached out her hand. 'It must have been so hard for you.'

'It's time they saw the light of day.' Her mother wiped the corner of her eye with a hankie. 'One or two may need bringing up to date, mind. Take them to Sophie Romerill – she'll know what to do. Now take off the dress and I'll press it properly. I'll lend you my mother's pearls and then you'll be the belle of the ball.'

Lydia slid the silk gently over her thighs. 'It's not a ball, Mama, it's a diocese dinner.' She'd had to invent the night out, but no one seemed to question the workings of the church these days. Besides, she needed to look the part to attract the Kommandant's attention. She would borrow some lipstick from Maggie (heaven knew where her friend managed to get it from) and then find some rags and curl her hair. But a family heirloom to seduce the enemy? The thought made her shiver.

Lydia swallowed the sherry in one gulp, keeping the revulsion from her face.

'Another drink, *Fräulein*?' The bartender eyed her curiously.

'Oh, yes, thank you. My friend must have been delayed.' She glanced down at her wristwatch. 'He's usually so punctual.'

The barman poured a sweet dark sherry into the curved glass and flashed her a knowing smile.

'There is no need to pay.'

'But, of course.' She lowered her eyes. 'I wouldn't dream of doing otherwise.' There was only so long she could sit here pretending to wait for her boyfriend without attracting the wrong sort of attention. She took out her compact and checked her lipstick.

'No. You not understand.' He was making her feel uncomfortable now. 'The drink is a gift from the Kommandant.' He gestured towards the table where Otto Kruger was sitting together with other Germans in uniform.

'So, *he* is the great Kommandant,' Lydia smiled. He looked old enough to be her father. 'I am honoured that he should take notice of me.'

The barman leaned closer. 'If your friend, he not come, the Kommandant, he invite you to his table.'

Nodding politely, she sipped at the sherry, checked her wristwatch again and slid down from the bar stool.

'May I, *Fräulein*?' The tall man who appeared out of nowhere had a bullish face and a false smile. 'I am asked by the Kommandant to invite you to his table.'

'That is so kind, but I was just about to leave. My friend, it seems—'

'It is not, *Fräulein*, how you say, correct, to say no to the Kommandant. Come this way, if you please.' Gently but firmly he grasped her elbow and led her across the room.

Lydia's skin prickled as the Kommandant's eyes swept over her. He was medium height with sharp features and a deep-set mouth, thin hair swept unnaturally across his forehead.

'You are a very beautiful woman, if I may say, *Fräulein* ... er...? Have we met before?'

'Le Page. Lydia Le Page. Indeed, we haven't, Herr Kommandant, though I've heard all about *you*.'

'Then I must, how you say, make amends. Please have another drink.' He raised his hand to the waiter.

Lydia lowered her gaze, her lashes grazing the top of her cheeks.

'I'd be delighted, Herr Kommandant. You are more than generous.'

Otto Kruger sat at the head of a raised table which was positioned directly in front of the piano. He addressed his companions.

'Please meet Miss Lydia Le Page who will be joining us for dinner tonight.' The officers stood up at once.

The Kommandant looped his arm in hers and pulled out a chair.

'Sit down, please, *Fräulein*.' He signalled to one of the waiters.

Fighting hard to contain her fear, Lydia took her place, a demure smile pinned to her face. A glance round the table revealed that the soldiers were well fed and groomed with no signs of the hunger facing her fellow islanders.

'I'm pleased to meet you, gentlemen,' she said. 'I hope you are finding our island hospitable.' They nodded politely and resumed their conversation.

Lydia feigned puzzlement as they discussed her in their native tongue. *'Was für eine schöne Frau!'* It was clear that they approved.

'So, Miss Le Page – may I call you Lydia?' The Kommandant gave her his full attention now. 'How long have you lived in Guernsey?'

'All my life.'

'Then I'm sure you can help us with some of the small matters that can still be, you know, confusing.'

'We must deal with this difficult time in the best way we can.'

'Exactly, my dear, exactly. And if pretty girls like you show such understanding, I'm sure we will all get along, how do you say?'

'Splendidly.'

The Kommandant's eyes narrowed. 'Indeed, *Fräulein*. Splendidly.'

Rising from her chair and murmuring an apology as the officers rose too, Lydia gestured towards the powder room and ambled over to avoid attracting attention from other tables. She pushed her way through the cubicle door and covered her face with her hands. Taking deep breaths, she tried to contain the deafening noise in her head. She *must* go through with this: it had taken weeks to prepare herself mentally and she wasn't going to give up now. Since the German officers had commandeered the Grand Hotel as their off-duty meeting place, several of the island's wealthier families had seen fit to join them. Part of her admired these islanders for refusing to be intimidated, but another part couldn't help thinking that they were buttering up the enemy. She shivered. If buttering up could avenge her father's death, then that's what she would do.

'Ah, *Fräulein*.' The Kommandant eyed her appreciatively when she returned to the table. 'You look more beautiful than ever. Come and sit down – the meal is ready.'

Lydia forced a smile. She may be hungry, but she had no intention of showing it.

Kruger gestured to the waiter to refill his glass.

'What is it, Lydia, that you do as a living?'

'My work is voluntary. I help at Torteval School, looking after the little ones when the teacher's busy.'

'Ah – you do this thing for no money! That is admirable, is it not?'

She nodded, biting into the smoked salmon.

'And you have family?'

'I live with my best friend and her parents. My own parents died a few years ago.' The lies came easily.

'That is sad, is it not? I will try to make you happy once more, *ja*?'

'You are doing so already, Herr Kommandant.' She raised her glass.

The main course consisted of lightly breaded veal with lots of fresh vegetables. Delicious as it tasted, the food seemed to lodge in her throat. What right had she to have so much when others had so little?

As they were finishing, a waiter approached the table and whispered to the Kommandant. He stood up immediately.

'Excuse me, *Fräulein,* I have to take a call on the telephone. I am sure my fellow officers will keep you entertained.' With a short bow, he was gone.

Lydia continued to feign ignorance as she listened to the conversation in German. The youngest officer, a tall man with blond hair and a gravelly voice, was explaining what he would like to do to her, given half a chance. They all sniggered.

Raising her eyes from her plate, Lydia cleared her voice.

'If you would kindly speak in English, then I could understand what you are saying.'

The blond officer winked. 'My apologies, *Fräulein*. Your meal is good, *ja*? We hope you enjoy it well.'

'Thank you,' she smiled back. 'The food is excellent.' *Better than your English, you two-faced rat,* she muttered under her breath.

Just then the Kommandant reappeared. 'It is pleasing they have kept you speaking with their little English, *Fräulein*. Forgive me for my absence.'

Gesturing to the blond officer, he leaned forward and whispered something unintelligible to him. The man saluted and hurried away.

'And now—' the Kommandant clicked his fingers, 'it is time for the champagne.'

'So, Lydia.' Arthur paced from one end of the vestry to the other. 'What did you find out?'

'Well, nothing, not yet, but I—'

'Nothing? But Kruger must have said something, surely?'

'Leave off, will you, Arthur?' Martin was sitting at his desk, trying to control his anger. 'For heaven's sake – she's only just met the man.'

'I'm sorry, I'm sorry.' Arthur held up his hands. 'You've done well, Lydia, really well. You've been introduced to the

Kommandant and he seems to have taken a liking to you. When are you seeing him again?'

'I'm not, not yet. He offered but I refused.' She frowned. 'I'm supposed to be a lady, remember?'

'Are you *sure* he didn't suspect anything?' It was Martin's turn to pace the room.

'Absolutely sure. He was a real gentleman. Or at least he acted like one. I heard his officers discussing me in German, though. They'd no idea I understood what they were saying.'

Martin's face softened.

'You need to gain their confidence. When they think they can trust you they'll be even more careless.'

Lydia's hand flew to her mouth.

'I've just remembered something. The Kommandant left the table to take a telephone call. When he got back, one of the officers excused himself and left immediately.'

'So something *is* brewing!' Arthur looked jubilant now. 'I knew it.'

'Right,' Martin interrupted. 'Let's leave it at that. Good work, Lydia.' He looked at his watch. 'Take the rest of the day off and I'll see you at the meeting tonight. As for you, Arthur – I need a word.'

As Lydia closed the door behind her, Martin's voice hardened.

'Whatever happens, I don't want Lydia compromised.'

'It's a bit late for that.' Arthur scratched his head. 'You knew what she was getting herself into, and so, I presume, did she.'

'That's as maybe, but I want you to look after her, guide her. She has no one else to confide in.'

'I'll do whatever you say, but the girl's got spirit. I think she can handle Kruger.'

'It's going to get a lot tougher, tougher than any of us imagined. Everyone's actions must be covered.'

Arthur was listening intently now. 'You know something, don't you? What is it?'

'You'll find out soon enough. In the meantime, the prayer group must never know about Lydia's part in all this. If anyone sees her with him, make them swear on their lives to keep quiet, then report back to me. Is that understood?'

'Yes, boss.' Arthur gave a mock salute. 'Understood.'

CHAPTER 13

It was well after midnight when Lydia got back to Maggie's. Stumbling over the rear porch she felt her way to the kitchen door.

'Boo!' Maggie appeared out of the shadows. 'Where have you been at this hour?'

'You startled me,' Lydia gasped. 'What on earth are you doing lurking in the dark?'

'I wasn't lurking. I was waiting for you.'

'Well I'm here now. Is everything okay?'

'It's fine, but there's something I need to tell you.'

Easing herself into a chair, Lydia rubbed her grazed ankle.

'It must be important for you to wait up. So go on.'

'I'm not really sure how to say this.' Maggie absentmindedly sucked her thumb. 'But people are *talking* about you.'

'Talking about me? Since when did you listen to gossip?'

Her friend crossed to the sink, filled the kettle from the cold tap and set it down on the range.

'They are, well, they're calling you a Jerry Bag.'

'That's ridiculous!' Lydia stiffened. 'Why ever would they say that?'

'I've no idea. I know it's not true, but someone reckons they saw you with, erm, a German officer.'

Lydia jumped up.

'A German officer?' She could hear the fear in her own voice. 'That's nonsense, it really is. What would I want with a Jerry? You know how I feel about them.'

'Of course I do.' Maggie put her arms protectively round her friend. 'But *you* know what folks are like round here. Grace Leale had her hair cut off last week, and her face painted with coal. They say she's having a German baby.'

'Oh dear, poor girl.'

'She's all right, I think. Her hair quite suits her short and—'

'Oh, Maggie, whatever am I going to do with you?' Lydia smiled, despite herself. 'I meant about the baby.'

'Oh well, yes, the baby. There'll be a few more of those born out of wedlock, I shouldn't wonder, before the war's over.'

'Mmm – perhaps. But for now, I'd ignore the gossip, and get on with your life. Smile at the enemy and don't make a fuss – it's the only way to survive.'

'Is that what they mean by collaboration?' Maggie persisted, her eyes wide with curiosity.

Lydia pretended to yawn. 'No, that's a different thing alto-gether.' The more she lied the worse she felt. 'I'm tired, I'm afraid. I didn't get much sleep last night. Don't worry about that drink. If you don't mind, I think I'll go straight up to bed.'

'Okay – but be careful, please.' Maggie gave her a hug. 'I don't want anything bad happening to you.'

'It won't, I promise. Goodnight.'

Lydia climbed the stairs, her thoughts in turmoil. Who could have seen her with the Kommandant? All the guests at the dinner that night had been German or German sympathisers and she saw no one else she knew, apart from one or two local dignitaries. Even the hotel staff were Jerries these days. Reaching her room at the top of the house, Lydia locked the door firmly behind her.

Arthur had warned her about idle gossip. What did she expect? She was a collaborator now. She threw her bag on to the tallboy and aimed a kick at the bottom drawer.

Peeling off her jumper and skirt, she climbed into bed and pulled the eiderdown over her shoulders. The warm September days had given way to autumn nights and she could feel a chill in the air. Soon they'd be facing their second winter under the Nazis and still no victory in sight. Lydia stared at the ceiling, distorted images crowding into her head. If she kept her eyes open for long enough, hopefully she'd ward off the dream.

Lydia woke with a start. She dressed quickly, let herself out of the house without making a sound and set off for town. The wind was fresh and the steel blue sky edged with fine wisps of cloud. Approaching the entrance to Cambridge Park she heard the sound of footsteps and glanced round furtively.

'Arthur – thank goodness it's you! I thought someone was following me.'

'I was, I mean I am.' Arthur fell into step beside her. 'It's not easy keeping track of you these days, especially in that outfit.'

'That's the idea.' She tugged at her navy wool coat. 'It makes me feel invisible. Is anything wrong?'

'No, don't worry. I just wanted to tell you our plan worked – Otto Kruger is smitten with you – truly smitten.'

She walked on ahead. 'How on earth did you find out?'

'Let's just say I've made a few enquiries. Believe me, you're safe, at least for now. The Kommandant suspects nothing.'

'I hope you're right.' Lydia sighed. 'I wish I could say the same about Guernsey folk. They're calling me a Jerry Bag already.'

'Don't worry. You can't keep secrets on this island. Anyway, it might even help our cause.' He gave her hand a sympathetic squeeze. 'Better a harlot than an informer.'

She attempted a wry smile. 'But who could have seen me?'

'Anyone – take your pick. Just carry on as if nothing's happened and, when in doubt, deny everything. They'll soon find someone else to talk about. Which reminds me—' he fumbled in his pocket, 'does the Kommandant know where you live?'

She nodded. 'Yes. He's seen my papers. Why do you ask?'

Arthur pulled out a cigarette, striking a match as he cupped it in his hands.

'When he contacts you – and he will – you must agree to meet him again.'

'I'll do my best, though I'm still not sure what's expected of me.' A gust of wind lifted her hair. 'I was studying to be a pharmacist, not a spy.'

'Don't worry. We'll brief you beforehand. You're not in this on your own, remember.'

'Okay, but how do I know when I'll see *you* again?'

'You don't, I'm afraid.' He inhaled the smoke with practised ease. 'Now, is there anything else before I go?'

She glanced at the cigarette. 'Can I have a try?'

'I thought you didn't smoke?' He passed it to her.

'I didn't.' She inhaled deeply. 'But I do now.'

CHAPTER 14

October 1941

As the weeks passed, Lydia spent more and more time with the Kommandant. Sometimes he would take her for a ride in his official car – an imperious-looking black Humber – always with the same sour-faced driver.

They would motor to Jerbourg and walk together along the clifftops, gazing out towards the coast of France where Hitler's army kept its stronghold. When they were alone like this Lydia would glean what she could about the numbers of aircraft on the island, or the latest regiment to be shipped in, careful to couch her questions with a smile and an innocent sweep of her lashes. If he tried to kiss her she would pull away, protesting they might be seen. She needn't have worried. People no longer pointed the finger, or called her a Jerry Bag, for fear of losing their lives. Otto Kruger was not a man to be crossed. Deep down, however, Lydia knew that tongues were wagging faster than ever.

One cold October afternoon they left the car and walked over the causeway to Lihou Island, an outcrop of rocks on the far west point of Guernsey, only accessible at low tide. Before the war the ruined twelfth century Priory of St Mary attracted many visitors, but these days it was used by German soldiers for target practice with heavy artillery. Striding alongside the Kommandant, Lydia embraced the rasping wind that rendered conversation impossible.

After twenty minutes they arrived at the furthest edge of the island, favoured by locals for its collection of rock pools, sparkling now in the winter sun.

'Tell me about these waters.' Kruger's face moved closer to hers. 'I hear they are famous.'

'The pools all have names. The one over there is the largest of all.' Lydia stretched out her hand.

'Ah yes, and what is it called?'

'It is known as the Venus Bath.' She hesitated. 'It is named after the—'

'There is no need to explain.' His eyes danced with amusement. 'Venus is the goddess of love, is she not?'

Lydia nodded, staring across the space that separated her from home. A sudden sense of fear made her shiver.

'You are cold?'

'Just a little, it's nothing.'

'But you are shaking, *Fräulein*. We must find shelter.'

'No, I'm fine, really.' She forced a smile.

'Then I will keep you warm.' Removing his gloves, the Kommandant bent forward and cupped her chin in his hand, his fingers stroking her neck as his lips found hers. His tongue explored her mouth as the full weight of his body pressed against hers.

Panic rose like bile in her throat. How could she escape from this vile man in this godforsaken place? Pushing her back against a rock, he thrust his hand clumsily through the lapels of her coat and down into her blouse, then bent his head greedily as his lips followed.

'The tide,' she shouted, wrenching free and waving towards the shoreline. 'Beware of the high tide. We must go back before the water rises.'

'You did not enjoy that, *Fräulein*?' His eyes pierced hers. 'You are a little frightened of me, perhaps?'

'I'm worried about the tide, that's all… People have been cut off before now and there's a risk of—' She was babbling, she knew, but she couldn't stop. 'If you wish to … er … kiss me, at any other time that is—' In desperation she gestured into the distance. The Kommandant's driver was waving furiously, his animated cries distorted by the wind. 'Do you think perhaps we should go?'

Otto Kruger replaced his gloves with a slow, almost mocking air.

'You are right. It is, indeed, time for us to leave. But soon, my dear Lydia, we can be together, the two of us alone. We can be somewhere a little more comfortable, perhaps. You understand?'

She nodded, unable now to hide the colour flooding to her cheeks.

'I have, how you say, embarrassed you, *Fräulein*?'

'Just a little.' She busied herself buttoning her blouse. The tide had saved her this time – but what about the next?

Sophie Romerill, Guernsey's finest seamstress, had lived in a cottage on the west coast of the island for as long as anyone could remember. Approaching the garden gate, Lydia noted the place had seen better days. Paint was peeling from the window frames, weeds were sprouting through the eaves and a broken-down chimney pot sat at a crazy angle on the roof. She gave a sharp rap on the door.

Slightly built with a head that seemed too big for her shoulders, the old woman was covered in pins and pieces of coloured ribbon, her white hair held back from her face by an old cotton scarf.

'Mrs Romerill? I'm Lydia Le Page – Emily's daughter.'

'Come in, my love. I've been expecting you.' She gestured to a narrow hallway that led into the parlour.

Lydia's eyes widened. The room was crammed with mismatched chairs, brightly coloured cushions and a variety of ancient bookshelves crammed with dress patterns. A glass-fronted cupboard full of ornaments stood one side of the hearth, while a carved oak plant stand and battered leather pouffe filled the other. In the centre stood a faded horsehair sofa.

'Find a seat,' Mrs Romerill said genially, 'and make yourself at home.'

Lydia perched on the edge of the pouffe, absorbing everything in sight.

'I have to say you come very well recommended.'

'Thank you, my dear, but there's not much call for tailoring now. I make do and mend as best I can just to keep the roof over my head.'

'And that's exactly why I'm here, Mrs Romerill. I've got some clothes that need altering – beautiful dresses and skirts that belonged to my late aunt. They've been packed away in a dusty trunk for heaven knows how many years.'

The old woman's eyes lit up. 'I'd be very happy to help.'

'There are satin shifts from the twenties, with scalloped edges and handkerchief hemlines, and a real silk chemise... I couldn't believe my eyes when I saw them.' Lydia lowered her voice. 'I was only a baby, you see, when my auntie died, in a motor accident, and we've never really spoken about it since. All these years Mama kept the clothes hidden away and now she wants me to have them.'

'You're a very lucky girl, but don't bring them all at once, mind, or someone'll rob them for the black market.'

'Don't worry, I can look after myself,' Lydia said with rather more confidence than she felt. 'Can I come again tomorrow?'

'You can, my love. We could do with a friendly face around here.'

Lydia stood up. 'Then tomorrow it is. And thanks, Mrs Romerill, it's been a pleasure to meet you.'

'Call me Sophie, please, and a pleasure it was to meet you, too.'

*

At three o'clock the following afternoon Lydia knocked on the cottage door. Getting no reply, she followed the gravel path round to the back garden and peered through the kitchen window.

Sophie Romerill was leaning against the sink, her eyes swollen with tears. Spotting Lydia, she wiped her face with the back of her apron and opened the door.

'What is it, Mrs Romerill, er, Sophie? Has something happened?'

'They've been here – those people from the Aliens Office. They say I'm a Jewess.' She pulled out a handkerchief. 'I'm sick to the pit of my stomach. Whatever am I to do?'

Lydia put her arms round the woman's frail shoulders.

'But I don't understand. Why have they picked on *you*?'

Sophie gulped. 'My parents were Austrian Jews. They lived on the island for six years before going back home. By that time, I'd met and married my husband. He was a Guernseyman, Church of England through and through. He's dead now, God rest his soul.' She covered her face with her hands.

'Did you explain all this?'

'Oh yes. I told them my parents were long since dead and that my late husband was a Gentile, but they wouldn't listen. They want me to prove I'm not Jewish, but how can I do that?'

'They can't make you into something you're not.' Lydia desperately hoped she was right. 'Just hold up your head and say nothing.'

'I've got to put a notice in my window reading "Jewish Undertaking".' The old woman was mumbling to herself now. 'They were good, honest, humble folk, kept themselves to themselves. If I leave here that's the end of it. I'll die in a concentration camp. I'll never come home again.'

'Listen to me, Sophie. I know some people who may be able to help you. Come to Torteval Church on Sunday morning. We'll find a way out of this, I'm sure of it. No one's going to send you away.'

'You're a good girl, Lydia. Your ma said so and it's true.' Sophie wiped her eyes with the back of her sleeve. 'Come on now and show me the dresses. Do it quickly, mind, or I'll ruin them with my tears.'

Two hours later Lydia set off back along the coast road, thoughts racing round her head. The persecution of the Jews in Europe was widespread, but here in Guernsey? How could a handful of innocent people do any harm? Pulling her coat sleeves down over her knuckles, she battled against the early evening wind. Someone had to protect Sophie Romerill. She would speak to Martin herself tomorrow. He would know what to do.

Lydia's heart hammered as Martin spoke from the pulpit, his voice hard with anger.

'Ask yourselves why you are here today.' His eyes scanned each one of them. 'Is it out of habit? A chance to wear your Sunday best, maybe? Or is it because you are frightened of the enemy and worried about the future? How many of you can hold up your hand and say "I am here because I care. I care about what happens to my fellow men, about the war that is devastating Europe. I care that bombs are being dropped all over Great Britain, that people are dying and I can do nothing to help them"?'

A barely contained whisper of dismay ran round the pews. Some of the regulars coughed nervously while others shifted in their seats. Old Mrs Deveraux, who was sitting by the main door, lifted her walking stick with an angry flourish, pulled herself to her feet and shuffled outside.

'If anyone else feels they are not up to listening to what I have to say, then please leave now. This is a house of God and a place for freedom of will.'

No one moved.

Martin's face was inscrutable as he held the Bible aloft.

'What is war? There are numerous references to war in the Old Testament. The best-known is Ecclesiastes Chapter Three, Verse Eight. "There is a time to love and a time to hate, a time for war and a time for peace". *Now*, I tell you, is a time for war. Which means that each one of you should do everything in your power to thwart the enemy. Do it humbly and proudly. Do not bemoan your situation, your lack of food or the removal of your loved ones to a place of safety. Be good to your fellow islanders, give them love, loyalty and whatever kindness you can find in your hearts—'

Lydia turned to look at the bemused faces around her. While one or two nodded in approval, many were tutting or shaking their heads.

'*Let us be strong together—*' the rector's voice grew louder, but Lydia was no longer listening. Why did he have to incite them? Why couldn't he show that he really was on their side? That he was doing all he could to bring down the enemy? She wanted to ask him but there was no point. Whatever the consequences, Martin Martell would do things his way.

Lydia watched from a distance as the congregation melted away. Martin had disappeared. Darting forward, she ran through the porch and banged on the vestry door.

'Can I come in?'

'Hello. I thought you'd gone home. What can I do for you?'

'I enjoyed your sermon, even if nobody else did.' She gave a wry smile. 'But that's not why I'm here. It's Sophie Romerill. They're threatening to deport her.'

Martin gestured to a chair as she recounted the story.

'I'll help if I can,' he said when she'd finished, 'but it won't be easy.'

'Thank you.' Impulsively, she threw her arms around him. 'I knew you would.'

He untangled himself and rested his arms on her shoulders. 'Is there anything else you need?'

'Nothing.' She fixed her eyes on his. If only that were the truth. 'Nothing at all.'

Edna Gallienne was peeling parsnips in the kitchen when Lydia arrived home.

'Is Maggie upstairs?' she asked, warming her hands on the range.

'Probably – though heaven knows where. I'm darned if I know what's come over that girl these days.'

Lydia felt a stab of guilt. She'd been too wrapped up in the prayer group lately to spend time with Maggie.

'Maybe I could have a word?'

'Would you, dear? I'd be ever so grateful.' Edna tipped the peelings into a separate pan. 'Maggie's hardly ever at the shop now. She leaves at noon and doesn't come back till we close.'

'She's probably just feeling bored, Mrs Gallienne. Bartering's hardly her idea of fun.'

'She could be a lot worse off.' Edna pulled a face. 'Some folks live in fear of their lives. That's not much fun either.'

'You're right, I know.' Lydia thought fleetingly of Sophie Romerill. 'But don't be too hard on her, please. She means well.'

'So what are you doing with yourself these days?' The older woman forced a smile.

'I've taken a break from teaching, but I'm sure I'll be back again. Right now, there's plenty to do at the church.'

'With the Reverend Martell? I've heard a lot about him – a charming man, so they say. He seems to have everyone's interests at heart.'

'He's a perceptive man.' Lydia chose her words carefully 'He's doing his best to make everyone's lives a bit easier. The older members of the congregation don't like him – they think he's trying to modernise the church. He stands in the pulpit and asks them to consider why they are there at all. But what he's doing isn't just about the church, it's about survival.' Lydia hesitated, realising she'd said too much.

'If you say so, my dear.' Edna Gallienne was lost in her own thoughts, oblivious to the rosy blush that had spread across Lydia's cheeks. 'Would you like to join us for some soup?'

'Thanks, Mrs Gallienne. I'll go up and see Maggie first.'

Lydia ran up the stairs two at a time, her heart racing faster than her feet. The less she said about Martin the better. She may have had her doubts about him, but that was in the past; these days he was in her thoughts for very different reasons. If only... Putting the next thought aside she knocked on the bedroom door.

CHAPTER 15

'You can't hide it from me, Lydia Le Page,' Maggie shook her head. 'I've known you for too long.'

Lydia raised her eyes. 'Hide what?' They were sitting together on Maggie's bed, candlelight casting peculiar shadows on the walls.

'You're seeing someone – *I know you are.*' She put her thumb in her mouth. 'Is he a German officer?'

'Where on earth did you get that idea?'

'Someone mentioned it when they came into the shop. So please tell me. I have to know the truth!'

'Is that what this is all about?' Lydia was shouting now, fear fuelling her anger.

'What *what's* all about? Have you been talking to Ma again?'

'She's just a bit worried about you, that's all, Maggie. She hardly sees you these days.'

'Don't change the subject. Just tell me the truth. Are you having a fling?'

'There's nothing to tell.' Lydia lifted a brush from the dressing table, absentmindedly dragging the bristles through her hair. 'I'm sorry, but you must trust me. I swear I'm not doing anything wrong.'

'You're not the same since you came back.' Maggie's lip trembled. 'You always were serious, but now you're secretive, too. We used to have such a laugh, you and me, and I thought, what with you living with us and everything, we could have had some fun. Or at least make the best of this blasted war.'

Lydia kneeled down and grasped Maggie's hands. 'I need you to trust me, please. I would never do anything to hurt you.'

'I do want to trust you, really I do, but—'

'Good – then that's all there is to it.' She stood up. 'Your ma's made some tomato soup. Will you come and join us?'

'I'll be down in a minute.'

Lydia ran down the stairs, her heart hammering against her ribs. She had lied to her best friend, her mother and, yes, even to Martin. If only she knew how to lie to herself.

'How's Mrs Romerill these days?' Edna handed Lydia a steaming bowl of soup. 'I hear she's been altering your auntie's clothes?'

'Sort of, yes. She's a brilliant seamstress so I'm told, and not short of work, but she's got a lot on her mind.'

'It's that wretched Jewish business, isn't it?'

Lydia nodded. 'She's scared out of her wits. She sits at home every day waiting for the soldiers to drag her away.'

'Who'd have thought it would come to this?' Edna fetched a cake tin from the top shelf. 'Take her a slice of my soda bread, will you? I used the last of the flour, but it's still fresh. And if that daughter of mine doesn't show up soon, I'll give her supper away an' all.'

Lydia's trips to Sophie's home became a welcome escape from the reality of her own life. Arriving at the cottage early one afternoon, she let herself in through the front door as usual, undressed and slipped into the long blue evening gown. Glancing round she saw the old woman smiling at her from the sitting room door.

'Sophie! I didn't hear you come in.'

'You do look a picture in that dress, my love,' the old woman smiled. 'The hem should be finished today.'

Lydia swished the silk organza as she stepped up on to the stool.

'Of all Aunt May's dresses, this is my favourite.'

Sophie nodded approvingly. 'The blue sets off your colouring.'

'And matches my sapphire ring.' Lydia held out her hand. 'That belonged to my aunt, too. But that's enough about me. How are you today?'

'Aw, you know how it is. There's gossip a-plenty since that notice went up on the door.'

'Because they think you're Jewish? What difference is that supposed to make?'

'None to you and me, dear. But some folk look at me strangely now, like I might cause them trouble.'

'Take no notice. Besides, the rector will help you, I'm sure of it. He won't let them send you away.'

'Hold still, or you might regret it,' Sophie attempted a grin, her mouth still full of pins.

'Lydia smiled back. 'Make sure you don't swallow that lot! Which reminds me, I've brought some of Edna's soda bread. Would you like a piece?'

'That I would.' Sophie pulled herself up with a groan. 'I'll put the kettle on to boil, and don't you dare move, my girl, till I get back.'

Early the next morning Lydia crept out of the house and cycled through the empty lanes to Torteval. She hadn't heard from Martin since the day of the sermon, but she had to tell him what had happened. After several knocks he finally answered the door.

'Hello, Martin. I'm sorry to bother you, but—'

'Lydia! What are you doing here at this unearthly hour?' He ran his hands through his uncombed hair. 'Come in, please. Is something wrong?'

'It's Maggie. She suspects something. I just don't know what to do.' The words tumbled out. 'She thinks I'm having an affair with a German officer.'

Martin let out a low whistle.

'I thought this might happen. You've denied it, I presume?'

Lydia nodded. 'I told her not to listen to idle gossip. Maggie can be scatterbrained at times but she's not stupid. I *am* living in her house, after all.'

'You'll just have to invent something to keep her off the scent.' He motioned her through to the drawing room. 'It shouldn't be too difficult.'

'I'm not so sure about that. Or I wouldn't be here.'

Martin picked up a file from his desk and flicked through the pages.

'I've got an idea. Why don't you tell her it's me you're sweet on? That should throw her off the scent.'

'That's ridiculous.' Lydia's face burned with embarrassment. 'Why would I say that?'

'Because it's plausible, I suppose.' Martin looked up. 'And it would make your life much easier. Don't look so horrified, please. Sit down and I'll get you a drink.'

Lydia shook her head. It would take more than a cup of coffee to appease her.

'What a wonderful imagination you have, Reverend Martell. Maybe you should have been a playwright. You've clearly missed your vocation.'

A roguish grin appeared on his face. 'At least it's a credible lie.' He peered into the mahogany-framed mirror above the mantelpiece. 'I'm not that bad looking – at least when I've had a shave.'

Lydia stretched to her full height. 'How could you joke about this? *You* asked me to join the prayer group. *You* got me into this mess, so for heaven's sake don't make fun of me now.'

'I'm sorry,' he said, his face contrite, 'but if Maggie thinks I'm the object of your affections, she won't believe a word about the Jerries.'

'Okay, let's suppose I was – er—' she struggled to find the right words, '*holding a candle for you.* Why would I keep it from my best friend?'

'All sorts of reasons. You're worried about the difference in our ages, you think it's improper to have these feelings at such a difficult time... You know the sort of thing.'

'Oh yes, I know the sort of thing, all right.' The sarcasm came easily now. 'I don't know why I didn't think of the idea myself.'

'Don't be angry with me.' Martin reached for her hand. 'We have to do this. It's the only way to get through.'

Lydia wrenched herself free. 'I'll bear that in mind. And now, if there's nothing else, perhaps you'll excuse me?'

'Only on one condition.' He followed her to the front door. 'Say you're not cross with me. You may not believe this, but I wouldn't hurt you for the world.'

He looked so sheepish standing there, sleepy and unshaven, that her resolve weakened.

'Okay, you're forgiven, but just this once, mind.'

'Thank you. And Lydia – if things were different, I'd—'

His final words were lost as she slammed the door shut behind her.

Lydia arrived back at The Vrangue before breakfast. The house seemed unnaturally silent as she filled the copper kettle to the brim, brought it to boil it on the range and emptied the steaming water into the old iron bath. She didn't trust the gas geyser and anyway they were only allowed two inches of water for bathing these days. Stepping gingerly into the tub, she could still hear Martin's voice going round in her head. *I wouldn't hurt you for the world.* Her stomach lurched at the memory.

She cupped the water in her hands, trickling it over her shoulders and down the smooth white skin of her breasts. Clutching a sliver of soap, she cast her mind back to those far-off summers spent with Papa at Sea Breeze. Together they would pick the ripening tomatoes in the sticky heat of the greenhouse, grading them by size as the fruit dropped through rows of specially designed wooden filters. Next, the trays of fruit were put into baskets and stacked in the packing shed ready to ship to England. As the sun went down, father and daughter would play hide and seek among the trees, Lydia shrieking with laughter when her giggles gave her away. Exhausted, she would follow Papa to the kitchen door where he scrubbed her hands with soap and water in an old metal dipper, patting them dry with a clean flannel. To this day the smell of carbolic, a heady mix of fresh air and disinfectant, could transport her back to her childhood.

Lydia opened her eyes and shivered; the water in the bath was stone cold. Reaching for a threadbare towel, she wrapped it tightly round her. She could cope without soap or hot water and manage with very little food, but sometimes the empty space inside her heart seemed just too much to bear.

Back in the kitchen Lydia refilled the kettle and set it on the range.

'Morning, Mrs Gallienne,' she smiled as the older woman appeared in her dressing gown.

Edna yawned. 'You were up bright and early. Where on earth have you been?'

'To the rectory, that's all. I had some papers to return to Martin.'

'At this hour?' she tutted. 'I'd have thought he'd have less on his plate these days, what with the school – not to mention the church – being half empty.'

'Well, you're wrong, Mrs Gallienne. People need him more than ever while the Jerries are here.'

'Wretched Germans. There's one for every two islanders, so they say. They're making our lives a misery, but praying won't change anything.' She pointed to the oven. 'I've made a bread pudding for supper tonight with some stale scraps from the larder. It's food in our bellies that'll save us in the end.'

Edna reached into her apron pocket, 'This letter came for you earlier. It looks official. I hope it's not bad news.'

Lydia carried the envelope into the dining room and closed the door behind her. Hands shaking, she broke the seal.

Your presence is requested at dinner with
the Kommandant, Major Otto Kruger, at the Grand Hotel
on 30 November 1941 at 7.30 p.m.

She crushed the card in the palm of her hand, a wry smile crossing her lips.

Lydia bumped into Flo Brouard outside Le Riche's store.

'A penny for your thoughts.' The old woman winked. 'Though I reckon they're worth a lot more.'

'I was miles away, sorry.' She smiled. 'How's my dear mama? Not still unwell I hope?'

'She's busied herself making a rag doll for young Nellie, Jean Le Tissier's girl. The poor mite's pining for her brother who's in England. It's just a few scraps of cotton, mind, but the child's face lit up when she saw it. Anyhow, enough of my chatter. Where've you been hiding? We don't see much of you these days.'

'I'm doing my bit at the church.' Lydia sighed inwardly. She couldn't afford to be spotted at Flo's; if the Jerries found out she was there it would only arouse suspicion. She hoped one day that Mama would understand.

'What brings you into town, then?' Flo was still talking.

'I've brought some old books to barter. I want to get a present for Mama in exchange.'

'Hmm… It's not safe round here these days. A real hive of activity it was before the enemy arrived, but now there's no one about.'

'Jerry Bag, Jerry Bag … She's a Jerry Bag.' A scruffy boy, barely ten years old ran from the store, spitting out the words like venom.

Bewildered, Flo scanned the empty street.

'He can't mean you, can he, my girl? He must've mistook you for someone else.'

Lydia stiffened. 'Of course, he doesn't mean me. Ignore him. He's just being stupid. There's a troublemaker in every class.'

The older woman shook her head. 'And you should know. Which reminds me. I hear you're not teaching any more. What a pity. I thought you liked it?'

'I did – I mean, I do. Anyway, I haven't left. I'm just having a few weeks off. Martin – the Reverend Martell, that is – wants me to concentrate on parish visits.' It sounded lame, she knew, but it would have to do for now.

'How is the rector? Well, I hope? Tell him to come and see us again. We'd like that, your mama and me.'

'He's very busy, right now, Mrs Brouard, but I'll ask, I promise. I'd best be off. Keep safe.'

'And you, my love.'

Lydia spent the next few hours mulling over her meeting with

Flo. Thankfully the older woman had dismissed the whole thing as a foolish prank, but not before a flash of doubt had crossed her face. Would Flo repeat what she had heard? Not to Mama, of course – her mother had enough on her plate. But what about Maggie, or even Mrs Gallienne? How long before someone else pointed the finger? Lydia's life, once so simple, had blurred around the edges till she barely recognised herself. She didn't know who to trust any more. One thing was certain: she needed to speak to Maggie before it was too late.

'Can you keep a secret?'

'What is it?' Maggie looked up from the battered magazine she was reading.

'It's Martin. I think you might've been right about him after all.'

'Me, right?' Her friend giggled. 'Tell me more.'

'I'm starting to see him in a different light. He's kind and thoughtful and, well, he does do a lot of good.'

'You mean you *do* fancy him? You're a dark horse. Why didn't you say?'

The colour rushed to Lydia's face. She was finding this difficult enough.

'I do have feelings for him, yes. I did try to tell you, but you weren't listening.'

'That's smashing news. Does he feel the same?'

'Sort of, yes, but it's a bit more complicated than that. A lot of people respect him, and it wouldn't look good if—' Her voice trailed away. 'Besides, there's a war on, and, well, I'm a lot younger than he is.'

'He can't be more than thirty-two if he's a day. I'm happy for you, really I am.' Maggie pressed her finger to her mouth. 'And I promise with all my heart that I won't say a word.'

'Thanks – that's such a relief. I knew you'd understand.'

'You bet I do.'

'Ah, *Fräulein*, you are beautiful. I am happy, once more, to have you at my dinner table.'

'And I'm honoured to be here, Herr Kommandant.' Lydia flashed him a smile.

'Next time I will send my driver to pick you up. There will be a next time, *ja*?'

'If that's what you wish, but there really is no need.' The last thing she needed was an official car arriving at Maggie's home.

'Ah, I see. You have, perhaps, another form of transportation. A vehicle you are hiding from the Kommandantur?' His eyes glinted.

'Not at all, Herr Kommandant. I wouldn't dream of breaking your rules. I am happy to walk these days as our island's such a beautiful place to be.' She lowered her lashes. 'I see you have ordered some more champagne. I am flattered and you are very generous.'

'And you are very lovely, Lydia.' He raised his glass. '*Prost*! To us.'

Lifting her glass, Lydia gazed around the room. There were fewer diners tonight – mainly middle-aged couples who mixed with the German officers with ease. These people were not intimidated – they had every intention of getting on with their lives. For the first time since the Occupation, Lydia felt in control. She smiled back at the Kommandant, whose eyes, she noticed, had remained on hers.

'What is it you are thinking?'

'I was thinking how fortunate I am to be here tonight.'

'That is good. And now, I wish to know more about your Guernsey people.'

'We see ourselves as independent,' she chose her words carefully, 'living, as we do, so much closer to France than Britain.'

'But you speak English? That makes you an English woman, does it not?'

'It makes us British, but much of our culture comes from the French. We are, in our own way, unique.'

'Unique? What is this?'

'Special. Not quite like anyone else.' She paused. 'Do you miss your country, Herr Kommandant?'

His eyes narrowed. 'I miss my family, yes. But I am an officer – we do not talk of such things. And now, would you like to dance?'

She smiled and stood up. 'It would be a pleasure.'

They waltzed to the sounds of Strauss, their faces so close she could feel the warmth of his breath. She willed herself to keep calm. As the evening wore on, the clink of glasses or a sudden peal of laughter would take her back to a life that seemed gone forever.

'You are tired now, *Fräulein*?' A sly smile crossed the Kommandant's face.

'Too much champagne, perhaps?' She lifted her glass and pretended to yawn. 'I think it is time I went home.'

CHAPTER 16

Christmas 1941

'Your family – they have lived always on the island, Lydia?' Kruger's eyes penetrated hers. They were taking afternoon tea at the Old Government House Hotel, a popular meeting place for German officers.

'Yes – we've been here for generations,' Lydia nodded. 'I'm a Guernsey girl through and through.'

'A Guernsey donkey?' The Kommandant flashed his yellowing teeth. 'That is right, is it not?'

'Donkeys, yes, that's what we locals are called.' *Damn him – how come he knew so much?*

'You are, shall we say, fortunate, to live here, Lydia. My soldiers, they think they have come to paradise.'

'Yes, it is certainly very peaceful.' She bit her lip. *Peace? God help her if he thought she was poking fun.* 'I mean, well, it's a place we're all very proud of.'

'I understand.' His thin lips creased into a smile. 'Please do not trouble yourself. Our countries are at war, Lydia, but all of us wish for peace, do we not?'

'Of course.'

The Kommandant eyed her curiously. 'Are you feeling unwell, my dear? You look perhaps, a little flushed.'

'I have a slight headache, that's all. It's nothing.'

He pulled out a large cigar and cut the end with a penknife. 'I have some information that will make you feel better. You are a clever girl. Am I right?'

'I'm not stupid.' Her hand shook as she raised the china cup to her lips.

'You need not worry, Lydia. This is, you know, a compliment. I have a very special task for you in mind. I want you to be my English assistant at the Kommandantur. How is it you say – short time?'

'Part time.' Her skin felt clammy. *What else did he know? Had he blown her cover?*

'Ah yes, part time. You help me with important work and you will be excused some of the things that happen to,' he hesitated, 'more unfortunate islanders. You are pleased, yes?'

'Very pleased.' Her stomach knotted with fear. 'Are there any other Guernsey folk working at your headquarters?'

'No, but that need not concern you. We will see more of each other now.' His mouth curled at the edges. 'I will pay you well, my dear.'

'That is so kind of you, Herr Kommandant.'

'I've asked you before, my dear. Call me Otto, please, when we are on our own.' He smiled smugly. 'I am giving you a position of trust. Every day you will open my correspondence, that which is written in English, and every day you will make the replies. You understand?'

'I understand. I won't let you down.'

'I have given instructions that you will be treated with respect. But if ever I find out that you have—'

'You can trust me,' she cut in. 'My loyalties, Otto, lie with you. But now, please forgive me, I must go. I'm expected at church.'

'Ah, the church. You enjoy these activities. You help the young children, yes? Those who are left behind?'

Lydia swallowed hard. 'I look after them during the Sunday service. They get a bit restless after the first two hymns so we take them into the hall to colour or make Christmas cards... Sometimes we take a trip out on weekdays too.' She knew she was gabbling but she couldn't stop herself.

'The children, they come second, *Lydia*, will they not? Your place is beside me from now on. You will come to my home very soon and discuss the matter further?'

Lydia pulled her gloves from her bag and stood up.

'I'd be delighted. In the meantime, thank you so much for the tea, Herr Kommandant. I bid you good day.'

She crossed the room in what felt like slow motion, and emerged at last into the winter sunshine, narrowly missing a milk lorry. Lydia cursed out loud. It was eighteen months since the bombing and now the island faced a second Christmas under Nazi rule. If she obeyed Kruger's orders she'd be working for the enemy. And if she didn't? Either way she was damned.

Walking down the Esplanade past Town Beach, Lydia headed out towards the open-air bathing pools. Built almost a century ago, the pools at La Vallette were filled with sea water that ebbed and flowed along with the tide. These days they were closed to the public to prevent islanders escaping to the French coast. Lydia watched as the wind whipped the surface into a teeming frenzy of foam, like hundreds of white horses riding the waves. She could hear the thudding of hooves, her head spinning as the noise reached a crescendo.

Lydia steadied herself on a rock. Did Kruger really need her help? Or was it a trap? She'd soon find out.

CHAPTER 17

January 1942

'Good morning, Fräulein Le Page.' The Kommandant's face broke into a smile. 'Welcome to my office.'

He was wearing a greatcoat with a leather belt buckled over the top and a diagonal strap across his chest. Her body stiffened. She'd never seen him in full military dress before.

'Good morning, Herr Kommandant.' Lydia felt like a child on the first day of school. 'I am honoured to be here.'

'You like it, *ja*?' He removed his coat with well-honed precision, hung it on the bentwood stand in the corner, and sat down behind the large oak desk.

Nodding politely, she gazed around the room. Everything was impeccable. A portrait of Hitler dominated the far wall with photographs of high-ranking German officers positioned at a suitable distance beneath. Books – scores of leather-bound books – covered every available space, some in glass-fronted cabinets which appeared to be locked. Her eyes fell upon a large steel filing cabinet with a framed map of Guernsey above.

'It is—' she searched for the right words, 'very grand.'

Mistaking her fear for first-day nerves, the Kommandant rested his hands on her shoulders.

'You will make my coffee now and have some also as it is your first day. That is an easy task, is it not?' He directed her to a small anteroom with a stone sink, a single gas ring and a small wooden table and chair. On the table stood a metal coffee jug, a tin of ground French coffee and several coffee cups, each inscribed with a swastika. A foot-square window, high above, let in the only light.

Lydia filled the jug with water and set it on the gas ring, which she lit with the match provided. She watched, motionless, until the water boiled. Next she measured out two dessert spoons of coffee, drawing the fragrance into her lungs before returning the jug to the ring. Placing the coffee, sugar and milk on the engraved silver tray she returned to the Kommandant's desk.

'*Danke schön, Fräulein.* That is splendid. I have already outlined your duties to you, have I not? In addition to dealing with my correspondence I wish you to speak, when necessary, to the Controlling Committee of Guernsey, the Guernsey Police and the Aliens Office. You understand?'

She nodded.

'You do not speak German, *Fräulein*, I am correct in that?'

'I'm afraid not, Herr Kommandant.'

'That is good. However, you will on *no account* look at my personal correspondence. To do so would result in—' He lowered his eyes and drew a finger across his throat. 'I'm sure we understand each other?'

Lydia nodded and followed him, mechanically, to her own desk across the room. It contained a telephone, a file marked *English Correspondance* (spelt incorrectly, she noted), a leather blotting paper holder, a pen and pencil and a framed photograph of Adolf Hitler.

Just then the Kommandant's phone burst into life, filling the silence between them.

Gleaning little from the conversation that followed, Lydia tried to concentrate on the file in front of her. By the end of the morning her head was throbbing and the set smile on her face had disappeared. She had read carefully through the correspondence (mostly formal letters from the States of Guernsey) before drafting replies, placing a question mark in the margin against any attempt by the sender to communicate in German. The Kommandant spent most of his time in meetings, calling back only briefly to pick up some paperwork. She stayed at her desk throughout in case she was being watched, and kept her head down, showing scant interest in her surroundings. She was deep in thought when the door burst open.

'Fräulein Le Page?' The soldier clicked his heels. 'The Kommandant says you will leave now. You will attend at the same time tomorrow morning. Come with me to the exit. Do you have your pass?'

Lydia nodded. Grabbing her hat and coat, she followed him wordlessly through the maze of corridors to the back of the building. The soldier stopped only to salute his superiors, his heels clicking mechanically as he raised his hand. Once outside, Lydia walked slowly past the guards and out into the road, her eyes blinking in the sunshine. Her steady walk turned into a trot and before she realised it she was running like a child, past the town church, along the Esplanade and towards home.

It was gone six o'clock when Lydia got to the Regal Cinema where a long queue had already formed. Clutching her ticket, she found an empty space three rows from the back and sat down.

Several minutes later Arthur slipped into the seat beside her.

'Turned out fine again today,' he said as he folded his mac on his lap. 'Needn't have brought this with me after all.'

'Better safe than sorry.' She nodded politely, as if to a stranger.

'It's an English picture tonight, I believe,' he persisted, slipping her a note under the raincoat.

'That's why I'm here,' she replied, keeping her eye on the

screen. 'I don't understand a word of German but that's almost all you get, I'm afraid, these days.'

'Would you like a sweet?'

'That's very kind.' She sneaked a look at Arthur's face. His eyes were ringed with dark shadows. 'But if you don't mind, I'd like to watch the picture now.'

'Of course, I hope you enjoy it,' he nodded as the lights went down and the screen flickered and burst into life.

REBECCA
With LAWRENCE OLIVIER and JOAN FONTAINE
Directed by ALFRED HITCHCOCK

Lydia watched as Maxim De Winter, played by the handsome Olivier, strolled on to the set. She knew the story, but was extremely glad of the respite. She settled back in the chair, her mind temporarily distracted. The next time she glanced at Arthur he was sound asleep.

Five minutes before the interval Lydia excused herself and moved silently along the row and out into the foyer. The powder room was deserted. She pushed open the cubicle door and locked it firmly from the inside. Opening Arthur's note, she read it twice, her eyes moving rapidly over the page. Then she tore it into tiny pieces and flushed it down the lavatory.

CHAPTER 18

Lydia fumbled with the back door lock, banging her elbow on the metal handle.

'Blast the blackout,' she cursed, edging her way around the kitchen table and into the hall. 'Is anyone home?'

'I'm up here.' Maggie's voice echoed from beyond the stairwell. 'Ma and Pa are in bed. I'll be down in a jiffy.'

Lydia stared upwards, adjusting her eyes to the darkness. A ray of torchlight appeared out of the gloom followed by a pair of sturdy legs.

'I'm so glad you're back.' Her friend's breath came in sharp bursts as she clattered into the hallway. 'Put the kettle on, will you? There's something I need to tell you.'

Lydia reached for the caddy and scraped up the last of the tea leaves. Mrs Gallienne had shown her how to make nettle tea for when they ran out of the real thing, but she shuddered at the thought. Hopefully, the Jerries would be long gone before she had to drink that disgusting stuff.

'So what is it you have to tell me that's so important?' she asked, pouring boiling water into the old brown pot.

'Hitler wants to deport you.' Maggie absentmindedly sucked her thumb.

'Deport me! What on earth do you mean?'

'Well, not you exactly, but anyone born in England, or caught here at the outbreak. They're sending them to German prison camps.'

Lydia swallowed. 'Where did you hear this?'

'Look!' Maggie held up the evening paper. 'It's here in the *Star.*

"By order of higher Authorities, the following British subjects will be evacuated and transferred to Germany. Persons who have their permanent residence not on the Channel Islands. All those men not born on the Channel Islands, who belong to the English people and their families."'

'Oh, Maggie, you really had me worried for a minute. I might have been at college in England when war broke out, but I'm a Guernsey girl born and bred. This is my permanent residency. Besides, their English is awful. It doesn't even make sense.'

'I do hope you're right,' Maggie sniffed. 'I couldn't bear to lose you again.'

Lydia's mind was racing. The Jerries couldn't possibly know she was living in England before they landed. Anyway, they *must* have checked her false credentials somehow before giving her the job.

Out loud she said, 'Now come on, drink your tea while it's hot. It's the last of the ration.'

'All right, but I don't trust Hitler, or that horrid Kommandant.' Maggie pulled a face. 'I hope they both burn in hell.'

Lydia walked through the sparsely lit corridors to the library. She'd been at the Kommandantur for three weeks now and was gradually getting to know her way around. She'd been warned which areas were off limits, but the imposing oak-panelled library was not one of them. The hotel's reading room before the Occupation, it now housed thousands of books, mostly German, but also French, Russian and Italian. At the far end of the library a cream marble fireplace was filled with wooden logs which were lit every afternoon, despite the fuel shortage, and radiated much-needed warmth. These days the library included a stationery store housed in one of many anterooms; it was here that Lydia had business. She pushed open the door to find that the sentry's chair was empty. Holding her pass and requisition documents tightly in her hand, she stared round the room. Paper, envelopes, pens, pencils and endless brown files were piled high to the ceiling with labels depicting their contents. To the left of the door a locked metal box appeared to contain the official notepaper of the Third Reich. Her pulse quickened. If only she could get her hands on that.

'What are you doing, *Fräulein*?'

Lydia jumped as the soldier appeared at the door.

'I'm waiting to be served.'

You wait out here,' he scowled. 'What is it you want?'

She handed him her documents.

He scanned them briefly. 'This I will find. You get for the Kommandant?'

'Yes.' She nodded.

'Then go back. I will come when I am ready.'

She let herself out of the library and walked quickly back to her office. That was a close shave. She would have to be more careful in future.

It was gone five o'clock when young Tom from Torteval Farm arrived with a message for Lydia. She hadn't seen Martin since she'd told him about Maggie and wasn't even sure she wanted to, but she had to obey orders. Hurriedly she scribbled a note to Mrs Gallienne, retrieved her father's bicycle from the shed and set off on the three-mile journey.

'What's wrong?' Lydia asked, as soon as he opened the door. She followed Martin into the study.

'I've made some enquiries about Sophie Romerill and it's not good news, I'm afraid.'

Lydia bit her lip. 'What do you mean?'

'It seems some whistle-blower gave her name to the Jerries and she's on their list of suspected Jews. Once that happens, there's no going back.'

'But it's all in her past, surely?'

'It's not that simple. The only thing Mrs Romerill can do is deny her ancestry, but it won't be easy. Do you want me to go and see her?'

'Would you? The poor woman's terrified. She's convinced she's going to be deported.'

'She may well be, I'm afraid. They're already sending the British-born islanders away.'

'I know. Poor Maggie was worried it might include me. Why are they doing it?'

'To avenge the German civilians now interned in Iran. Twenty Channel Islanders must go for every single one of them.'

'That's terrible.' Lydia swallowed back tears. 'How will they choose?'

'It's random so it could be anyone, I'm afraid. Women and children included.' He turned his back to her. 'But there is another reason I asked you here.' Lifting a file from the safe, Martin spread the contents over his desk. 'Take a look at this. It's the latest intelligence from Britain. Hitler's plans for the island.'

'Plans? What do you mean, plans?'

'There's no easy way to say this – Hitler wants to Germanise Guernsey.'

'*Germanise* Guernsey?' A bolt of fear shot through her. 'What on earth does that mean?'

'It means he intends to move the islanders out and the German people in.' Martin avoided her eyes.

'But that's crazy – he can't evacuate the whole island, can he?'

'I'm afraid he can do what he likes. He's waited a long time to get on to English soil and now, it seems, he's determined to stay put.'

'So you think England is the real target?'

'I suspect that's the master plan. If the island was successfully *peopled* by Germans, Hitler would gain on two counts. First, it would be seen as a major coup, and secondly, he'd have a new German state close to the English and French borders. Guernsey's probably just a dry run.'

Lydia shivered. 'That's madness, surely? It sounds like a picture at the Regal. Besides, where would we all go?'

'To Jersey? Or France, maybe? We only know part of the plan. It's vital we find out the rest.'

'And how are we supposed to do that?'

'Well, that's where you come in, Lydia. We need you to gain access to the Kommandant's personal files.'

Her skin felt taut, as if her flesh was trying to escape.

'But I've only just started the job. I, well, I need to familiarise myself first.' The shock had numbed her senses. She was playing for time, and he knew it.

'That won't be easy, I'm afraid. For all I know the whole thing could be a plant, just to put us off the scent. But we have to be sure.'

'So how will I recognise these files?'

'Our intelligence is good. You'll be fully briefed, I promise. Look, if there was any other way, believe me, I wouldn't ask.'

'And what if I refuse?'

'I don't think you will, Lydia.' His voice hardened. 'You knew what you were letting yourself in for when you joined the prayer group.'

'Don't patronise me, Martin.' Anger erupted inside her. 'You had your eyes on me all along, didn't you? Good old Lydia – she'll do perfectly. She'll seduce the Kommandant, then, dear Lord, we can all be saved.' She spat the words out of her mouth like a bad taste. 'I actually thought you felt something for me. How stupid I must have been.'

'If you're scared, just say so.' His voice remained calm.

She wiped her face with the back of her hand, struggling to suppress the tears.

'For your information, Martin Martell, I'm not scared. I'm utterly terrified.'

'It's okay, Lydia.' His arms slipped round her. 'Please don't cry.'

She bowed her head as the tears flowed freely, soaking through his shirt to his skin.

'I'm sorry.' His voice was breaking now. 'I'm so, so very sorry. I have to be hard on you, don't you see? You're stronger than I'll ever be.' Lifting her chin, Martin traced his thumbs across her cheeks, his touch so tender she wondered if she was dreaming. 'Don't cry,' he whispered, stroking her hair. Then, very gently, he tilted her chin and kissed her lips.

Martin felt as if he had been hit by a lorry. His head ached, his limbs trembled, and he couldn't think straight. Whenever he thought of Lydia he saw only Janet's face: Janet crying, Janet cowering, Janet looking right through him as if he didn't exist. What the hell was happening to him?

He thought back to the day when he'd lost Janet for good.

'We can always postpone the wedding till you feel better,' he'd said. 'We've got all the time in the world.'

Janet had stared right back at him, her eyes crazed. 'Are you refusing to marry me?'

'Of course not, I just don't think we're ready.'

'You don't think *you're* ready, you mean. I'll sue you for all you're worth. That'll put paid to your precious future.'

Wincing at the memory, he stood up and poured himself a whisky. Lydia didn't need her life ruined too. Only the cause mattered now.

CHAPTER 19

Lydia slipped out of bed and padded towards the attic window. It was barely dawn, yet birds filled the air with song, unencumbered these days by the noise of traffic. Shafts of sunlight appeared over the rooftops and for the first time since the Occupation she felt a surge of joy.

She could picture Martin now, his thumbs stroking the tears from her cheeks, his eyes bright with emotion. She wanted so much to hold him close, feel his naked skin against hers, to kiss his face, his eyes, his body... Lydia shut her eyes, shocked by the vision in her own mind; nothing had prepared her for this. Smiling softly, she crossed her arms over her chest, holding on to the memories.

So much had changed. Here she was, about to risk her own life, as well as the lives of others around her, and nothing seemed to matter but Martin.

Papa's voice resounded in her head. *'Don't misjudge the power of love. It can hit you when you least expect it.'* She was her father's daughter in more ways than one. How she wished she could talk to him now.

Brushing these thoughts aside, Lydia hurried to the first landing and tapped on Maggie's bedroom door. A sleepy voice beckoned her in.

'There's something I have to tell you, Maggie, and there's no easy way to do it.'

'What is it? What's happened?' Her friend was wide awake now.

'I'm working for the Kommandant.'

Maggie's face crumpled. 'You can't be serious. After all you said! Tell me you're joking, please.'

'I can't. I'm afraid I have no choice. If I disobey his orders, or break the rules, I'll be shot.'

Maggie leapt out of bed, her skin the colour of newly fallen snow. 'Shot?'

'Yes, I'm afraid so. It's a crime to disobey the enemy. They shoot their own soldiers for insubordination. I'm sorry, but it really is best that you hear the news from me.'

'But why you?' Her friend's eyes narrowed. 'All this talk about being sweet on the rector when it's the Kommandant you've been seeing. Go on – admit it!'

'Shush – your parents will hear. I have been seeing him, but not in the way you mean. Otto Kruger noticed me at the dinner dance, you know – the one where I wore the crepe de Chine dress? He made some enquiries and then I was approached.' She hated lying but she had no choice.

'You shouldn't have gone to that stupid dance.' Maggie was crying now.

'There's no point going over that again. Martin's been very understanding about it all. I'm already on temporary leave from the school and he's promised to find a replacement.'

'I'd rather *die* than work for that wretched Kommandant.'

'As I said, I might well have to.' The corners of Lydia's mouth twitched. 'But you're wrong about Martin. I really do love him.'

Just then Edna Gallienne's voice echoed up the stairs.

'Are you awake, Lydia? I've a note here from the Reverend Martell. Young Tom from Torteval brought it just now.'

Lydia ran downstairs and grabbed the envelope. Tearing it open she scanned the contents.

An extraordinary meeting of Torteval Prayer Group
will be held at The Rectory at 2 p.m. this afternoon.
Your prayers are urgently sought.
Reverend Martin Martell
Rector of Torteval

'Is something wrong?' Maggie appeared at the sitting room door.

'It's nothing. We're having a meeting later, that's all, at the rectory.'

'An excuse to see Martin?' Maggie's voice was loaded with sarcasm. 'I'm sorry, but for someone who's supposed to be besotted, you don't look very happy. I might appear simple to you at times, but I know something's going on.'

Lydia wasn't listening. What had happened? The prayer group never met at such short notice. She glanced at her watch.

'I'd better get there early. I'm sure it's my turn to make the tea.'

Martin appeared at the door, his eyes scanning the hastily assembled group. Lydia watched as he circled the room, whispering to some, reassuring others, seemingly oblivious to her presence.

At last he saw her, his face set, his smile too bright as he moved forward to shake her hand.

'Ah, Lydia – thank you for coming so promptly.'

Her heart plummeted. What did she expect? A fanfare of trumpets? An orchestra of angels? This was a business meeting, for heaven's sake. He'd clearly forgotten the kiss already.

'Is something wrong?' She came to her senses at last.

Martin nodded. 'It's Arthur. He sends his apologies, I'm afraid. Two soldiers found him at Icart Point last night after the curfew. He said he was baiting a wild rabbit and didn't realise the time but our friends at the Kommandantur didn't like this explanation, so they asked him back for a little chat.'

The colour drained from Lydia's face. Now she understood. If Arthur was in danger, then so were they all.

'So who will I rely on now for my intelligence?'

'I will keep you informed until further notice. You will be allocated another contact whether or not Arthur returns.'

'I see. Will this change our plans?'

'Our plans will go ahead on schedule, with one or two changes to the rules. Is there anything else?'

She shook her head. Losing Arthur was a huge blow but she couldn't admit it to Martin.

'Forgive me, but I can't stay on for the meeting. I promised to call in at the Emergency Hospital. They're really short-staffed at the moment.' It wasn't a very good lie, but it would have to do.

'Ah yes, the hospital. Your friend, Mrs Romerill, has been admitted, I believe.'

Lydia nodded. 'They came to see her again from the Aliens Office. She did as you said and denied everything, but the shock was too much. The doctors may have to send her to the asylum.'

'It's probably as well.' Martin's eyes gave nothing away. 'There are worse places she could be. And now, if you will excuse me?'

The world turned grey as she watched him cross the room. So this was how it felt to be rejected. For a moment she was a child again, playing in the sand with her father on Chouet bay. Together they gathered smooth flat pebbles from the shoreline, each one polished to perfection by the tide. With a flick of the wrist Papa skimmed them over the water, watching as they hit the surface then bounced back again and again. Lydia tossed her precious stone into the waves, an unspoken prayer playing on her lips. The black and white pebble formed a dazzling wide arc before plunging noise-lessly into the ocean. Finally, she understood what failure meant.

'Is anything wrong, my dear – you look a bit pale?' A shrill voice brought Lydia back to the present.

'I'm fine, thank you, Mrs Guille. It's just a headache. Now, if you don't mind, I'm expected at the hospital. Will you excuse me?' She had to leave. She couldn't stay in the same room as Martin a moment longer.

Gathering her thoughts, Lydia slipped from the room and let herself out the rectory door. So Arthur was in custody – the news was worse than she'd feared. She had lost an important contact as well as a valued friend. He'd been careless, maybe, downright stupid even, but could they deport him for breaking the curfew? Maybe it was safer for him to be out of action for a while. The Jerries would be watching them all more closely now.

'Ah, Lydia. You are early this morning, are you not? You could not sleep, *vielleicht*?' Otto Kruger's mouth creased into a grin.

'Not at all, Herr Kommandant. I slept very well. It's just that I have a lot to do and want to make sure I do it properly. Shall I get your coffee now?'

'You know how I like it, yes?'

Nodding, Lydia hurried away. At least she'd managed to look round the office before he'd arrived. She'd shown her pass to get in this morning as usual, but the guard on the door just waved her through. She'd deliberately flirted with the same guard once or twice before and he seemed to have taken a liking to her.

The Kommandant's desk was locked at all times and the key kept in his wallet. The filing cabinets at the end of the room were easy enough to open but she hadn't had an opportunity to look at them. The English correspondence was left in her in-tray, but contained little of interest, while the German letters were opened with a silver paper knife by Otto Kruger himself.

Lydia poured the strong rich coffee from the pot, her taste buds watering.

'What a beautiful day,' she said, placing the tray in front of him.

'Indeed it is. And now, Lydia, I have a task for you.' He handed her a box file. 'You will find inside letters from those island people who wish, shall we say, to advise the Kommandantur of any wrongdoings against the Reich. Some people prefer not to give their names, but for those who do, I wish you to make the reply.'

'Thank you, Herr Kommandant. I will see to it right away.'

Her heart fell as she looked through the file. A few islanders, it seemed, were willing informers. Unlawful possession of crystal sets was the biggest crime reported, along with stealing food from the Germans and openly criticising the enemy.

A familiar name caught her eye.

'Sophie Romerill, dressmaker of this parish, is a practising Jew. Don't believe anything different.'

The letter was anonymous, of course. Lydia felt sick. Why would anyone want to ruin the life of a vulnerable old widow?

She glanced towards the Kommandant's desk, then dropped the letter into her bag. Watching his brow furrow as he studied his paperwork, she felt a surge of strength.

'Damn the lot of you,' she muttered under her breath. 'We *will* win this bloody war.'

CHAPTER 20

Lydia blinked as the familiar house came into view. Sea Breeze stood proudly on the clifftop, pink granite walls sparkling in the winter sunshine. A single tear squeezed from the corner of her eye, trailed down her cheek and dropped on to her collar.

She could hear Papa's voice in her head. *'Come on, Liddy, you can do it.'*

Leaning back against the beech tree, she breathed deeply, trying to stem the panic. 'It's okay, Papa,' she whispered.

She knocked firmly on the door, waiting for the inevitable creak as it opened.

'*Ja?*' The soldier scowled.

'I have an appointment at two o'clock with Kommandant Otto Kruger.'

'Enter.'

Lydia stepped into the entrance hall, her heart banging against her ribs. The polished oak staircase rose up to the landing where she'd played as a child on rainy winter afternoons. While Mama dozed in the drawing room, she would slide down the banisters, shrieking with delight as she landed with a thump on the rug.

'*Fräulein?*' The soldier's voice interrupted her thoughts. 'You come through now.'

Otto Kruger removed his cap, a broad smile on his face. 'Welcome to my home. Or should I say my *Guernsey* home, Lydia. You like it?'

Lydia clutched her coat to her chest, afraid he would hear her heart thudding. She cast her eyes far out into the distance. 'The views are lovely.'

'The best in the island, I am informed. You are shaking, Lydia. Are you cold? Come nearer the fire.'

'No, no, I'm fine, thank you. I have a headache coming on. Perhaps I could sit down?'

He gestured towards the sofa. 'We have plenty of time, how you say, in our hands?'

'*On* our hands.' Lydia jumped as the clock struck two.

The Kommandant laughed. 'That, as you English say, is a *father* clock, is it not?'

'A *grand*father clock.' It had been in her family for many years. She stared at the mantelpiece, stripped of her mother's vases, the wooden bowls trophy Papa had won at Beau Sejour, the hand-painted woodpecker she had been given as a child. In their place were photographs, presumably of Kruger's family – blond-haired boys, a middle-aged woman (straight-faced and severely dressed) – and an assortment of trophies which, she suspected, had been requisitioned from other people's homes.

Was he married? Did she care?

'This is my mother, and my sister, Eva, with her children.' He followed her glance. 'You like them, *ja*?'

Images of Lydia's childhood flashed into her mind, fusing together like a double-exposed film.

'You must miss them. But I'm sure you'll be back home soon.'

His eyes narrowed. 'That is for the Führer to decide. And now, I need to tell you my plans, *ja*? I am going away for one week.'

'Going away?' Lydia held her breath.

'Yes – to Jersey. In some days' time.'

Jersey! She forced a smile. Maybe the intelligence was right.

'Is it a holiday you are taking, Herr Kommandant?'

His face darkened. 'No, not a holiday. I have business there. But you need not trouble yourself with that.'

'Shall I come into the office in your absence?' She kept her voice steady.

'That will be necessary. I have instructed Leutnant Wolf to watch over you and he will talk to me by telephone all the time. Now tell me – do you know Jersey?'

'I've been to St Helier once or twice but I don't know it well.' She lowered her lashes. 'There is what we call friendly rivalry between the two islands.'

He eyed her curiously. 'Guernsey donkeys, Jersey donkeys, no?'

'Oh no. There are no Jersey donkeys.'

'But you are, how you say, "one happy family?"'

'Oh we get on, don't get me wrong, but we have our own foibles. Jersey people are known as *crapauds*, or toads.' Lydia ignored the confused look on his face.

He shook his head. 'I shall know more about these Jersey people when I get back, will I not? Then, perhaps you and I can have a day out together again. You can show me, once more, the sights of your island?'

'It will be a pleasure.'

Otto Kruger picked up a sheaf of papers and began firing instructions at her in faltering English.

Lydia had stopped listening; her mind was racing. One week. One whole week! That ought to be enough to find what she needed. Leutnant Wolf, no doubt, would be keeping a close eye on her but she could deal with him. Feeling exhilarated, she tried to concentrate on the Kommandant's words.

'Is there anything you do not understand, *Fräulein*?' he said, at last.

She shook her head. 'I am happy with my instructions, Herr Kommandant.'

'That is good. Now, before you go there is an important—' he glanced at his notes, '*function* I wish you to attend with me. It is organised by the German authorities for the States of Guernsey. We expect the Chairman of the Controlling Committee, the Chief of Police and other, er, dignitaries, to attend.'

'Thank you, Herr Kommandant. I'd be honoured to accept.'

His thin lips twisted into a smile. 'You have a formal dress, Lydia?'

'I have one or two, what we call family heirlooms.' She hesitated. She'd already said too much.

'Splendid. My driver will collect you, at a time to be arranged. And now, if you will excuse me?'

'Of course.'

Within seconds the sour-faced soldier appeared and escorted her back to the entrance vestibule. He opened the door in silence and slammed it shut behind her.

Lydia walked down the path and on through the gardens – now overgrown and knotted with weeds. She allowed her eyes to linger for just a moment, then turned abruptly and made her way back to town.

'So what's the occasion this time?' Maggie stood at the bedroom door.

'A grand dinner for the States dignitaries.' Lydia patted a curl into place. 'The Jerries want to butter them up in the hope that flattery will gain them favour. It's supposed to be a "model occupation", don't forget.'

Maggie kicked off her shoes and crossed her legs beneath her.

'What does that mean – *model occupation*? I've seen it in the *Star* a few times, but I still don't understand.'

Lydia pulled her hair to the back of her head and twisted it into a bun. 'It's the first time in history that Germans have occupied English soil. The chairman of the Controlling Committee thinks we should accept the situation with dignity – you know, stiff upper lip and good old English spirit.'

'Is he right, do you think?'

'Maybe. Openly showing contempt could make life a lot more difficult than it is already.' She picked up a piece of cork, singed at the edges, and dabbed some colour over her brows and eyelashes.

'Is *that* why you're going along with it? Working for the Kommandant, going out with him on dates?'

'For the last time, I am *not* going out with Otto Kruger.' Lydia sighed. 'I am accompanying him to the Channel Islands Hotel tonight because I don't have a choice. Anyway, you know very well my affections lie elsewhere.'

A loud bang on the door made Maggie jump. 'That must be Corporal Schmidt.' The Kommandant's driver was a regular visitor to the house in the Vrangue. 'Ma doesn't like it, you know, him coming here—' her voice tailed off.

'Do you think I don't know that? I've talked to them both, your ma and your pa, and explained I'm only following orders. They're trying their best to understand but they're scared, like the rest of us.'

'So what shall I tell the driver?' Maggie's face was defiant.

Lydia glanced at her watch. It was seven fifteen and the dance didn't start till eight.

'Tell him I'll be down in five minutes, will you, please?'

'So who'll be there tonight?'

'The chairman of the controlling committee, with his entourage, of course. Oh, and anyone whose name sounds important.'

'Will there be lots of food?' Maggie never could curb her curiosity.

'There will.' Lydia held up her evening bag. 'You'd be amazed how much I can fit in here.'

Grinning to herself, Maggie turned and ran down the stairs.

'You look wonderful tonight, Lydia!' The Kommandant's eyes gleamed. 'The prettiest lady in the room. I am very fortunate for you to accompany me.'

'Thank you.' She curtsied briefly. 'I am honoured to be here.'

Lydia glanced round the ballroom. A solemn-looking quartet played in the corner while several couples, mostly elderly, danced self-consciously to the unfamiliar tunes. The top tables were decked with candles and fresh flowers, ready for the Kommandant and his party to sit down.

Recognising some of the official guests, Lydia smiled politely in acknowledgement. She was here as the Kommandant's assistant, nothing more.

She waited patiently until everyone present had moved inexorably down the receiving line. Glancing sideways, she saw that Otto's eyes were already upon her.

'Ah, *Fräulein* – shall we dance?'

Lydia took his hand, conscious of his face against hers as they moved across the floor.

'You are extremely beautiful tonight.' His voice tremored. 'Have I said that before?'

'Yes, you are very kind.'

'No, not kind, I speak the truth. My wife, she died five years ago – a problem with her heart – and since then I have looked at no other woman.'

'I'm so sorry.' To her surprise, Lydia felt a brief stab of

sympathy. He looked defeated somehow, as if the loss of his wife had lessened him as a man.

'No matter. I know that I am older than you, but I trust that my age does not trouble you too much.'

'Of course not.' She eyed the swastika on his arm and her resolve strengthened. This was no time for sentiment. If the Kommandant had feelings for her, then surely her mission would be easier.

'I have a big house in Düsseldorf.' He held her gently and swirled her round. 'There is a garden with *der Brunnen* –how you say – a fountain – and many rooms. Sadly, there are no children. Maybe you will come and see it one day?'

Rolling her head back as the music soared, she avoided his eyes. 'Maybe, one day.'

Later, after the meal had ended, Otto's henchman appeared at the table and passed him a note. The Kommandant stood up, bowed and excused himself from the room. Seizing the opportunity to eavesdrop on the conversation around her, Lydia listened without speaking. To her disappointment the officers' talk was inconsequential.

'You would like a drink, *Fräulein*?' The Leutnant's face glowed with false camaraderie.

'A glass of water would be welcome.' This man clearly hated her, and the feeling was mutual.

'You are enjoying your time at the Kommandantur?' A few drops of water from the jug splashed on her hands as he leaned over.

'It's a job I am pleased to do.' Lydia wiped her fingers with a napkin.

'Major Kruger thinks he is fortunate to have you in his office, *Fräulein*, but I—' He stopped short. 'Ah, here he comes now.'

She sighed with relief at the Kommandant's timely return, eager to know why he'd left.

'Ah, Lydia, I have something to tell you. My driver, Korporal Schmidt, is ill and has asked to be excused. He will not be able to take you home.' The Kommandant withdrew a cigar from his breast pocket. 'You will stay with me at the hotel tonight, *ja*?'

Lydia's body froze.

'That's kind of you, Herr Kommandant, but there really is no need. I couldn't possibly put you to all that trouble.' She knew she was stalling, but for once her mind was completely blank.

'It is, as you English say, no trouble at all. I have already made the necessary arrangements.'

'I, er—' the rest of words lodged in her throat. Fear had silenced her voice.

'And now – more champagne?'

She watched, mesmerised, as the bubbles surged to the top of the glass. Clutching the narrow stem as if it might give her courage, she raised it up and poured the golden liquid down her throat.

'I think you should maybe sip it, my dear. That is the correct way.' His face broadened into a smile.

'How very silly of me.' The colour rose in her cheeks. 'I was so thirsty I must have got carried away.'

The Kommandant beamed.

'Then I shall order another bottle.'

Lydia gazed round the sumptuous room. The only light came from two burgundy silk lampshades on either side of the bed, throwing ghostly shadows across the walls. Chinese rugs decked the floors and ornate cushions were scattered around. At the far end stood an antique mahogany wardrobe with a matching oval mirror on a stand. Fragile with fear, Lydia knew there was no escaping now.

Slowly she removed her jacket and hung it in the wardrobe, then unzipped the silk eau-de-nil dress, letting it fall to the floor. Tugging at her throat with clammy hands, she managed to release the clasp on Mama's beloved pearls. Finally, she undid her stockings, pulled her chemise over her shoulders and slid, trembling, under the starched sheets.

The sound of footsteps echoed down the corridor. There was silence, and then the door handle turned. Shrinking into the pillow, she closed her eyes, listening to the sounds of Kruger removing his uniform. Seconds later he got into bed beside her. She could still run away, tell him it was all a mistake. She still had a choice. She shivered. She'd known all along it would come to this. The hours of making small talk, smiling prettily at the enemy, gleaning information while obeying the rules of the Kommandantur.

The Kommandant's hoarse voice broke into her thoughts.

'You are shaking, my dear. Don't be frightened.' He leaned towards her, his body casting a distorted shadow on the wall behind them.

'I'm cold,' she lied. 'I want you to hold me close.' In her mind she imagined Martin, his eyes burning into hers, his fingers tracing a path from her eyes to her mouth, before stroking her throat and moving inexorably down.

'Relax and it will not hurt. I promise I will make you happy tonight.' The Kommandant's voice floated above her, his body like a falcon ready to pounce on its prey. The noise in her head grew louder till she heard someone scream…

She arched her back. Please God it would soon be over.

CHAPTER 21

Martin threw open the rectory door. 'Lydia. Come in, you look frozen. Where on earth have you been?'

'Just walking – up the Val des Terres.' She shivered, despite the winter sun. 'I needed some time to myself.'

'The Val des Terres? But that's miles.' He glanced at the clock. 'It's half past three. Have you eaten today?'

'You sound just like Mama.' She followed him through to the kitchen and warmed her hands on the range. 'I'm just a bit under the weather, that's all. It's probably a touch of flu.' *He defiled me. And I let him.*

'Sit down and I'll make you a drink. I've got some lemon crystals in the pantry and there's sugar left over from the last meeting.'

'Thanks.' She sat at the rectory table and rested her head in her hands.

Keep away. I'm soiled. Soiled by the Kommandant – soiled by the Nazis.

'There.' He put the steaming glass in front of her. 'I think you should rest before you go home. Why don't you lie on the sofa in the drawing room? I'll get an eiderdown from the spare room and make sure you're not disturbed.'

She nodded, too tired to argue. *Don't be kind, I can't bear it. I'm a slut. A Nazi whore.*

He stood up and ran a nervous hand through his hair.

'Whatever it is that's bothering you, I hope you'll be able to tell me when you're ready.'

Lydia lay back on the makeshift bed, her mind full of self-loathing. She stared at the ceiling where naked cherubs with feathered wings adorned the frieze, like butterflies from heaven. How could she justify what she had done? She remembered Martin's words, thrown at her in anger, '*You knew what you were doing when you joined the prayer group—*' A silent sob escaped from her mouth. Did she? And much worse, did he? Would he have asked her to join the Resistance if he knew it would come to this?

Looking back to her first days in England, how naïve she must have seemed. Brought up with every comfort imaginable, protected by her parents in a tight-knit community, she knew nothing of politics, literature or life outside in the real world. Few women had the chance to study at college and she had taken it all for granted. She had made friends, even had the occasional boyfriend, but nothing serious. She shut her eyes tightly, still trying to block out the memory of the previous night.

An hour or so later, after a fitful sleep, Lydia woke to the sound of rain beating against the drawing room window. She clambered off the sofa and ran upstairs to the bathroom, dousing herself in cold water till her skin tingled. Taking a deep breath, she dried her face, smoothed the creases from her blouse and made her way down to the study.

'Come in.' Martin's eyes gave nothing away. 'Are you feeling better?'

'Much better, thanks,' she lied, sitting down in front of him. 'It was kind of you to let me rest. I was wondering, have you heard any more about Arthur?'

'He's in Laufen internment camp in Germany. It's one of the better camps from what I can tell.' Martin shuffled the papers on his desk. 'I'm glad to see you've got some colour back in your cheeks.'

'I wish I'd realised he was in trouble.' Lydia bit her lip.

'You couldn't have, none of us did.'

'But I *knew* there was something wrong. He *told* me.'

'Told you?' Martin raised his eyebrows. 'Why didn't you say so before?'

'Because he asked me not to. We met at the Regal – just after I started at the Kommandantur. Arthur said I would be safe as long as I was careful; he'd done his homework and so far no one suspected me at all. Then he passed me a note.'

'What did it say?' Martin stood up and paced the room.

'That I mustn't speak to him, or mention his name to anyone, until further notice. If I saw him in town I must ignore him and cross the street. If I disobeyed, then my life – and his – would be in danger.'

'You did right not to tell me. Arthur must have had his reasons.'

Lydia stared at the floor. Why did he make her feel so inept? Sometimes she wished he'd get angry with her again. Anything was better than not knowing how he felt.

'I think I should go now,' she said. 'The Kommandant's going to Jersey next week, and I've lots to do before then.'

'I'm sorry, of course you must go. I should have been more considerate. But before you do—' He pulled her to him for the briefest moment. 'Just be careful – that's all.'

Lydia arrived home as Maggie was heading out of the door.

'Where are you off to?' she asked genially.

'To see a friend.' Maggie avoided her eyes. 'Won't be long.'

'Anyone I know?'

'Why do you ask?'

'Only that I hardly ever see you these days. You wouldn't think we lived in the same house.'

Maggie scowled. 'Maybe we'd see more of each other if you didn't spend so much time with the Kommandant.'

'Shush, please. It's work, not pleasure. Believe me, I have to do it.'

'*I have to do it,*' Maggie mocked. 'For your information, Major Kruger is not just tough on the islanders – some of his soldiers are badly treated, too.'

'How do you know that?' Lydia was listening intently now.

'I've just heard, that's all. Anyway, could we talk about this later? I'm in a hurry.' Maggie put her words into action.

'Shall I see you at teatime?' Lydia ran to the door but Maggie had already disappeared.

Lydia's heart plummeted as she stood on the rectory doorstep. She'd rather be anywhere but here. The door opened before she had a chance to knock.

'Lydia, hello.' Martin smiled in welcome. 'I'm glad you could make it. There's someone here I want you to meet.'

She followed him into the drawing room, cheered by the sight of a friendly face.

'Hello, Mrs Mellanby – Irene – *coumciq lafaire va*?'

The older woman stood up.

'I'm very well, my dear, but you can speak in English now. You're among friends.'

'It's just a habit, I'm afraid.'

Martin looked from one to the other. 'Please, do sit down.' He gestured towards the low mahogany table which was set, as usual, with a matching silver coffee pot and hot water jug alongside fine porcelain cups and saucers. 'Help yourselves. And now I need you to listen very carefully.'

Lydia did as she was told. She knew that look well enough by now.

'I have decided that you,' Martin gestured towards Irene, 'will take Arthur's place until further notice. This, as I'm sure you know, will involve a great deal of responsibility. When Lydia needs any information you will get it to her, night or day, whatever the consequences.'

Irene nodded. A shrewd woman in her early forties, she exuded old-fashioned common sense that Lydia found comforting.

'We are comrades already,' the older woman beamed. 'I'm sure we'll get on famously.'

Lydia really missed Arthur, especially as it seemed so hard to talk to Martin these days. At least now she would have someone to confide in.

For the next half-hour the two women talked as Martin looked on, nodding now and then in approval. Irene ran the family baker's shop in Smith Street where the lack of basic ingredients had badly affected trade. These days she sold jars of bramble jelly, brown flour rock buns, carrot jam and her own tomato bread, the recipe for which was a well-kept secret.

Irene's father had been an intelligence officer in the Great War and she'd grown up enthralled by his tales of bravery and valediction. Keen at first to follow in her father's footsteps, Irene had fallen in love with a local blacksmith and chosen to stay at home instead. It was only now that she regretted the lost opportunity.

As they finished talking, Martin left the room and returned clutching a black folder.

'What I am about to tell you is highly confidential.' His face appeared grey in the half-light. 'You, Lydia, have some prior knowledge of this, but neither of you must speak of it to anyone, even under threat of your lives. Do you understand?'

They both nodded.

'We have reason to believe that Hitler plans to ship every Guernsey man, woman and child over to Jersey. In time, our people will be deported to France – and all over Europe – to ensure they do not attempt an uprising or try to regain what is rightfully theirs. Guernsey will become a military base for German soldiers and, eventually, civilians will settle here too – selected citizens who will herald the beginning of a new Aryan race. A mass rebuilding process will take place until the houses, churches, schools and public buildings bear no visible sign of their heritage. Furthermore, in accordance with Hitler's decree, all history books, newspapers and public records will be destroyed and a new German "Utopia" created in which children – white, blond-haired children – will be indoctrinated from an early age. These plans must be thwarted at all costs or Guernsey, as we know it, will disappear.'

Lydia gave an involuntary shiver. So this was what Hitler meant by the 'Germanisation' of Guernsey. It was far worse than she'd feared. She glanced sideways at Irene whose face betrayed nothing.

'How do you know all this?' the older woman said at last.

'I can't tell you that, I'm afraid, but our sources are excellent. And now to the main reason for our meeting.' Opening a file marked *Church Organ Fund*, Martin turned to Lydia. 'There's a vital task we want you to undertake that will involve gaining access to the safe in the Kommandant's office. We have to find the exact details of Hitler's plans for they affect the lives of everyone on the island.'

'How do we know the plans are there?' asked Irene.

'You'll just have to trust me on that.'

'Do we know the combination of the safe?' Shock had finally loosened Lydia's tongue.

'We do. That's the easy bit.'

'How did you get it? And what if it's not the right one?'

'You ask too many questions, Lydia.' Martin shook his head. 'Just listen to me, please. The safe is in the wall at the back of Kruger's office hidden behind a large map of the island. You will be told exactly what you are looking for and we expect you to photograph as much of the information as you can.'

'When am I to do this?'

'As soon as possible. This is our best chance, while Kruger's still in Jersey.'

'There's just one problem.' Lydia kept her voice steady. 'Kruger's henchman doesn't trust me – he's made that very clear. Leutnant Becker will be watching my every move.'

'Then we'll just have to distract him, won't we?' Martin drummed his fingers on the table. 'Let me worry about that. You'll be fully briefed in the next twenty-four hours.'

'And what about me?' asked Irene.

'You must watch and wait. Stay away from the shop and speak to no one until I make contact again. Say you are ill, make an excuse, but keep out of sight. Meanwhile I'll put the plan to the others.'

Lydia eyed him closely. He didn't need anyone's consent. He was the boss and she knew it.

CHAPTER 22

Lydia woke with a jolt and rubbed the sleep from her eyes. She couldn't escape the nightmare – the implacable sea that still haunted her dreams. As a child she had loved the smell of the salt, the roar of the ocean, the sun that shone through clear water on to the golden sand. It had seemed the summer days would never end. But at night the sea took on a different guise: dark, heavy and mysterious. At night the sea crept silently, slyly, over her face until she drowned.

Making her way downstairs, she heard singing coming from the kitchen. She painted a smile on her face and threw open the door.

'Someone sounds happy.'

'I *am* happy.' Maggie was chopping cabbage into a large mixing bowl. 'You see, there's something I've been meaning to tell you.'

'We could do with some good news for a change.'

'I've met someone, someone really special.'

'That's wonderful.' Lydia threw her arms round her friend. 'Who is he? Do I know him?'

'His name is Kurt. He's very thoughtful and, well, I don't know how to explain it really. He's, well, courteous, exceptionally kind and as worried as we are about the war.'

'Kurt?' Lydia's face paled. 'A soldier? How did you meet him?'
'I was riding my bike near Candie Gardens a few weeks ago. It was just before curfew and I was worried I might be caught.

Anyway, I collided right into him and nearly knocked him over. He picked me up and gave me a plaster for my knee. He had such a sweet smile. Oh, Lydia, I can't believe he really is the enemy.'

'And you've seen him since?' The look of horror was lost on Maggie.

'Oh yes, the next time he saw me we stopped for a chat. I was just coming out of Creaseys and he was walking towards the town church. There were two of them. Kurt bowed ever so slightly and asked my name. I told him and he introduced himself, and his friend – Jurgen, I think he was called. Then he bowed again and said "Goodbye" in that funny accent and then they just walked away.'

'Is that it?' Lydia let go of her breath.

'No, not exactly.' Maggie's face reddened as she grabbed handfuls of cabbage and rolled them in seasoned flour. 'Don't be cross with me, please. He's wonderful and so different from anyone else I've ever met.'

'You mustn't do this, Maggie, can't you see? It will bring you nothing but heartache.'

'It's too late now to change my mind. I think I'm in love with him.' She put the cabbage cakes on a baking tray and slammed the oven door shut.

'Please, just listen to me.' Lydia begged. 'If anyone finds out they'll—'

'What? Cut off my hair and cover me with tar and feathers?'

'They'll call you a Jerry Bag… You'll be ostracised.'

'Don't lecture me with your posh English words,' Maggie was shouting now. 'You're a fine one to talk! *You're* sleeping with the Kommandant!'

Lydia gasped. 'How could you say such a thing? That's not true, and you know it.'

'Do I? It's okay for *you* – is that what you're saying? But now *I'm* in love with a German the rules have changed.'

'In love? You can't possibly think I'm in love with the Kommandant?'

'What am I supposed to think?' Maggie pouted. 'What other explanation can there be? All this talk about Martin – it's just a smokescreen, isn't it?'

Lydia buried her head in her hands. 'You don't know what you are saying. The war's turning friends into enemies. What will happen to us all?'

'Nothing's going to happen until you start telling me the truth.' Maggie scowled. 'And now, if you'll excuse me I've got things to do.'

Wearily, Lydia pulled open the back door and sat down on the step. She should never have lied to her best friend, she knew that now. She'd been crazy to think she could get away with it. And now Maggie was in love with a German soldier.

'Ah, Fräulein Le Page. You are here once more, I see?' The officer's stocky frame filled the doorway of Kruger's office.

'Good morning, Leutnant Becker.' Lydia kept her voice light. 'Would you like me to make you some coffee?'

Ignoring the question, the officer moved menacingly towards her. He was tall, much taller than the Kommandant, with a sallow face and stark blue eyes.

'I wish to make it clear that you are here because the Kommandant wishes it.' He grasped her wrist and twisted it up against his jaw. '*I* do not approve of your presence. You understand, *ja*?'

Wincing, she wrenched her hand away.

'I understand.'

'Good. There is no need of coffee. You are here to work.' His eyes narrowed to a squint. 'I will be watching you, *Fräulein*.'

Lydia held her breath until the sound of his boots had disappeared down the corridor. The fear that clawed at her gut was all too familiar these days. Gazing round the Kommandant's office she scrutinised every detail. On his desk pens and pencils were positioned at exactly the same angle while each shelf was an exercise in precision: hardbound books standing bolt upright, their titles displayed in alphabetical order. Every document, new or old, had its rightful place. Why did she feel he was watching her still?

Sitting down at her own desk she flicked through the in-tray. Whatever his reasons for being in Jersey, the Kommandant had left a huge pile of work and clearly had every intention of keeping her busy. On top of the pile was a list of buildings where V for Victory signs had been daubed around the island. Her task was to contact all the addresses where occupants fell under suspicion, whether schools, shops, or private individuals, and send them a warning. Only last week someone had painted a bright blue V on the walls of the Emergency Hospital, a harmless act of passive resistance, and one she secretly admired. Many islanders had home-made V badges hidden in their gloves or under their lapels, all of which did wonders for morale.

Lydia fed some paper into the typewriter. She hated helping the enemy. She hated being called a collaborator. It was time to concentrate on the real task in hand.

At precisely four o'clock the following afternoon Lydia peered through the window of the Kommandant's office. Two local fishermen were arguing about their share of the day's catch, their voices rising high on the wind. This was her cue.

Shutting the office door with a heavy clunk she walked to the far side of the room, listening for sounds of movement in the corridor. The Kommandant's desk was partially obscured by a large metal bookcase packed solid with hardback copies of *Mein Kampf* and memorabilia from the Great War.

Lydia slipped behind the desk and stood level with the large framed map of Guernsey. She gave it a sharp tap and watched it slide to one side. Reaching for the dial on the front of the safe, she keyed in the combination, holding her breath as the seconds ticked by. A single click – then the heavy door swung open in her hands. Adrenalin kicked in as she stood on her tiptoes and felt inside. First came a large bunch of keys and then she saw what looked like hand-drawn plans of the aerodrome. Underneath were pages and pages of correspondence dated before the war and an old-fashioned barometer wrapped in brown paper. In a corner of the safe a used brown envelope was stuffed with German marks along with a bundle of blank identity cards. There was no trace of the dossier on Hitler's plans for Guernsey. Painstakingly she searched through the rest of the contents.

Lydia froze. Did she hear footsteps? Blood still pumped though her body, but her legs refused to move. If they found her now they would shoot her. Jolted back to reality, she leaned back, closed the safe door and slammed the picture frame into place before kicking out wildly with the back of her calf to create a distraction. Losing her balance, she toppled backwards across the tooled green leather desk. Pens, pots, papers and letters cascaded down, streaming out over the floor in an orgy of confusion. She stared at the chaos with frightened eyes – would it be enough to save her?

The door flew open.

'What do you think you are doing, Fraülein Le Page?' A familiar rasping voice filled the air.

'I have had a fall, I'm afraid, Corporal Reinhart.'

'I can see that with my own eyes. But how?' Seconded from the barracks at Vazon Bay, Gelda Reinhart was disliked by almost everyone she met, but Lydia had tried to keep on the right side of her.

'I think I must have blacked out.' She rubbed her eyes with the back of her hand.

'Blacked out? What does this mean?' The corporal's hair was cropped short like a man's and her pink eyes bulged with curiosity.

Rolling over away from the safe, Lydia pulled herself up.

'It means I fainted. I have not eaten today, Corporal. I felt dizzy and the next thing I knew—'

'Yes, yes, *Fraülein*, but why do you not eat? You are allowed food when the Kommandant is away – is that not so?' She gestured towards the floor. 'You will clear *der Quatsch*, how you say, the mess, and I will send somebody to help.'

'I would rather do it myself, thank you.' Lydia cleared her throat. 'I know where it all belongs.'

The corporal smiled, waving her hand towards the desk.

'The Kommandant will know nothing of this. It will remain between the two of us. In return, you will keep me on Major Kruger's, how you say, good books. You understand?'

Lydia nodded in relief. Right now she'd agree to anything.

Leaving work at the end of the day, Lydia hurried to the telephone box by the bus terminus and dropped her bag on the floor. She had no idea if she was being followed. She flicked through the directory, pretending to search for a number while she collected her thoughts. Had she really escaped the fracas at the Kommandantur unscathed?

When Corporal Reinhart left the office, a smirk etched on her face, Lydia had cleared up the mess without further interruption, meticulously restoring everything to its rightful place. Humming under her breath to calm her nerves, she double-checked the Kommandant's desk – pens, pencils, papers, a glass paperweight and a statue of a German eagle with a swastika in its claws, all in their original place, the twisted brown cord of the telephone lying just as he liked it, at right angles to the door. The map of Guernsey she'd swatted at had, miraculously, swung back into place over the safe. With one backwards glance, she grabbed her hat and coat and walked the hundred or so yards to the main entrance. Trying her best to appear nonchalant, she chatted idly to the soldier on duty before showing her pass and strolling out of the building.

Was the corporal playing games with her? Lydia raised her eyes heavenward. If the Jerries wanted to arrest her, she wished they'd just get on with it. Replacing the directory, she glanced down at her watch: six thirty p.m. Perhaps she hadn't been followed, after all. She would find another phone box and then ring the rectory.

Lydia leaned heavily against the harbour wall. The crippling fear had eased now, but the bitter taste of failure seared the back of her throat. A loud squawk pierced the air as a lone seagull landed on the parapet, a welcome splash of light in the all-encompassing gloom.

'Lydia! Thank God you're safe.'

Martin's face appeared in the shadows.

'Yes, I'm safe.'

'I came as fast as I could.' He sounded distraught. 'I've borrowed the horse and trap to take you home.'

'That's kind of you, Martin, but I didn't mean to alarm you.' Kindness was the last thing she needed right now.

'You look exhausted,' he whispered. 'What happened?'

'I searched the safe but the papers weren't there. Just some boring correspondence and a bunch of old keys.' She smiled ruefully.

'You did your best. So why are you so upset?'

'As I closed the safe, I heard Corporal Reinhart marching

down the corridor. I pretended to trip over to cover my tracks.' She quickly recounted the story.

'Are you hurt?' he asked when she had finished.

'No, but that Reinhart woman suspects something, I'm sure of it. I've probably ruined things for all of us.'

'Hold on, hold on.' Martin's voice was gruff. 'You did your best. The papers could be hidden anywhere, for pity's sake.'

'In the Kommandant's home, you mean? At Sea Breeze?' She blinked back tears. 'Is that what you're trying to say?'

'Don't even think about it, Lydia. The miracle is you *didn't* get arrested. That's all that matters to me.'

She looked at him closely now, his dark hair in disarray, his grey eyes bright with emotion.

'All that matters? But I thought—?'

'Sometimes you think too much. I was convinced something had happened.'

His hands gripped her shoulders. 'And that ... well, that's more than I could bear.'

'What do you mean? I don't understand.'

'You don't, do you?' He shook his head. 'You really can't see what's right in front of you.' Closing his eyes, he moved forward and rested his head on her chest. 'I love you, Lydia Le Page. Christ only knows how much I love you.'

Desire, which had lain dormant too long like snowdrops in summer, surged through her body with such force that she broke free from his grip, a sharp cry escaping from her lips.

Gently lifting her chin, he stroked his thumbs over her cheeks.

'Don't cry, my beautiful, brave girl. Please don't cry.' He pulled out a handkerchief and gently dabbed her face.

'Why didn't you say this before?' Lydia's voice was barely a whisper.

'I tried to, remember, the night before Arthur was arrested, but if I'd told you how I felt, would you have believed me?'

'I'm not sure.'

He shook his head. 'I'd denied it, even to myself. And now I'm worried I've left it too late.'

She wanted to beat her fists on his chest, to shriek out loud, *of course it's too late, you stupid man, you're in love with a Nazi whore.* Just then a truck full of soldiers appeared out of the dark, moving noisily down the Esplanade towards them.

'Come on.' Martin's voice was thick with emotion. 'I'm taking you home.'

The night air was freezing by the time they reached the pony and trap. Gently Martin lifted Lydia into the seat and tucked a woollen blanket round her knees. Without a word he drove through the empty lanes, his body not touching hers. Lydia closed her eyes, unable to comprehend what had happened between them. All she could hear was the sound of hooves and the rhythm of her own heartbeat.

Twenty minutes later she woke with a start. Martin had pulled on the reins bringing the trap to a standstill and was staring at her as if for the first time.

'What is it?' She turned round to face him.

'I want to kiss you, no, I *need* to kiss you, dear Lydia. Is that so very wrong?'

'No,' she whispered, feeling the warmth of his breath on her face.

His lips, at first, were tentative. Then he kissed her again, more urgently now, his tongue caressing hers.

'Stay with me my beautiful girl, stay with me always.' The words echoed in the stillness of the night.

Though her mind was telling her to stop, every fibre of her body disagreed. She loved this man, she knew that now, but the love, the desire, the crushing need to be a part of his life had come too late for both of them. She had given herself to Otto Kruger and that was where she belonged.

'I need time,' she said at last, pulling herself away from him. 'Please let me have some time.'

He nodded; his eyes gave nothing away. 'Of course. I will take you back home.'

Later that evening, lying in bed with her eyes wide open, Lydia wondered if she would ever sleep again. Every sense seemed heightened by these new emotions; the meaning of life rewritten in a strange yet vibrant prose. Tomorrow no longer mattered. Tonight she was in love.

CHAPTER 23

Early the following morning Lydia was filling the kettle at the kitchen sink when Edna appeared in her dressing gown, her face flushed.

'You'll never guess who was at the front door just now.' The older woman tutted. 'The Reverend Martell, no less. He came with this letter for you.' She dropped an envelope on to the table.

Lydia steadied her hands on the sink. 'At this hour? He must have something urgent for me to do.'

'Well, whatever it is, he looked very solemn. Turning up like that without so much as a smile. I don't know what's happened to manners these days.'

'I'm sure he didn't mean to be rude. He has a great deal on his mind at the moment.'

'So you keep telling me, but I'm darned if I know what it is. He's running a church, not the British Army. Make me some sugar-beet coffee, there's a good girl, as soon as the kettle's boiled. I'm going upstairs to get dressed.'

Shutting the kitchen door behind Edna, Lydia tore open the envelope.

My dearest Lydia

I have an important mission to undertake so it may be a while before I see you again. I'm sorry I couldn't explain more last night

but I need you to keep strong for both of us. Carry on with your work and remember, wherever I go, you are here inside my soul.
Yours always,
Martin.

Lydia screwed the note into a ball and threw it on to the range, watching as it flared briefly in the hot coals. Had something happened? Or was he just giving her time to sort out her feelings? Whatever the reason, she prayed he wasn't in danger.

Wrinkling her nose, she poured boiling water on to the dried sugar beet and then carried the tasteless liquid through to the parlour.

Mechanically she walked back into the hall and shouted up the stairs, 'Your coffee's in the parlour, Mrs Gallienne. I'll be off to work now.'

The overnight frost had disappeared and the north-easterly wind smelt of burning wood. Lydia cursed as a lorry careered towards her; how she hated traffic driving on the wrong side of the road. Soldiers on motorbikes tore recklessly around the island's narrow lanes, which were littered with German road signs, while the locals – the few still allowed petrol – carried on as before. It was a miracle no one had been killed.

Approaching the Esplanade, Lydia glanced at the clock on the Weighbridge. How much longer could she put off going to the Kommandantur? After yesterday's disaster she would probably be sacked or even arrested and neither prospect held much appeal. If only Arthur was still here. He would have reassured her, or at least told her what to do.

'Please, Martin,' she whispered under her breath, 'please don't come to any harm.'

As she reached the bottom of the Pollet, Lydia caught sight of

Maggie standing in a shop doorway. Waving to catch her attention, she spotted a soldier pedalling furiously in the opposite direction. Was that Kurt? Were the two of them still together? Somehow she'd hoped they'd finally seen sense.

'Hello, Maggie,' she called out. 'You were up early this morning. I didn't hear you leave.'

'I wasn't at home last night.' Maggie stared down at her feet. 'Told Ma I was staying with a friend.'

'Are you sure you know what you're doing?' Lydia asked, crossing the road.

'I can look after myself, thanks. You might be cleverer than me, Lydia Le Page, but you're not my keeper. Anyway, shouldn't you be with the Kommandant?'

'The Kommandant is away in Jersey,' Lydia replied without thinking.

'Oh, what a shame. You must be so lonely. Do excuse me or I'll be late for work.' With that Maggie turned and stomped off down the street.

Lydia let out a sigh. What right did she have to criticise anyone? She was in love with the rector of Torteval, sleeping with the German Kommandant and any day now might well be shot as a traitor. One thing was certain: she would find Hitler's plans for Guernsey whatever Martin said, even if it meant breaking into Sea Breeze. She still had the key to the back porch so with luck it wouldn't come to that. Decision made, she quickened her pace and headed towards the Kommandantur.

The house on the cliff was bathed in silence as Lydia approached the back gate. Edging towards the rear porch, she stumbled, biting hard into her tongue. She could feel the beads of sweat glistening on her brow as the key slowly turned in the door. Thank God they hadn't changed the lock. She crept into the parlour, straining her ears for sounds of movement, then through the entrance hall crouching down to peer through the leaded window. The soldier on guard was dozing in the winter sun, his rifle perched at an angle at his feet. As soon as she reached the drawing room, she was overcome with bittersweet memories. There beside the inglenook fireplace stood her father's writing desk, just as it had when she was a child. She could almost see the smoke rising in grey swirls from the bowl of his beloved briar pipe.

A deafening crash shattered the silence, followed by the sound of splintering glass. Lydia stood motionless, her heart thudding. Dashing back into the hall she grasped at the cellar door, tumbled down the steps and landed spread-eagled on the floor. Was it an intruder? Or had the Kommandant returned? She listened in vain for the sound of footsteps.

After several long minutes her eyes adjusted to the dark. Rubbing her bruised leg, she felt her way around the basement, tripping over several upended boxes. They were full of German reference books and requisitioned wireless sets along with a strange assortment of metal tools. Stopping now and then to listen for sounds of movement, she heard nothing but an eerie silence.

Up ahead a chink of light appeared through the cellar window, barely visible through the tangle of weeds. There beneath the window ledge stood a small wooden cupboard covered in dust and cobwebs. Lydia studied it closely, a far-off memory unfolding somewhere deep inside her. Dusting the cupboard down with her handkerchief, she reached out and twisted the metal key, gently rocking it back and forth until the lock surrendered. As the door gave way the sweet smell of hyacinths overwhelmed her.

Every winter when she was small, Papa would plant three hyacinth bulbs in a brown ceramic bowl that once belonged to

Grandmama. With all the reverence of childhood, Lydia would place the bowl in the wooden cupboard, shutting the door firmly to keep out the light. Next her father would hide it away under the stairs. At the beginning of February Papa retrieved the cupboard and lifted the ancient bowl out of the gloom. From the brown and wizened bulbs, green shoots sprouted like moisture rising from desert sand. Lydia watered the plants each day, gazing in awe at the star-like flowers in glorious shades of pink and purple. This, she knew, meant spring was on its way.

Now, all these years later, Lydia stared in disbelief at her find. Tugging at the cupboard door she cursed under her breath as a slat came away in her hand. She crouched down and peered inside, but the cupboard was empty. Stung by disappointment she replaced the slat, her hand catching on something wedged underneath. Easing it to the safety of her palm she saw that it was an old brown envelope folded in two, barely the size of a postcard. She peered at the familiar black handwriting. Though faded and torn, the letter clearly bore her own name.

Just then the cellar door creaked, like a bough bending in the storm. Lydia thrust the envelope under her sweater. She must have been crazy to think she could get away with this. Her body rigid, she watched as two small eyes appeared out of the dark. Relief had never felt sweeter. Scrambling up the cellar steps she grabbed the ball of black fur, sobbing as the kitten rubbed its wet nose against her face.

After several minutes had passed she pulled open the cellar door and peered out into the hall. A flower vase lay in pieces, its broken blooms scattered over the wet carpet. Creeping round the debris, she ran into the drawing room and crouched down behind the velvet curtains. From there she could see the lone sentry, helmet pulled down over his eyes, his hand still clutching his rifle as he slept. Inside, the house was silent except for the tick of the grandfather clock and the eerie echo of her beating heart.

Lydia moved from room to room, staggered by the chaos the enemy had caused. It was as if the tide had altered its course, surging up the cliffs, and into the house, whisking away the memories she'd cherished for so long. After a fruitless search of the ground floor she ran upstairs, checking cupboards and drawers, anywhere she thought the papers might be. Back in her old bedroom the emotion became too much. She knelt down and wept; her mission had been in vain.

Lydia crept through the back porch, her throat taut with fear. Glancing from side to side she ambled back to the cliff path so as not to arouse suspicion. Then, fuelled by adrenalin, she ran non-stop till she reached Maggie's home.

The house in the Vrangue was empty. Seizing the moment, Lydia bound up the stairs, shook off her shoes and slipped into bed, her father's letter clutched in her hand. She lifted the counterpane, placed the envelope on top of the sheet and carefully removed the contents.

December 24, 1930

My dearest Liddy

Please forgive your old Papa for what I am going to say. Your Mama and me, we might have been wrong but it was all done out of love. I am going to copy out a bit of your school report from when you were seven years old. The words are too posh for my liking, but it's how I will always remember you.

'Lydia is an inquisitive little girl. She is bright and intelligent with a great capacity for making friends. She is rarely satisfied with a simple explanation. If she fails to understand a concept

she will ask, and ask again, and keep asking until she's convinced she has the right answer. It is altogether a pleasure to have her in my class.'

That is the brave little girl I'm writing to now. I'll be gone from your life when you read this, but, Liddy my girl, you'll stay with me into eternity.

Now there's something I have to tell you, something I should have said a long time ago. I hope and pray it won't hurt you too much. You were born in England on Christmas Eve, 1918, to Emily's sister, May, and her husband Walter Weissman, who had some important job in an Austrian bank. As you know they were killed in an accident in the South of France. You were nigh-on eighteen months old when we adopted you as our own.

I know this will come as a terrible shock. We always meant to tell you, your Mama and me, that you were not our own flesh and blood. We had tried for so long for a child of our own but it was not to be. We thought you were a gift from God. As you grew up, we blocked it from our minds until, in the end, we almost believed you were ours.

Can you forgive us? There were many times, dear Liddy, when I wanted to tell you the truth, but I promised your Mama I wouldn't for as long as I lived. Now, at last, it's time for you to hear it.

I hope one day you'll be blessed with a child of your own. Then maybe you will understand what we did.

Your loving Papa, always.

Jack Le Page

Lydia lifted her pillow and placed the letter underneath. Pulling the eiderdown over her face she cried until her eyes were dry and her breath came in muffled gasps.

'Oh Papa,' she whispered, 'how do I know who I am?'

CHAPTER 24

Emily wrung her hands together till they were raw; something was wrong and she knew it. She hadn't seen her daughter since Christmas and the longer the silence lasted, the worse it seemed. Lydia was out most days, so Edna said, spending her evenings on church business or else shut in her room. It was bad enough losing Jack, but now it felt like she was losing her daughter too. Sometimes in her darkest moments she wondered if the three of them had ever really belonged.

Gasping for breath, Emily hauled herself out of the chair. She had one of her funny turns coming on. She grabbed the last of the smelling salts, wrenched off the cap and breathed in deeply, her heart flapping like a fledgling flying the nest. Overcome with tiredness, she made her way to the bedroom, tugging at the buttons on the collar of her blouse. She rolled on to the bed, slid the eiderdown over her shoulders and closed her eyes. She would rest for an hour till her breathing settled down. Then she would put on her hat and coat and go and find Lydia.

Lydia was just leaving Maggie's house as her mother appeared at the gate.

'Mama, you frightened me. What on earth are you doing here?'

'What do you think? I've come to see you. You've been avoiding me, so don't deny it. What have I done?'

'You know very well what you've done.' Lydia eyes flashed. 'You should have told me.'

'Told you what?'

'About my father!'

Bewildered, Emily shook her head.

'What is there to tell? *Mon Dieu* – you know more about him than anyone.'

'No, Mama. I'm talking about my *real* father.' She lowered her voice. *'The one who was a born a Jew.'*

Emily steadied herself on the gatepost as the colour drained from her face.

'Hush, dear girl. Who in heaven's name told you that?'

'Your own husband, that's who – the man you married. He wrote me a letter. I found it by accident the other day.' She knew it was cruel, but she couldn't help it.

'A letter … but … how?'

'He wanted me to know, didn't he? But you wouldn't let him tell me.'

'Where on earth did you find this letter?' The old woman's eyes filled with tears.

'It doesn't matter now. The important thing is that he wanted me to have it.'

'Let's not talk about it here, please. As far as I'm concerned, I'm still your mother. Can we go into the house, please?'

'We can.' Lydia unlocked the front door. 'But don't think you can silence me that easily.'

Head bowed, Emily followed her in. 'Your papa and me, whatever you may think, we made the decision together.' Her words came out in a whisper.

'Of course you did.' Lydia's anger had found its own voice. *'I* didn't have a say in the matter.'

'You were much too young to understand, don't you see? At

first I pleaded with Jack not to tell you. Then, as time passed, it got harder and harder to face up to the truth.' Emily wrung her old lace handkerchief between both hands, perspiration gathering in droplets on her forehead. 'Oh, *ma petite*, we didn't want to spoil your happiness.'

'*Your* happiness, you mean.'

'We did what we thought was best for everyone.'

'By hiding who I really was? Shame on you, Mama. I had a right to know.'

Just then Edna's voice cut through the air.

'*What on earth's going on?* You'll wake the entire neighbour—' She stopped short. '*Emily – are you all right?*'

Lydia spun round.

'Mama, what is it, what's wrong?' She reached out as her mother slumped to the ground.

The doctor's voice was reassuring.

'She's in shock, that's all. She'll be better when she's rested.'

Lydia cradled her mother in her arms, unable to control her tears.

'It's my fault, doctor. I said something she didn't want to hear.'

'There's no need to blame yourself, my dear. I have examined her heart and lungs. She has a bad chest but nothing untoward. Your mother has already lost her husband and her home. Such events can trick the body into showing all kinds of unpleasant symptoms.'

'So she will get better? Is that what you're saying?'

He nodded. 'Don't be too hard on yourself. We are living in difficult times.'

Lydia smiled wanly. Platitudes were the last thing she needed right now.

*

Several hours later as the light faded, Lydia faced the enormity of what had happened. At the age of forty Emily Le Page had adopted her dead sister's baby, overwhelmed as she was by grief, and innocent in the ways of motherhood. Poor Mama didn't deserve to be treated this way.

Lydia had been cruel and selfish, turning on the very woman who had raised her as her own. She longed to tell all this to Martin, but then hadn't she betrayed him, too? She had slept with Otto Kruger: there could never be anything between them now. She was a different person with a new life and a new set of values. One thing was certain. Martin's life was already in danger. He must never know her father was a Jew.

'Why have you been avoiding me?' Martin frowned as he paced up and down the drawing room. 'I've been back a week and you haven't spoken a word.'

'I'm not avoiding you.' Lydia stared out of the rectory window. 'I've been busy at work.'

'Tell me, what's wrong?'

'I can't, I'm sorry.' She had come here on impulse hoping to make her peace and now she regretted it.

'Say something, please – anything is better than silence.' Grasping her shoulders, he pulled her to him. 'I love you, Lydia, for heaven's sake, you *must* know that. I love your strength, the way your eyes crinkle when you're—'

'Stop it, Martin, please. It's no good.' She bowed her head. 'I can't do this.'

'Why not? You feel the same about me, I know you do. Look at me and tell me you don't love me.'

'I care about you, Martin, really I do.' She covered her face with her hands. 'But, well, the truth is – I think my future lies with Otto.'

Incredulity swamped his face. 'That bastard Kruger? Don't make me laugh! Oh, come on, Lydia. You can do better than that.'

'He's going to take me back to Germany after the war.' Lydia studied her fingernails. 'There's nothing left here for me now. We can start a new life—'

Martin grabbed the cloth and ripped it from the table, sending cups, spoons and saucers crashing to the floor.

'Don't lie to me, Lydia. If you don't feel the same then say so, but don't insult my intelligence. What in God's name has the man done to persuade you?'

Lydia's eyes flashed with rage. 'How dare you say those things to me? Are you suggesting I can be bought?' Clenching her hands, she launched forward, thumping his chest till her breath came in gasps and tears trickled down her cheeks. Why did he have to make it so painful? Why couldn't he just let her go?

Martin stood there, his body rigid, arms by his side, waiting for her anger to subside. Then, bowing his head, he turned and left the room.

'I'm worried about the Reverend Martell.' Irene ran a duster over the shop counter. 'I can't get any sense out of him any more.'

Lydia feigned surprise. 'Why, what's wrong?'

'I think he's getting careless, too careless for his own good.'

'In what way? I admit I haven't seen much of him lately.'

'Well, I have. I called at the rectory yesterday and it wasn't a pretty sight. In all my life I've never seen such a mess – books and papers all over the place, unwashed cups, and clothes in a heap. Between you and me I'm not even sure he'd had a wash, never mind a shave. I know it's none of my business, dear, but have you two fallen out?'

Lydia bit her lip. She could trust Irene, she knew that, but when it came to Martin, she didn't even trust herself.

'Not in the way you mean,' she said at last. 'It's just that, well, working for the Kommandant is taking all my energy right now.'

'And your senses, from the sound of things. You look drained, my love, completely worn out. Are you sure there's nothing you want to tell me?'

'To be honest, I'm worried about Sophie Romerill.' Lydia was glad of a chance to change the subject. 'It's bad enough threatening to send her to Germany, but now they've requisitioned her home. I had a look yesterday and it's been looted. There'll be nothing left when she gets out of hospital.'

Irene pursed her lips. 'I reckon she won't be here for much longer. She's a Jew, isn't she? Like as not the Jerries will send her packing.'

'Her parents were Jewish, from what I can gather, but not practising Jews. Besides, she's a sweet old woman and wouldn't hurt a fly. Someone with a grudge against her must have informed the Jerries.'

'That's as maybe—' Irene hesitated. 'They shoot the Jews in Germany, you know. Load them up in a van, put them in front of a firing squad and shoot them.'

'But they'd never do that to *our* people, would they?'

'They'll do whatever Hitler orders, I'm afraid. The Kommandant might seem civilised, hosting dinner dances, smiling at young babies, but don't be fooled by all that. Kruger's pure evil underneath.'

Lydia closed her eyes. She didn't need reminding. Even now she could see the lust in his eyes, feel his body bearing down on hers.

'Are you unwell, my dear?'

'Just a bit dizzy, that's all.'

'I'd get along home if I were you.'

'I will, if you don't mind, Irene. Oh, and thank you for telling me about, well, you know, the rector. I'll see what I can do.'

CHAPTER 25

Emily's eyes were pleading.

'Don't be angry with me, Lydia, I beg you. You're all I've got left now.' The old woman's hands lay motionless on the counterpane, blue veins bulging through the pallid skin. Two days had passed since she'd fainted. Although the fever had gone, her health had scarcely improved.

'I'm sorry for what I said—' Lydia wrung her hands together, 'and for the pain it caused you, but how *could* you both keep such a devastating secret?'

'Because we loved you. In the beginning, you see, we didn't want to risk hurting you. And then, as time went on—'

'Didn't want to hurt me!' Lydia's words came out in a strangled squeak. 'I'm not really Lydia Le Page, am I? I'm no longer a Guernsey girl. My real parents are dead and I'm a Jewess living on a Nazi-occupied island!'

Emily leaned back on the starched white pillow, the little colour she had left draining from her face.

'Never let anyone hear you say you're a Jew – do you hear me? It's much too dangerous. They'll send you away. You must carry on as if this hadn't happened. Your papa would never have wanted—'

'But he wasn't my papa, was he? That's just it. I loved him like a father, I miss him like a father, but – oh,' she hesitated. 'You're not my real mother either. Why didn't someone just tell me the truth?'

'It was my fault, Lydia.' Emily's voice was barely a whisper. 'I made Jack keep the secret. He wanted to tell you so many times, but I begged him to wait a little longer.' She covered her mouth and coughed, a dry hollow cough that made her chest rattle.

Lydia poured a glass of water, put her arms round her mother's shoulders and lifted the glass to her lips.

'Of course he wanted me to know. He must have done, or he wouldn't have hidden the letter.'

'Tell me about the letter.' Emily lay back on the pillow and closed her eyes. 'Where did you find it?'

'Let's not talk about it now. You're not well, Mama, and I shouldn't be upsetting you like this.'

'Please, my girl ... I need to know.'

Very gently she took hold of the old woman's hand.

'I broke in to Sea Breeze. It was stupid, I know, but the Kommandant was away and I wanted to see what they had done to our home.' This was not the truth, but it would have to do for now. 'I still have the key to the back porch – you know how Papa always insisted we had a spare – and—'

'You stupid, stupid girl,' Emily started to splutter. 'Do you want to get yourself killed?'

'Listen to me, please, Mama.' Slowly, and without emotion, Lydia related what had followed.

Tears streamed down Emily's cheeks as the story unfolded.

'He found a way to tell you, didn't he, from beyond the grave,' she whispered. 'My poor dear Jack, he had the last word in the end.'

'He was right, you know he was. Go to sleep now, and we'll talk about it in the morning.'

'How is your mama?' Flo looked up from her knitting.

'She's sleeping now, Mrs Brouard. We talked and I'm sure we've still got a lot more to say, but that's for the future. The fever's passed, and she just needs plenty of rest.'

'Don't be too hard on her,' Flo said sadly. 'She loves you dearly. A kinder soul you couldn't wish to meet.'

Lydia's body ached with exhaustion. Who else, she wondered, knew the truth about her past? Desperate as she was to know, she daren't risk another confrontation. Instead she just nodded.

'I'm off now back to Maggie's.'

A shadow of a smile crossed Flo's face. 'Don't blame yourself, my love. You didn't ask for any of this. You'll see, it'll sort itself out in the end.'

'You're a good friend, Mrs Brouard, and my mother needs you right now. I'll see you in the morning.'

Two weeks later Emily's strength started to return.

'I've kept something for you, Lydia,' she said as the two of them sat in Flo's parlour, shafts of light poking their way through the curtains. 'Photographs of your *real* mama when she was a little girl, right up to when she got married.'

Lydia hesitated. 'Do you have some of me as a baby, you know—' Her voice trailed away.

'With your mama and papa? Yes, I do. They're all in the envelope on the table.'

She pulled an old cardboard photo frame from the pocket of her cardigan.

'This one is my favourite. Don't open it till you're on your own. It belongs to you now.'

Lydia's hand flew to her mouth. 'I've just realised something!'

'Whatever is it?'

'The dresses. I've been wearing my real mother's dresses.'

Emily pressed her fingers hard against her lips. 'I thought it was what you'd have wanted. You remind me so much of May at your age.'

Lydia squeezed the older woman's hand. 'Don't upset yourself. Tell me what she was like.'

'Not at all like me. She felt trapped in Guernsey, poor soul. She dreamt of going to England and travelling the world. And then she met your papa. I remember her so full of energy, always smiling, always wanting to know what was round the corner. Sometimes she seemed much older than her years. It was as if she knew she hadn't got long on this earth and wanted to live every moment as if it was her last.'

Lydia swallowed back tears.

'And my father?'

'Oh, he was such a charmer, forthright and intelligent. He swept your mother quite off her feet. He was tall – about six foot two, with dark, slicked back hair and a moustache. He'd moved to England to escape the persecution of the Jews and made quite a success of himself – something to do with banking. Oh, Lydia, your mother loved him from the minute they met – she was just so happy.'

'Did she, er, plan to have me?' Lydia bit her lip. 'Was I, you know, a wanted child?'

'You were a surprise, I think, but a lovely one. They idolised you, the pair of them. You'd have thought they'd invented parenthood the way they fussed over you – it was a joy to see, believe me. Your mother was kind-hearted, too. She knew it hurt your papa and me that we couldn't have children of our own so she brought you home to see us as often as she could, to make us feel part of the family.'

Lydia closed her eyes. 'I should remember something of those days, shouldn't I? Something about my old life?' So many things were beginning to fall into place: the feeling of belonging the first time she arrived in England, the look of fear that flitted sometimes over her mother's face, her father's extraordinary devotion

– all of these made sense now. It was as if she had wiped the steam from the mirror only to see the truth staring back at her.

Emily's voice had faded into the distance now. 'You were much too young to remember.'

When Lydia woke, she was on her own. Carefully she spread the contents of the battered brown envelope over the dining room table. There were several photos of her birth mother with her father – a handsome man with a serious expression softened by wide, questioning eyes. In another shot a young Lydia, barely able to walk, was clutching on to her parents' hands.

Then came the familiar one of the newly married couple; Walter Kreisler and May Le Page together. A framed copy had been in the drawing room at Sea Breeze for as long as she could remember. She could see her own likeness in her father now – the square chin, the slight turn of the head – why hadn't she noticed it before?

Finally she pulled out the photograph Emily had given her: a woman with sleek dark hair falling into gentle curls round her face, smiling down at the baby in her arms, her eyes radiating love.

'Hello, Mama,' she whispered, over and over again, as if the words could transcend time.

She sat quite still as daylight turned to dusk, surrounded by faded prints that filled her mind with memories no one had ever shared. When she stood at last, her eyes long devoid of tears, she knew what she had to do.

Emily Le Page was sitting in the drawing room, staring out of the window with a look of bewilderment on her face. Kneeling down, Lydia cupped the blue-veined hands in her own.

'Thank you, Mama,' she whispered, 'thank you for making me who I am.'

The old woman turned, her waxen cheeks stained now with colour.

'Mama? Does that mean I am still your mother?'

'Of course you are, and always will be. You must never think anything else.'

'Oh, Lydia.' Emily took her daughter in her arms. 'I love you, my dear, darling girl.'

'Thank you for coming, Lydia.' Martin's voice was hollow. 'I need to tell you the truth before I go.' They were standing in his study, fear almost tangible in the half light.

'What do you mean, before you go? What's happened? What have you done?'

'They've finally got me. They know who I am. Just listen, please. It's only a matter of time now. It was stupid. I don't know what came over me. The Jerries were following me when I picked up the latest news from the Allies. I should've just left it and gone back later, but I took the risk. I thought I'd shaken them off, so I stopped for a drink at the town pump. They caught me red-handed with the evidence in my bag. I told the Leutnant – self-opinionated bigot – that no one else at the church was involved, but I'm not sure he believed me.'

'But—'

'Please. We haven't got much time. I want you to promise that you'll carry on with the prayer group, for your own sake, and the safety of everyone else.'

Her heart did somersaults. He spoke as if he were dead already.

'I will, I promise. But are you sure about this? They can't shoot you just for gathering the news, can they?'

'They can do what they like, Lydia. You should know that better than any of us.'

She lowered her eyes. 'How long have you got?'

'Not long.'

'So why didn't they arrest you on the spot?'

'I've got twenty-four hours till I'm deported.' He grimaced. 'The dog collar does have its uses.'

'Oh, Martin—' she sobbed as her arms went round him. 'How will I know that you're safe?'

He reached out and touched her cheek, stroking away the tears. Then, grasping her fingers, he drew them slowly to his mouth.

Her head fell forward on to his chest as desire flooded through her.

'What is it?' he whispered.

'I don't know – my legs feel weak.'

Pressing his fingers to her lips, he carried her through to the drawing room, lowering her gently on to the sofa.

'Don't leave me,' she whispered. 'Hold me, please.'

He removed her necklace and gently undid her bodice, kissing each button in turn as it gave way to his fingers. Slipping the dress over her shoulders, he tugged at her chemise, staring, mesmerised, as the white skin of her breasts emerged.

Free from restraint, her hands grasped his collar, tugging at the vestment that separated her from his skin.

'No, Martin, wait.' Her cry pierced the silence. 'I've done this before—'

'Sshh… Do you think I don't know?' He stroked her hair. 'It's my fault, and mine only. I couldn't protect you. I couldn't save you from him. It's a nightmare I'll carry to my grave.'

'But I'm a wh—'

He clasped his hand to her mouth.

'You're a woman, Lydia, a wonderful, sweet, caring woman and I love you deeply. Now I want you to love me before it's too late.'

Closing her eyes, she gave in to his touch, desire and sorrow melting into one.

CHAPTER 26

Something had happened to Martin. Something had happened, and she knew it. Lydia ran outside, oblivious to the clouds that filled the blackened sky. Pulling her coat over her shoulders, she raced down the path along Guelles Road, and out towards St Martins, her tears lost in the downpour that soon drenched the night. She ran until her bones ached and her body begged her to stop.

Two hours later she reached the grounds of the rectory, ducking down exhausted behind a hedge. The rain had begun to ease now and she could hear an engine running and the sound of muffled voices. She pulled out a handkerchief and wiped her face dry, her breath still rasping in the back of her throat. A German soldier shouted orders and the house was swathed in light. Peering through the leaves, Lydia saw Martin emerge, escorted on either side by two soldiers. His eyes were blazing but his mouth was set into a defiant smile. She clasped her hands in front of her, fighting the urge to call out his name.

The soldiers pushed him roughly into the jeep, laughing and jeering in broken English, their guns glinting in the artificial light.

'You are man of the cloth, eh? The holy collar will not save you now.'

Lydia held her breath, her heart still thumping. Where were they taking him? Would he be interrogated? She sank back on to the wet ground, feeling exhausted as the damp seeped into her flesh.

She could still picture Martin on the day they first met, his face full of concern as she lay sprawled on the ground in front of him. She hadn't known what to make of him at first. Looking back, it was clear now she'd ignored her own feelings despite the many signs: her stomach flipping over when they met, the sudden outrage at something he'd said, the constant desire to say his name.

She'd thought him invincible as, almost imperceptibly, he had taken the place of her father. But Martin had been careless, reckless even, and she needed more than anything to know why. It was too late to ask him now.

The doors of the jeep clanged shut as it set off down the lane; Lydia held her breath until the soldiers were out of sight. She glanced round furtively, pulled herself up and then brushed the mud from her clothes. Stifling her sobs, she made her way back to the road and started the long walk home.

'We're starting a petition for the Reverend Martell,' Irene said with a defiant smile. 'We're getting all the parishioners to sign it. He is our rector, after all, and the custodian of our school. Whatever the charges, we must deny them.'

'A petition?' Lydia swallowed hard. 'What will that achieve? This is the enemy we're talking about. They're not reasonable people. Why should they listen to us?'

'It was *the enemy* who wanted a "model occupation", don't forget. They're the ones who took pictures of smiling babies and shook hands with our policemen. Two-faced bigots. They can't have it both ways.'

'But they've arrested him now. He'll be sent to an internment camp, surely?'

'Don't you worry about that, my girl,' Irene winked. 'The

Reverend Martell is a man of God, don't forget. Why would a holy man get mixed up in acts against the enemy?'

Lydia felt a flicker of hope. 'Where will you take the petition?'

'To the Kommandant, of course. The last thing he needs is a revolt on his hands. When he sees how many folks are rooting for Martin, he might just reconsider. You keep out of it, mind. The less you know about any of this the better.'

Lydia tried to remember Martin's words. *They caught me red-handed with the news from Britain – I've only myself to blame.* Maybe if she'd been more understanding. Maybe if she hadn't shut him out.

Out loud she said, 'Okay. Do your best, Irene, we don't have much time left.'

Within twenty-four hours they had rallied support from all over the island. Words were exchanged on doorsteps, out in the fields, in schools, shops, doctors' surgeries and anywhere a sympathetic ear could be found. Preparing as they were for another frugal Christmas, the people of Guernsey took time out to help. To Lydia, alone in her room, time stood still. She could only wait and hope. It was more than her life was worth to get involved.

At four o'clock in the afternoon the Reverend William Le Riche, Acting Rector of Torteval Church, delivered the petition to the Kommandantur. Half an hour later Lydia was summoned to the Kommandant's office.

Otto Kruger threw the petition on to his desk.

'You are aware that this man,' he scowled, 'this *Martin Martell*, has been arrested for crimes against the German Reich?'

'I have heard this, yes.'

'Do you know the extent of his crimes, *Fraülein*? No matter, I will tell you. He acquired false news of Allied successes in

Europe with the intention of distributing this to the island people. And now, the people, they wish for him to be spared.' He gestured to the paper in front of him. 'I have here what you call a "petition". For a man who is new to the island it is, perhaps, a little extreme?'

Lydia didn't trust herself to speak.

'Come along now, *Fraülein*.' His smiled widened. 'Is there something that you are not telling me?'

'Not at all, Herr Kommandant. You can do what you like with the rector, as far as I'm concerned. I may have worked for him once, but he is of little importance.' She had nothing to lose now.

'He is a traitor. Do you hear me – a traitor!'

'You must do as you think fit.'

'*Fit?* What does that mean, *Fraülein*? This Martell collects untruths about Allied victories with the intention of telling others. He may be a "man of the cloth" as you English say, but he is still a traitor.'

'Of course.' She glanced towards the kitchen. 'Perhaps I can get you a drink?'

'Damn the drink, Lydia, and damn your rector.' The Kommandant scowled. 'I intend to send him away. He will get what he deserves.'

'You're not eating your soup, my dear.'

'I'm sorry, Mrs Gallienne.' Lydia's face reddened. 'I'm not very hungry.'

'Not hungry?' The older woman spluttered. 'Here we are, not knowing where the next meal's coming from and you're *not hungry?*'

'I shouldn't have said that, it was wrong.' She cast her eyes down to her plate.

'You're lovesick, I'll be bound, lovesick for that rector of yours.

It's a pity he couldn't keep his nose out of other people's business, then he might still be here with us.'

'That's not fair, Ma.' Maggie leapt to her friend's defence. 'Martin was trying to give people hope. He's a hero, if you ask me.'

'So it's Martin, is it now? What's happened to your manners, girl? There's a lot of folks need saving round here and the rector's only one of them.'

'You're right, Mrs Gallienne,' Lydia interrupted.

'I know I'm right. Some folk are dying of hunger. Occupational malnutrition, they call it – bah! As if we need fancy words. I wonder what your fine rector would make of that.'

'He understands hunger, whatever you may think. I saw him give his week's ration to a poor mother who was sent to prison for heckling the Jerries.'

'The *poor mother* I saw him comforting the other week? I must say, he did look very understanding.'

Maggie banged her fist on the table.

'How can you be so cruel, Ma? The man helps people because he cares. Tell her, Lydia, tell her.'

Pushing back her chair with as much dignity as she could muster, Lydia stood up.

'Thank you for the soup, Mrs Gallienne. And now, if you'll excuse me, I have a headache coming on.'

Reaching the top of the stairs, Lydia hesitated. The prayer meeting was being held at Irene's home tonight. If she left now, they'd have time to talk before the others arrived. She grabbed her coat and sneaked out of the back door, the worn soles of her shoes slipping as she ran through the frost-covered streets. It was Christmas in two weeks' time – their third under German rule. With Martin gone, who would stand up for them now?

*

Irene Mellanby lived in a rambling Victorian house on Grandes Maisons Road, half a mile from St Sampson's Harbour.

'Thank goodness you've come!' Grabbing Lydia's arm, Irene pulled her into the vestibule. 'They've found out about GINA. Someone left a news-sheet in the library and a blasted soldier discovered it.'

'Do they think Martin's behind it?'

Irene shook her head. 'They can't prove it, thank goodness. The British news they found on him was handwritten. But they knew he'd been listening to the radio. And for that, ostensibly, he's been sent away.'

Lydia began to shake.

'Are you sure he's left the island?' Why did she cling on to hope? Hadn't she seen it with her own eyes?

'I'm afraid so.' The older woman's voice hardened. 'Which means, more than ever, that *we* must carry on. From now on the Guernsey Independent News Association has nothing to do with us. This is a respectable prayer group, and that's how it's going to stay.'

Lydia gave a wan smile. 'You're right, I know. It's just that—'

'He'll be back, you'll see. He's stronger than any of us realise. Now come on – help me with the refreshments. It's cocoa substitute tonight, I'm afraid. Either that or my rhubarb wine!'

The prayer group was unusually subdued. They began, as usual, by singing God Save the King, and then raised a toast to the rector's safe return. A series of readings and prayers followed in case they were being watched; it was far too risky to do anything else.

Lydia couldn't concentrate. Martin had been deported. Irene Mellanby's words kept tumbling round in her head. A loud bang drowned her thoughts as the drawing room door flew open and four armed soldiers burst in.

'Put your books down, hands up,' shouted the leader, firing a shot into the air that deafened all of them. The bullet ricocheted off the ceiling, sending clouds of dust all over them.

'How dare you?' Irene's voice was indignant. 'This is my home, a private residence, and we were trying to say our prayers. What right have you to intrude?'

'We have reason to believe that you have been harbouring a criminal, a man who has committed a crime against the Third Reich.' The soldier in charge spoke good English.

'The only crime here is being committed by you, Leutnant. Look at these people. Do they appear to be the sort who would harbour a criminal?'

'Shut up, you stupid woman.' The Leutnant poked his gun in her chest. 'And empty your pockets – *NOW*.'

Irene removed her hankie from the pocket of her dress, together with a hymn sheet and a bottle of smelling salts. Defiantly she placed them on the table in front of her.

'Is there anything else?'

Clenching his fist, the officer swept the offending items off the table.

'Damn you,' he muttered, pushing Irene into a chair.

'Leave her alone, will you?' Lydia leapt forward. 'She's done you no harm. Why can't you show a little respect?'

An evil grin appeared on the Leutnant's face. Throwing his arm around her waist he sneered, 'Ah … this must be the Kommandant's lady friend. I have heard much about you.'

Lydia didn't flinch. 'Remove your filthy hand if you know what's good for you.'

He trailed his fingers upwards to stroke her chin. 'You think you're safe, but you won't be after this, *Fraülein*.'

'For your information, the Kommandant knows that I belong to this prayer group. I think you'll find it is not me but *you*,

Leutnant, who will fear for your safety. And now, if you don't mind, I suggest you leave.'

The soldier backed away with a mock salute. Grabbing the wine bottle, he motioned his men to the door.

'*Auf Wiedersehen, Fraülein.*'

Old Mr Falla was the first to speak.

'I misjudged you, Miss Le Page. You saved us all with your brave words. I see you have your father's spirit.'

'Thank you, sir.' Lydia wiped her brow with a handkerchief. 'I hope this means you won't be leaving the prayer group?' She glanced round the room. 'Or any of you, for that matter?'

'Not in a month of Sundays.' The old man shook his head. 'They can shoot the lot of us for all I care, but I'm damned if they'll win this bloney war.'

Dusting herself down, Irene Mellanby stood up and raised an invisible glass.

'Here's to our maker.'

By the look on her face she didn't mean God.

CHAPTER 27

January 1943

January brought one of the coldest winters Guernsey had ever known. Frost clung to the trees like silver stardust while streams that once meandered aside country lanes were frozen solid. How beautiful it all looked, Lydia thought wistfully, as she made her way to work.

Arriving at the Kommandantur at last, Lydia's heart felt colder than the ice under her feet. She showed her pass to the guard on duty and, with a quick nod, made her way slowly up the stairs.

The Kommandant was already at his desk, surrounded by trays of paperwork.

'Good morning, *Fraülein*.' He stood as she entered. 'I hope you have enjoyed your holiday. I have an important meeting to attend to this morning. You will do your correspondence then wait for me. You understand?'

Lydia nodded as he left the room. It was almost a month since they'd first slept together and now he didn't even smile. Did that mean he suspected something? A frisson of fear ran up her spine. No doubt she would find out soon enough. Meanwhile there was far more correspondence than usual to deal with after the Christmas break and she had no choice but to get on with it.

Picking up several letters from the centre of the pile, one envelope in particular caught her eye. It was written in scruffy handwriting and addressed *To Who it May Concern*. Slitting it open with a paperknife, she pulled out a note scribbled on the back of an old shopping list.

TELL THE COMANDANT HIS POSH ASISTANT IS
A JEW. WHAT WOUD HITLER MAKE OF THAT?

Instinctively Lydia flung the note across the desk, her eyes darting round the empty room. Who could have done this? Someone must know the truth about her real parents, someone who had a grudge against her. Steeling herself to think straight, she considered the options. She could burn the message on the gas ring in the kitchen, though the smell would probably arouse suspicion. She could hide it in the office somewhere or put it in her bag and hope she wouldn't be stopped and searched. But what if this wasn't the only copy? What if something similar had been sent to the Aliens Office or even to the police? Sophie Romerill was already under arrest. The few who had registered as Jews in 1940 had been forced to move home and sell their remaining possessions. One Jewish businessman had been taken to St Saviour's Mental Institution where he died from "insanity". Dropping to her knees, Lydia picked up the note, screwed it into a ball and slipped it into her handbag.

Half an hour later the door opened and the Kommandant entered the room.

'So, *Fraülein*, is it time for my coffee?'

She lowered her eyes, willing her hands not to tremble.

'It is indeed. Shall I make it now?'

'Now, yes. You may have some also, as it is your first day back.'

'That is very kind.' The room felt cold and damp after the winter break and she relished the idea of a hot drink. But coffee with the Kommandant? What did he want this time?

Five minutes later, with a feeling of foreboding, she carried the tray of matching coffee cups and saucers, milk jug and sugar bowl and placed it on Otto Kruger's desk.

'The coffee will be ready soon, but we don't have any biscuits today.'

'Never mind the biscuits. Sit down. There is something I must ask you, *Fraülein*, something that has just been brought to my attention.' He picked up his pen and held it for a second or two between his teeth. 'Where were you living before the Occupation?'

'At my friend Maggie's house, in the Vrangue.' Lydia held her breath. 'Why do you ask?'

He stood up, walked slowly to the door and looked out on to the deserted corridor. 'Is it possible you lived in *my* home, Lydia – the house named Sea Breeze?'

Her knees trembled. 'It is true, Herr Kommandant.' There was no point in lying. She just wanted it over with.

'Why did you not tell me this before? Why could you not tell me the truth?' A muscle twitched involuntarily beneath his left eye.

'I lied for your sake, Otto.' She felt a sharp pain, as if someone was stretching steel bands across her chest. 'If you had known who I was, you would not have wanted to see me again. I could not bear that. I did not want our friendship to end before it had begun.'

'And how do you feel about our "friendship" now?'

'It is even more special since we have—' she pretended to bite her lip, 'become closer. I hope I have done nothing to change that. I have, perhaps, been stupid, I can see that now.' Please God let him believe her.

'Where are your parents living?'

'My father is dead. My mother is staying with friends in—'

'No matter. She will be easy to track down if necessary. As for you – you withheld information from the German authorities and that is a crime.' He was staring at her now, his eyes seeming to penetrate her thoughts. 'I have decided, for the time being, that your former life in *my home*—' he emphasised the words, 'will remain a secret between myself and the Kommandantur. But if I find you have lied to me about *anything else...* I am sure you are aware of the consequences.'

Lydia sat motionless, stunned by the apparent reprieve.

The Kommandant sat down, propping his legs on the desk in front of him.

'One more thing, *Fraülein*. What do you know of—' he glanced down at his pad, 'a woman called Sophie Romerill?'

'She's a seamstress. She helps me with the clothes I wear when I – er – spend my time with you.'

'And did you know she was born a Jew? She's been ordered by the Aliens Office to leave the island.'

'They say she's a Jew, but she's not, I swear it.' Lydia smiled disconcertedly. 'Her late husband was, I believe, of that faith. Mrs Romerill has lived here all her life and is terrified of being sent away.'

The Kommandant lifted the silver cigarette box with both hands and offered it to her, a sly smile creeping over his thin lips.

'*Fraülein?*'

Lydia shook her head. 'No, thank you.'

'I will look into this matter.' He stood up. 'But the woman must prove her innocence – do you understand? I will not be made a fool of.'

'Of course, Herr Kommandant.'

'Now pour the coffee and get back to your desk.'

'Hello, my dear.' Irene's eyes were full of compassion. 'Come in. You look as if you need a good meal inside you.'

Lydia stepped into the darkened hall.

'I need someone to talk to. The Kommandant, he's just—'

'One thing at a time, my dear. Come into the sitting room.' The older woman pulled an envelope from her apron pocket. 'Martin gave me this for you before he was arrested. I couldn't give it to you earlier with the others looking on. Sit down and read it while I put the kettle on.'

Lydia's hands trembled as the page unfolded. It was his handwriting – she would recognise it anywhere.

My darling Lydia

Today I think only of you. How long will we be apart? If only I knew. How much do I love you? The answer holds the key to everything else.

I am writing this letter to say thank you; two humble, insignificant words that can never portray the true depth of emotion I feel. Thank you for loving me enough to lie for me, for pushing me away and causing yourself so much pain when happiness was within your grasp. How stupid I was not to see it. I was angry, so very angry, though God only knows that's not an excuse for my behaviour. Rage may be blind, but it seems I did not want to see. Now I know that your love is enough to live for.

Look at the moon tonight and, wherever I am, I promise I will see it too. Let it guide you through the darkness until we can be together again.

All my love

Martin

P.S. – Remember – the same moon shines in Jersey. Look once more and you will finally be safe.

Lydia read the letter, fighting back the tears. He loved her. What more proof did she need? And yet there was something about it that struck her as slightly odd.

'*The same moon shines in Jersey,*' he'd written. '*Look once more and you will finally be safe.*'

Martin hated Jersey and had vowed never to go back there. So why would he mention it now? He was trying to tell her something, she was sure of it – but what? She scanned the letter again.

'*The answer holds the key to everything else.*'

'Is everything all right?' Irene appeared from the hallway. 'It hasn't upset you too much, I hope?'

'No, Irene, just the opposite. I think Martin's trying to tell me something. I just don't know what it is.'

'There's dandelion tea in the parlour, and some barley-flour biscuits. Why don't you join me and things may fall into place?'

'Thanks. I'll be right with you.' Lydia picked up the sheet of paper. The key? The safe? Had Kruger taken the missing documents to Jersey? Or was Martin trying to tell her to look in the safe again? She jumped up and began to pace the floor. Why hadn't she thought of it before?

Waving the letter in the air, she burst into the kitchen, her thoughts coming out in a jumble.

'Read it please, Irene, I want you to. Then tell me what you think.'

Irene poured hot liquid into two mugs, balancing her spectacles on the end of her nose.

'You're right about what he's asking, Lydia,' she said at last. 'But I don't like it. I don't like it at all. You'd be mad to break into that safe again.'

'I have to, don't you see? It's what Martin wants me to do.'

'That's as maybe, but he won't be here when it all goes wrong. That man's turned your head, if you ask me.'

Lydia's face reddened. 'I know you mean well, but I also understand his reasons. This is much too serious to ignore. If we can get those plans to the British Government, we might be able to save Guernsey.'

'And how are you going to do that, my girl? Row them over to London yourself in a canoe? When Hitler wants something, there's no stopping him, so don't go getting any grand ideas.'

Pulling a face, Lydia swilled down the bitter-tasting drink.

'There are commandos for that sort of thing, aren't there? Surely it can be arranged. Don't you see – we've *got* to give it a go.'

'You'll be risking your life – and others' lives as well, don't forget.'

'We'll have no life at all if we don't do something. Please, Irene?'

The older woman pursed her lips.

'I'm sorry I was hard on you but I had to make sure you knew what you were doing.'

Opening the kitchen drawer, she pulled out a dog-eared book marked *Occupation Recipes* and flicked through it.

'You'd be amazed at the resources some of our members have. Batteries, bicycle, cable... Ah, here we are – Sam Doulon has a small Leica camera which would be ideal for your purpose. I'll arrange for him to get it to you. Then I'll need to know the day and time of your planned operation and the names of any German personnel who will be in the vicinity of the Kommandantur at the time. Is that clear?'

'Completely. Thanks, Irene.'

'And now, seeing as you don't appear to like my tea, I'll just have to drink the rest of it myself.'

CHAPTER 28

The following Monday morning Otto Kruger left his office at ten twenty-nine precisely for a meeting with the Chairman of the Controlling Committee and other senior members of the States of Guernsey. By a stroke of luck Corporal Reinhart had been drafted in to take minutes so at least she'd be out of the way. Lydia swept her eyes over the empty corridor; she knew exactly what she had to do.

Walking out of the office, a box file clutched under her arm, she made her way to the ladies' lavatories. After checking the place was empty, she locked herself into a small, dimly lit cubicle and retrieved the camera from a pocket sewn into her camiknickers. She pulled the chain, waited while the toilet flushed, placed the camera in the box file and ambled back to the Kommandant's office.

Lydia shut the door firmly behind her and stood behind Otto's desk. Tugging at the island map on the wall, she held her breath as the frame moved sideways to reveal the safe. She hoped to God they hadn't changed the combination. Easing open the solid metal door, she pulled out several loose items including a sheaf of Guernsey stamps, crudely stamped with a black swastika, and several identity cards. Underneath a bunch of keys she found a brown file she hadn't seen before, marked *STRENGES GEHEIMNIS*. Strictly private.

Biting down hard on her lip, she pulled the string and scanned the contents. Could this be what she'd been searching for? Stopping only to glance over her shoulder, she photographed each of the six pages, euphoria turning to fear as the seconds ticked by. She replaced the plans, closed the safe door and, with one deft movement, swung the map back into place.

Just as she finished, the telephone burst into life. Lydia stood motionless, her limbs locked with fear until the noise eventually subsided. Thank God there was no one around. After several minutes she left the office and crept back to the lavatory block, her pulse racing. Lifting her skirts, she pushed the camera into her underwear and, without a backward glance, fled the room.

She had just got back to her desk when a sharp knock came at the door.

'Come in.' Her voice came out in a high-pitched squeak. A junior secretary appeared carrying the Kommandant's mail.

Lydia waved her hand.

'*Danke schön*. Just leave it there. I will attend to it shortly.' She sank back into her chair, perspiration breaking out on her skin.

The rest of the morning passed interminably until Kruger returned at last.

'You are perhaps not well?' he asked, observing her flushed face.

'I have a headache, Herr Kommandant. I think I am running a temperature. I trust your meeting went well?'

'Running? We cannot have you doing that, *Fräulein*.' He gave a sly grin. 'We need you to lie down, do we not?'

She ignored his attempt at a joke. 'If I may be allowed to go home, I'm sure I will be better tomorrow.' Her shivers were genuine now, the camera hidden under her dress rubbing against the top of her thigh.

'If that is what you wish.' His eyes scanned the mail on his desk. 'Make sure you are here at nine a.m. prompt.'

As soon as she got home Lydia raced upstairs and flung herself on the bed, exhaustion tempered by panic at what she had done. She counted to twenty to calm her nerves, faltering as her body began to shudder. Swinging herself round she tried to sit up, but her legs refused to move. The ceiling moved sideways then spiralled towards her feet. Someone opened the bedroom door just as she slid to the floor.

'It's a good job Edna found you when she did, Lydia Le Page.' Irene scowled. 'You're your own worst enemy.' It was the day after the raid on the safe and she had called at the Vrangue with some caraway seed cake for the invalid. 'Have a cup of tea and get this down you,' she insisted, fussing like a mother hen.

'I'm fine,' Lydia waved her hands in the air. 'I only fainted. I just needed some fresh air, that's all.'

'Fresh air, my foot! Delayed shock, it was, if you ask me. As for those plans, whatever would have happened if you'd collapsed in the Kommandant's office? The Jerries would've found the camera and that would've been the end of you.'

'Well, they didn't, did they?' Lydia took a large bite of the cake. 'Mmm, delicious. So what happens next?'

'The papers are with Mr Sherwill now. The Controlling Committee will relay the information to the Cabinet Office in London.'

'Do you think Kruger is the brains behind it?'

'I doubt it. More like a stooge. Though they may blame him when they find out their plans have been intercepted.'

'And what if the Kommandant suspects me?'

'He won't. The man has a crush on you. Besides, the German Reich can hardly afford to lose face.'

'You're probably right.' Lydia sighed. 'Maybe I will have that tea after all.'

Irene opened her bag and handed Lydia a hip flask.

'Go on – have a drop of this instead. I'd like to be a fly on the wall when Hitler finds out his plans have been thwarted. He deserves a taste of his own medicine.'

Lydia breathed in the whisky fumes as her eyes strayed to the window.

'Thanks for that, Irene.'

'Shame on you, girl. You've not been listening to a word.'

'Sorry – I was thinking about Martin. He's a hero, isn't he?'

'He is.' Irene's face softened. 'And some might say you are, too.'

CHAPTER 29

March 1943

Lydia closed her eyes to block out the vision. Her body lay in bed with Kruger, but her mind was far away. She could see Martin now, dark hair tousled in the wind, his skin caramel against the stark white of his collar. He was standing on the edge of the Gouffre – a deep ravine on the south coast of the island – watching as the water seethed and bubbled below.

Then everything changed. With a jolt, Martin lost his balance and plummeted over the rocks, his frenzied scream mingling with the cries of the seagulls. Powerless to move, Lydia watched in horror as he disappeared beneath the waves...

'Maaaaaarrrrrtinnnnnnnn—' The word came out as a scream. Otto Kruger groaned as he lifted his body from hers.

'Shush, *liebling*, don't cry, someone may hear you. It was good for you, also?'

'I'm sorry?' For a moment she had forgotten where she was.

'You need not apologise, my dear. It is natural for you to express such joy, is it not? You are a very sensuous woman.'

Lydia sank back on to the sheets, perspiration oozing from her skin. She had leapt from one nightmare to another but still she *must* carry on; too many lives were at risk to stop now.

Lydia met the Kommandant on a regular basis, sometimes for a ride in his official car, sometimes for a meal, invariably ending at Sea Breeze. When the lights were dim and they'd run out of small talk, he would lead her to the bedroom where, without so much as a preliminary move, he would climb on top of her, gasping for breath in the dim light. At times like these she would focus her mind on other things: the Russian civilian workers who had arrived on the island barefoot and starving, the innocent Jews who had lost everything, the brave Guernseymen who might never come home…

Slipping out of bed, Lydia wrapped herself in a shot-silk dressing gown.

'I will pour you a drink,' she said softly, 'and then I must go home.'

'No, my dear. You will stay with me tonight. I have something to tell you. Come sit beside me.' He patted the silk counterpane. 'I have decided to release you of your duties at the Kommandantur.' Raising a cigarette to his lips, he sucked hard before exhaling the smoke through flared nostrils. 'It is, you understand, for your own safety. There are more important things now for you to do. When I leave the office at the end of the day I wish you to be here as my *companion*. Do you understand?'

His words clung to her skin like a blanket of wet snow.

'Yes, Otto. I understand.'

Early the following morning as the Kommandant slept beside her, Lydia slipped noiselessly out of bed. She dressed quickly and ran down the stairs, through the back porch and out towards Pleinmont Point, reaching the Fairy Ring just as the sun was rising. Sitting down beside the ancient stones, she clasped her hands together and broke down in tears. She had slept with Kruger in the name of the Resistance. Now she must continue to save her own life.

It was three months now since Martin had gone, the early

days of utter despair transforming into fear. Tugging at a tuft of grass, she watched the rough green blades as they scattered in the wind. She rarely attended church these days, feeling too much like a hypocrite to offer her thanks to God. Every other Sunday the Reverend Le Riche, Rector of St James, conducted the morning service at Torteval Church, but no one had taken Martin's place.

Looking skywards, Lydia breathed in the fresh air till her lungs felt fit to burst. She'd been thinking about the shortages at the Emergency Hospital. Staff were needed as well as supplies, according to the *Star*, with every available person working round the clock. Maybe she should volunteer. With her medical knowledge – and Otto away for most of the day – there must be something she could do. Her mind made up, she dusted herself down and made her way back to Sea Breeze.

A week later, wrapped in a warm coat and hat, Lydia set out for the hospital on her father's bicycle, the original tyres now replaced with old hosepipe. She battled hard against a strong westerly wind, her face glowing with the effort when she finally arrived.

The States of Guernsey Emergency Hospital was a four-storey building in the grounds of the Old Country Hospital, set up at the beginning of the Occupation to bring the island's medical needs together under one roof. Patients still had to pay for their treatment, unless they were receiving island assistance, but no amount of money could generate enough supplies for their needs. Lydia gave her name to the sullen-looking girl on the desk.

'I have an appointment with Matron at ten o'clock. I'm a little early, I'm afraid.'

'Take a seat.' The receptionist frowned without looking up. Lydia recognised her from a family with seven or eight children who lived on the edge of town. What right did she have to be scowling? The girl was lucky to have a job.

Half an hour later Lydia was shown in to Matron Le Brun's office.

'Ah, Miss Le Page. I'm sorry to keep you waiting. We're extremely busy, I'm afraid.' Matron's dark hair was scraped back from her face and topped with a starched white cap. Her complexion looked pale from lack of sleep, but her eyes were warm and friendly. Shaking Lydia's hand, she gestured to her to sit down. 'Now then, you said in your letter you wanted to offer your help. What, may I ask, are your qualifications?'

'Qualifications?' Lydia cheeks turned crimson. 'I don't have any as such, but I do have the right background and thought that, well, seeing as you are so short of help these days—' She knew she was babbling but she couldn't help it. What on earth had made her think it would be easy?

'Right background for what, exactly?'

'I'm studying to be a pharmacist. Or I was, before the Occupation.'

'That's very interesting. Where did you matriculate?'

'At Leicester College of Art and Technology, in the Midlands. I'm hoping to get a Diploma in Hospital Pharmacy.'

There was a short pause.

'I'm sorry to have to ask you, Miss Le Page, but do you have any paperwork to prove this?'

Lydia's heart took a dive; she was starting to feel like a criminal.

'I'm afraid not. You see, when I left England I fully intended to return.'

Matron's face softened. 'All our lives have changed, my dear. But I have to be careful who I employ, even more so now that the lives of so many patients are at risk. Some of them are very weak. Others are dying from malnutrition, or lack of insulin.'

Lydia leaned forward, clasping her hands in front of her.

'I want to help, Matron. My father died in this hospital last year and, well—' She hesitated. 'That's all in the past, but believe me I just want to do what I can.'

'I'm sure you do, my dear. It would be voluntary work to start with, you understand.'

Lydia nodded. 'I'd be more than happy with that.'

'Mm.' The matron picked up a pen. 'One more question. What can you tell me about the Pharmacy and Medicines Act?'

Biting her lip, Lydia scrolled back through her memory. Her student days might as well have been in another life.

'When I left England in 1940 the Act was still being drafted. The Government, as far as I remember, were trying to get rid of medicine stamp duty. They also wanted to stop the advertisement of products that claimed to treat certain, err, illnesses—'

'Go on, Miss Le Page. What sort of illnesses?'

'TB? Some forms of epilepsy? Oh, and anything that might bring about a termination – in other words, the abortion of a foetus.'

'Thank you. Your memory is clearly better than you thought. Come back a week today, at say—' she glanced at her diary, 'two o'clock, and I will show you around the hospital. And now, if you'll excuse me, I must get on.'

Lydia stood up, trying to contain her excitement.

'I'll do anything you ask.'

'Empty bedpans?' Matron raised her eyebrows.

'Anything.'

The ride home passed quickly as the wind gathered speed behind her. For the first time since he left, Lydia had spent an hour without thinking about Martin. Throughout the long days she had kept his image alive inside her head – like her own silent movie. Sometimes he would appear in the dark, eyes blazing, a mass of hair flopping over his brow. Then he would press his face to hers, his caresses telling her all she needed to know. But when darkness fell the inevitable questions began. Had he survived the journey to Germany? Was he starving? Or being tortured? Then the nightmares would begin all over again.

CHAPTER 30

Reg Gallienne was in the parlour puffing on a hand-rolled cigarette when Lydia appeared at the door.

'Hello, my love.' He glanced up from the *Guernsey Star*. 'How did you get on at the hospital?'

'I got a grilling from Matron.' She slumped into the chair beside him. 'But then what did I expect?'

'Nothing you couldn't handle, I shouldn't wonder. What happens now?'

'I'm going back next week to have a look round. I just hope she thinks I'm good enough for the job.'

'If you can work for that bastard Kruger, believe me, you can work for anyone.' He spat out a strand of wet tobacco. 'Good riddance to bad rubbish, that's what I say.'

'What do you mean, good riddance?' She sat up in the chair. 'Has something happened to him?'

'He's been given his marching orders, so it seems, and about time too. Here – have a look.' Reg held up the front page.

ADMIRAL FLEISCHER TAKES OVER AS
KOMMANDANT MAJOR OTTO KRUGER
SECONDED TO FRANCE

Lydia grabbed the paper from him, devouring every word.

She'd seen Otto just two days ago. Surely he must have known his fate by then?

'Are you all right, my love?' Reg frowned. 'You can't be sorry to see the back of that rogue?'

She shook her head, too dumbfounded to speak.

'You can get on with your life again now, my love. Hold your head up high. You'd make a grand nurse, if you ask me.'

'Thanks, Mr Gallienne.' Lydia finally found her voice. 'But it wouldn't be a nurse's job. Just an assistant of sorts. Helping with the laundry, changing the beds, all the things nobody else wants to do.'

'And you with all that medical learning. It's a crying shame, I say. Never did any book-reading myself. Ah well, put the kettle on, there's a good girl, and see if you can find where Edna's hidden the tea ration.'

Lydia filled the kettle with water and set it on the stove. Otto Kruger gone, and without a word? What could have happened? Had Hitler's plans for Guernsey reached England after all? Whatever the truth, nothing could dampen her spirits. At last she was free. Free from his fingers creeping over her flesh, free from the smell of his rancid breath, free from the weight of his body bearing down on hers. Like a child she danced round the kitchen, waving her hands in the air. This was the news she had longed for. Now she knew that Britain would win the war.

Lydia woke with a start. She had dreamt the Kommandant had burst into the office, in full military dress, and held a gun to her head. Papa was standing behind him under the portrait of Hitler. 'No, please, not my Liddy,' he was screaming. 'Shoot me instead.' There was a loud bang and then everything went black.

Wiping her forehead with the back of her sleeve, Lydia got out of bed and padded towards the window. What would happen to her now that the Kommandant had gone? Her relationship with Kruger had long been a matter of speculation on the island. So many people had seen them together it was impossible to dispel the rumours, though no one dared say anything to her face. Thank God that was over. She'd best keep out of sight for a while, at least until the fuss died down. But first she must speak to Irene. Dressing quickly, she scribbled a note in patois and crept out of the house.

A long queue had already formed outside the baker's shop in Smith Street. Nodding politely at the two women in front of her, Lydia was met with frozen stares. Unperturbed, she took out her shopping list and studied the contents. It was a full twenty minutes before she reached the counter.

'Morning, Miss Le Page.' Irene's expression gave nothing away. 'How's Mrs Gallienne today?'

'Not too bad, thanks.' Lydia handed over the note in her shopping bag. 'I've got some things jotted down, but we'd be grateful for anything you have.'

'I'll see what I can do.' Irene disappeared into the back room, returning a minute or two later. 'That's all I can manage, I'm afraid. I've marked the list for you. Now give my regards to Edna.'

Clutching the bag closely to her, Lydia headed across town. She needed somewhere private to read the reply. At the bottom of the High Street she cut through the arcade, climbed the stone steps and slipped into the deserted fish market.

It happened so quickly she didn't have time to scream. Armed with scissors and knives, the three women appeared from nowhere, grabbing her hands and tying them behind her back. Then they were upon her, pinning her to the ground, cackling like a coven of witches. They tugged and hacked at her hair, yanking it from her scalp, stuffing the tufts into her mouth till she almost choked.

'Jerry Bag, Jerry Bag, the Kommandant's girl,' they yelled in unison. 'Who's going to screw you now?'

Lydia swallowed a ball of hair and started to retch. Her attackers had covered their faces with scarves, but their eyes stared at her, cruel and mocking. If only she could speak.

'Oi – what do you think you're doing?' The man's voice boomed through the deserted halls. 'Let her go or I'll have you arrested.'

She lifted her head, desperate to identify her saviour. As quick as they had come the women disappeared, hoods flung over their heads, cursing furiously under their breath.

'Are you hurt, miss?' The policeman cut her free.

Lydia stared back, her mind blank.

'I don't think so.' Feeling for her handkerchief, she wiped the saliva from her mouth. 'I suppose it could have been worse.'

'It could that. At least you were spared the tar.' He grinned wryly. 'Just a minute, aren't you Jack Le Page's girl?'

Lydia nodded.

'Well, I don't know what you've been up to, miss, but I think I can imagine. I'd get off home if I were you and stay there. There's a lot of bad feeling about right now.'

She grabbed his outstretched hand and hauled herself up. Miraculously, the bag Irene had given her lay untouched on the ground. Removing her scarf from under her coat, she pulled it over her head, knotting it under her chin.

'Thank you, constable. I'm very grateful to you. And now I'll be on my way.'

Edna Gallienne stared in amazement as Lydia appeared for breakfast.

'My dear girl, whatever have you done to your hair? You look like a man!'

Lydia bit her lip. 'It's the latest fashion in England. All part of the war effort. I hear it saves a fortune in shampoo.'

'Bah, never mind fashion! They're too busy avoiding the doodlebugs over there, from what I can gather, to worry about their hair. Who on earth put you up to it?'

'One of the nurses at the hospital. I start next week and she said it would fit much better under my cap.'

'She should stick to what she knows in future, if you ask me. Whatever was she thinking of?'

'Well I quite like it, my girl,' Reg Gallienne winked as he came into the room. 'Makes you look like a pixie. Now, are you women going to gossip all day or can I have something to eat?'

After she'd washed the pots, Lydia set off from the house on foot and headed towards Les Banques. Reaching the end of Grand Bouet, she scrambled up on to the sea wall and breathed in the salt air. As a child she would come here with her friends at high tide to fling pebbles into the waves. Now she closed her eyes and stood with her arms outstretched, palms raised to the sky. In her mind she could see Kruger's naked body looming in front of her, feel the revulsion as his lips clamped down on hers. That man had made her a whore.

On Kruger's orders the occupying forces had opened a brothel at the far end of the island, shipping in 'working girls' from the Normandy coast. She'd heard say that the women refused to be kissed, averting their eyes till the business was completed. How she'd envied them during the long nights spent in Otto Kruger's bed.

Standing with her eyes heavenward, Lydia swayed back and forth in the wind, purging her soul of the sight of the man, of the feel, the smell and the touch of him. Because of him she'd endured the scorn on the faces of the people she had once called friends.

Because of him dear Papa had died, and Martin was languishing in some vile German camp. She would never, ever, forgive him for that.

'Nurse – come quickly.'

Lydia's pulse quickened. 'I'm not a nurse, I'm sorry, sir. How can I help?'

'My pillows need turning, can't you see?' The old man wheezed. 'I could die here in my bed and no one would notice.'

She patted his hand before plumping the pillows.

'There now. Is that better?'

'Hmm … I suppose so. What the devil are you doing, anyway, masquerading as a nurse?'

'I'm not *masquerading* as you call it, Mr, er—' she glanced at the name above his bed, 'Piriou. I'm just doing my best, in very difficult circumstances.'

'Difficult? Bah! I remember the last war. Nurses were nurses in those days. Get back to your duties, young lady, whatever they may be.'

Frustration overwhelmed her. What was she doing plumping pillows? If Matron wouldn't give her something useful to do, she'd have to take things into her own hands.

As the weeks slipped by Lydia learned how to boost the patients' morale by getting in touch with their families, organising sing-songs on a rainy day or keeping them company in the middle of a sleepless night. She soon became expert at distracting the ever-present soldiers who insisted doors be open at all times, even in the maternity ward.

One spring morning as Lydia headed for the sluice with a handful of soiled sheets, she began to question her own motives. What on earth was she doing here? What difference was she making to the war? For one selfish moment she wanted to cry out loud for the life she had lost. Then she remembered Martin, banished to Germany in some God-forsaken camp, and her heart flipped over.

'Pull yourself together, girl,' she mumbled under her breath. 'You're alive. You're clothed, and just about fed. What more do you want?'

As she turned the corner, Matron appeared at the end of the corridor.

'Ah, Miss Le Page, how are you today?'

'Very well, thank you, Matron. I'm getting to know the ropes.'

'I'm glad to hear it. So, tell me, would you like to do more?' The older woman fell into step beside her.

'I would like to feel more useful. Have you something in mind?'

'You're too good for bedpans, that's clear. We could train you up to be a nurse. It's hard work and you'd have to spend time observing on the wards. The hours would be much longer, there'd be lectures to cope with, not to mention the shortage of medicine.'

'Do you really think I could be a nurse?'

'Do *you* think you could, Miss Le Page? That's what really matters.'

'Yes, I do.' Lydia's face broke into a smile. 'Thank you, Matron. I definitely do.'

CHAPTER 31

December 1944

Maggie burst into the sitting room, her face streaked with tears. 'Come quick – it's Mrs Le Quesne.'

'What's happened? Where is she?' Lydia shot out of the chair.

'At home, asking for you. Tom brought me here in the trap.' Maggie pulled the crumpled paper from her pocket and held it up. 'It's awful, so very awful.'

The Red Cross message was handwritten in block capitals.

REGRET TO INFORM YOU GRANDDAUGHTER
KILLED IN ACCIDENT WITH MOTOR CAR.
FUNERAL TOMORROW LYTHAM PARK CEMETERY,
GOD WILLING. MORE DETAILS TO FOLLOW.
JUNE 19 1944.

'But this was months ago,' Lydia gasped. 'It doesn't even say if it's Wendy or Anne.'

'I know. Can you believe it? The poor woman's out of her mind with grief.'

'Damn the censors. Damn the Germans.' Lydia suppressed a sob. 'And damn and blast this bloody war. Come on, let's go.' They ran outside to where Tom was waiting.

'She never should've sent them away,' Maggie cried as they

hauled themselves up into the trap. 'Poor little mites. They should've stayed at home.'

'Shut up, Maggie.' Lydia's hands were shaking. 'You're only making it worse. The poor woman's in mourning. She feels guilty enough. The best we can do is comfort her now.'

'We're prisoners in our own island,' Maggie shrieked as the pony pulled out into the lane, 'and there's nothing we can do about it.'

'Here,' Lydia held out a hankie. 'It's no good crying. It's up to us to be strong.' Lydia could picture Hilda that morning, full of expectation as she opened her front door. The Red Cross messages from England had become her whole life.

Maggie blew her nose. 'I know I haven't always been the best of friends to you, but—'

'Look, I'm sorry I shouted,' Lydia cut in. 'Believe me, I'm scared enough for both of us.' She looked round at Tom, his determined face set into a frown. 'Now come on, we've got a job to do.'

When they arrived at the house, the lights were dimmed and the place was eerily silent.

'Where are you, Hilda?' Lydia's voice echoed through the empty hallway. She pushed open the drawing room door and made her way to the parlour.

Hilda Le Quesne was sitting on the stone floor, her shoulders covered by an old wool blanket. Rocking backwards and forwards, she whimpered like a newborn child.

Lydia crouched down beside the old woman and cradled her in her arms.

'It's me, Lydia,' she whispered. 'You look so cold sitting there. Why don't you come to your room and have a lie down?'

Hilda rolled over and let out a chilling scream.

'My babies – they've taken my babies.' Her body began to shake and her tongue hung loose from her mouth.

'Fetch Doctor Wren,' Lydia barked at Maggie. 'Get him here now, and don't take no for an answer.'

Could she be having a fit? Or was it severe shock? Remembering something she'd seen at the hospital, Lydia gave her a sharp slap across the face. Hilda stopped shaking at once and her eyes glazed over. Removing her own coat, Lydia laid it on the floor underneath the poor woman's head. All she could do now was wait and hope she'd done enough to save her.

'I've never seen anyone cry like that before.' Maggie shivered. 'I thought she was going to die.'

'So did I.' Lydia linked arms with her friend. 'That's why I slapped her face.'

They were walking down Tower Lane the following day. It was Sunday and church bells were ringing in the distance.

'You did the right thing. At least she's being looked after now.'

'Though heaven knows what state she's in. What were you doing at Hilda's, by the way?'

'Ma made a jam steam pudding and asked me to take it round. Mrs Le Quesne was about to open the Red Cross message when I arrived. I still don't understand why it didn't say more.'

Lydia squeezed her hand. 'Whoever had sent it couldn't possibly have known she had more than one granddaughter. Or maybe the message had been censored. We'll probably never know. Thank goodness we got to her in time.'

When Doctor Wren had arrived the previous day, he'd taken one look at Hilda and called an ambulance. Minutes later the poor woman had another seizure and was struggling to breathe.

'What brought this on?' the doctor asked, checking the patient's pulse. 'Did she faint?'

Lydia shook her head. 'She had some very bad news. By the time I got here she seemed to be in a trance. Will she be all right?'

'I'm not sure. Shock can do strange things to people. Can you find her some night clothes to take with her?'

Lydia had done as he'd asked, cursing herself all the time that she hadn't done more.

'At least she's in hospital.' Maggie's voice broke into her thoughts. 'That's the best place. You will keep an eye on her, won't you?'

'I'll call first thing in the morning before I start my shift. She's heavily sedated, so she may not recognise me.' Lydia shook her head. 'Come on, it's almost curfew. There's nothing else we can do now.'

'Surely you can find out *something*, constable.' Lydia leaned over the counter. 'Mrs Le Quesne is in a deep state of shock.'

'It's out of our hands, miss, I'm sorry. You know as well as I do that no communication is allowed with the mainland.'

'Indeed, I do, but this is an emergency. What about the Red Cross?' Lydia frowned. 'They sent the message in the first place.'

'But they don't write the messages, miss, and they don't censor them either. They come through International Headquarters in Switzerland. Let's just hope the lady gets more information soon. Is there anything else I can help you with?'

Lydia cursed under her breath as she left the police station. It had taken all her effort not to cry. It was heartbreaking enough to lose someone you loved, but not knowing which child to mourn – that was unthinkable. No wonder the poor woman was in such despair.

Maggie appeared in the parlour with an armful of turnips.

'Have you seen Pa? These should put a smile on his face.'

'He's upstairs listening to the crystal set,' Lydia said, 'though sometimes I wonder why he bothers. The Allies may be winning the war but we're no nearer to being freed.'

'Well,' Maggie grinned, 'at least we won't starve.'

'But that's just it. We probably will. We lost what few food supplies we had when the Allies invaded France. At this rate, there'll soon be nothing left.'

Maggie covered the turnips with her coat.

'I'd better hold on to these, then. They might be worth a bob or two on the black market.'

'You never take anything seriously, do you? We've hardly any bread in the house and what we have is mouldy.'

'I'm sorry, really I am, but someone's got to keep cheerful. They might not care a fig about us but surely the Jerries won't let their soldiers starve.'

'That's just it. They might not have a choice.' Lydia had been fretting about the shortage of food for several weeks now. Last time she had a bath, she'd been shocked to see that her curves had quite disappeared. Semi-translucent skin stretched across her collar bone and her ribs were clearly visible. In truth, she probably ate less than most. Since she'd started her training she sometimes felt too tired to eat. She gave the spare rations to Mama, who had a permanent cough and was feeling the cold now that autumn had set in.

The patients at the Emergency Hospital were more fortunate than other islanders. Most tomato growers still delivered to the sick, despite having their crops requisitioned by the Germans. Diabetics, however, were a continuing source of concern. It was impossible to give them a balanced diet with rationing so extreme. The elderly were by far the hardest to help, sometimes dying in their beds from lack of insulin. Everyone seemed powerless to save such lives.

Brushing these thoughts from her mind, Lydia smiled at Maggie.

'How's Kurt these days?'

'Shush.' Her friend glanced at the door. 'Don't let Pa hear you. It's been hard for the soldiers, too, you know. A friend of Kurt's was shot last week just for stealing an apple. They were forced to watch the execution.'

Lydia shrugged. She'd seen too much suffering to worry about a dead German soldier. Dropping her voice to a whisper she said, 'Do you two still feel the same?'

'I love him more than ever. He's so kind and caring. Don't be angry with me, please. I was wrong about the Kommandant and I'm sorry, but if the Germans lose the war I might never see Kurt again.'

'They *will* lose the war,' Lydia snapped, shocked by her own bitterness. 'What else did you expect?'

Just then Reg Gallienne appeared at the door.

'What's going on here? Do I hear raised voices?'

'Of course not, Pa.' Maggie held up the turnips. 'Take a look at these. Swapped my old bicycle pump for them. The stupid thing was useless, anyway.'

The old man's eyes lit up. 'Turnips. My favourite. What a good girl you are. We'll fry them for supper in linseed oil.'

'Linseed oil?' Maggie groaned, clearly glad of the diversion. 'Isn't that what you put on your cricket bat?'

'My cricket bat? Bah – that's long since gone for firewood. A couple of cloves in the oil will soon get rid of the taste.'

'I'll have my turnips boiled, Pa, thanks anyway.'

'Do as you like, my girl.' He gave her a wink. 'Anything's better than seaweed soup.'

While Maggie helped to prepare the supper, Lydia retreated to her room. With still no word from Martin, the waiting was taking its toll. Grabbing a brush from her dressing table, she dragged it through her hair until her scalp felt raw. She wanted to hurt herself, wanted the pain to be real, wanted anything that lessened her loss. He'd been gone for almost two years now; years of longing disguised as a dull pain that lodged under her breastbone and merged into everyday life.

Once she thought she saw him coming down the lane, a man with a furrowed brow and strong, angular gait. She'd rushed out of the door and down the path, her head dizzy, her heart crashing against her ribs with such force it almost knocked her off her feet. When she saw the stranger's face she turned away, crying till she had no more tears.

In the first weeks after Martin had gone she had tried desperately to discover where the Channel Islanders might be sent: Liebenau, Wurzach, Biberach? The internment camps all sounded the same. Some were for United States citizens, others for Commonwealth prisoners only. How was she supposed to know the difference?

A few Red Cross messages, it seemed, had got through from Laufen, but most of the other camps were swathed in silence. The few messages that did get through were heavily censored, making it impossible to discover what conditions were really like. Every day Lydia waited for a word from Martin – but the word never came. And so life had continued. Sometimes the sound of her muffled sobs would drift down from the attic at night. If Edna Gallienne heard them, she never breathed a word to anyone.

CHAPTER 32

The soldier appeared out of nowhere.

'Miss Le Page?'

Busy shopping for food on St Sampson's Bridge, Lydia feigned surprise. 'Yes, that's correct. Can I help?'

'I have been ordered to take you to Admiral Fleischer at the Kommandantur. You will come with me, please.'

She raised herself to her full height. 'Have you been following me?'

'My orders are to take you now, *Fraülein*.'

'But why would the Kommandant wish to see *me*?'

Ignoring her question, the soldier grasped her arm and marched her to his car – a black Wolseley parked across the road.

On the way back to St Peter Port Lydia gathered her thoughts. She hadn't met the new Kommandant and had no idea where he was quartered – Sea Breeze was used as an officers' mess these days. Did he know about the raid on the safe? Or had Kruger guessed something and given her away? Whatever the reason she must stay calm and deny everything. As the car sped round the corner, the Kommandantur loomed into view. Her chest tightened; she'd never wanted to see this place again.

Admiral Fleischer was in his late fifties with shaved grey hair and a broad flat nose that reminded her of a pug dog. He came straight to the point.

'You worked for Major Kruger, did you not?'

She nodded her head.

'You also spent time with him in a social capacity?' The new Kommandant's English was better than that of his predecessor.

'That is correct. I accompanied him to social events when required.'

The Admiral shot her a sly grin. 'I see. And what did you know of his business here?'

'Very little, Herr Kommandant. I was involved with his English correspondence for such matters as—' she fiddled with her gloves to stop her hands trembling, 'carrying out the Führer's orders for the Jews, or dealing with any disrespect shown to the German Reich by Guernsey people.'

'Did you show any of this *disrespect* yourself, Miss Le Page?'

'Not at all. I was very grateful to have paid work. I had no intention of abusing my position.'

The admiral shook his head. 'And if you did—' he glanced at the portrait of Hitler on the wall behind him, 'you knew what the consequences would be?'

Lydia nodded, too terrified to speak.

'Good. For now, I will give you a warning. You will say nothing to anyone about your time here with Major Kruger. Do you understand? You will say nothing of what you read, you saw or you heard.'

'Yes, Herr Kommandant.' The Germans were clearly getting desperate now that they were losing the war.

'Do you know why Major Kruger was moved to France? Did he tell you that he was being transferred?'

Lydia shook her head. 'I didn't know he had gone until I read it in the paper.'

She remembered the euphoria she felt at the news.

'That is good. My own preferred method is one of secrecy.

You islanders have no place here at the Kommandantur. Do you understand?'

'Yes, Herr Kommandant.'

'Now go.' He stood up. 'And if I ever hear your name mentioned again, I promise it will be the end of you.'

Lydia's legs buckled as they frogmarched her to the foyer. Summoning every last ounce of strength, she ran through the door and made her escape.

The prayer meeting was subdued.

'I am very sorry to have to tell you—' Irene's voice wavered. 'Arthur Le Moigne died in the Laufen Internment Camp, Germany. Arthur was a loyal and brave member of the Resistance who put the future of our beloved island above his own life. He will be remembered for his laughter and friendship, his devotion to duty and his innate sense of right and wrong. He will stay in our hearts forever.'

Lydia leaned back in her chair, listening to the shocked murmurings around her. Irene had broken the news to her just before the meeting started, but she hadn't even begun to take it in. She could picture Arthur now, asleep in the cinema beside her, looking less like a member of the Resistance than anyone she'd ever met. He'd been her friend as well as her ally, giving her the confidence to face the enemy and the consolation when she failed. It was hard to believe he had gone.

'We are also thinking tonight of our leader, the Reverend Martin Martell, who has not been heard of since he was deported to Germany in January 1943. Despite our best efforts, we do not know where he was sent, or what the conditions of his internment are, but we continue to pray for his safe return. Finally, I urge you all to keep your faith and carry on with the fight, as I know this is what both men would have wanted.'

Lydia shivered. She spoke as if Martin was already dead. Irene's voice continued in the background but she was no longer listening. Martin must be alive. Otherwise, what was the point of it all?

'And finally, we understand that the international ship *SS Vega* will be arriving in the islands within the week to bring food to our long-suffering people. Can we all stand and give three cheers for the Red Cross.'

'Come on, Maggie, have a look at this!'

The food parcel sat on the table neatly wrapped in paper and string. Lydia tore it open and spread the contents over the table, her eyes like two full moons guarding the earth. There was corned beef, butter, biscuits, jam, condensed milk, cheese and even a small bar of chocolate. Chocolate! She'd forgotten how wonderful it tasted.

'Look – real tea.' She flung the packet into the air. 'Seven pounds two shillings a quarter this costs on the black market!'

Swinging her legs off the sofa, Maggie stood up and gazed half-heartedly at the feast in front of her.

'That's an awful lot of food you've got there. Is there a parcel for me, too?' She stretched her arms in the air and yawned.

'Of course, silly. The Red Cross have sent one for everyone. I thought you'd be really excited. We haven't seen stuff like this in years.'

'I'm pleased, you know I am. It's the best thing that's happened in ages. It's just that, well—' Maggie's face reddened.

'Well, what?' Lydia undid the chocolate wrapper, her mouth watering.

'I've lost my appetite, that's all.'

'Lost your appetite?' Lydia grabbed her friend's shoulders. 'You can't mean it. We've been cut off for years and forced to drink nettle tea and eat seaweed soup. Now we've got food we could only dream of and you're not very hungry? Come on – at least have a taste of this – please?'

'I can't, really.' Maggie shook her head. 'It must be the excitement. What with the ship coming to our rescue and the Allies saying the war will soon be over, it's too much to take in.' She slumped back on to the sofa.

Abandoning the chocolate, Lydia made for the sink.

'Here – drink some water, then why don't you go and have a lie down? Maybe you'll feel better after a sleep?'

'You're a good friend, Liddy.' Maggie sipped the water gratefully. 'Isn't that what your pa used to call you? Do you think I could call you Liddy, too?'

'Of course you can.' Lydia swallowed the lump in her throat. 'It would make me very proud. Now go and put your feet up.'

Maggie turned as she reached the parlour door.

'Don't give up on me, will you?'

'Why ever should I?'

'Nothing, it's just that—' Her reply was lost as she disappeared down the hall.

Lydia finished unpacking the food parcel, her mind racing. What could be wrong with Maggie? Was she sickening for something? Or maybe...? She banished the next thought from her mind. One thing was certain: the Galliennes must never find out about Kurt. It would break their hearts if they knew their daughter was seeing a German soldier.

Several days passed and still Maggie's health did not improve. Pale and listless, she no longer perched on the parlour table after work, gossiping about her day; instead she made straight for her room, a worried frown on her face.

Early one morning, abandoning all hope of sleep, Lydia grabbed her dressing gown and headed for the kitchen. It was not yet dawn and the house was bathed in darkness. Reaching the first landing, she saw a chink of light coming from Maggie's room. Gently she pushed open the door to find her friend crouched on the bedroom floor. She had been sick into a bowl.

'My poor, dear Maggie.' Lydia stroked her friend's damp hair. 'You're having a baby, aren't you? I should have realised. Why on earth didn't you tell me before?'

Maggie nodded miserably.

'I was scared. I didn't want to believe it myself. Oh, Liddy, what am I going to do?'

'We'll get through it somehow, I promise. I'll get you a drink of water, then you get back into bed before you wake your ma and pa.'

'Thanks. I really don't deserve you.'

'Never mind that now. Just one question – does Kurt know?'

Maggie shook her head. 'I daren't tell him. He'll be so angry. Not with me, you understand, but with himself. But don't blame Kurt, please.' She choked back a sob. 'We were always so careful.'

'I'm not blaming anyone. But you *must* tell him, Maggie. He has a right to know.'

'They'll send him back to Germany if they find out. I'll never see him again—' Her voice trailed away.

'Listen to me. You can't keep this a secret. You *must* see a doctor, and then we can decide what to do.'

'I can't go to Dr Wren.' Maggie was crying now. 'He's sure to tell Ma.'

'Then come to the hospital. You'll be safe there. This isn't just about you, now – you must think about the health of your unborn child.'

Tears rolled down Maggie's face.

'Why are you being so kind to me? I'm sorry, you know, what I said about you and the Kommandant. I had no right to judge.'

'Don't worry about that now,' Lydia said, the image of Otto's face looming in front of her. 'We've been through it all before. Get back into bed. I promise I'll speak to Matron. And Maggie, is it really serious, you know, with Kurt?'

'I love him, if that's what you mean. You've no idea how it feels to love someone that much.'

Lydia forced a smile. 'That's good enough for me. Now try to get some sleep.'

As the weeks passed, Lydia helped Maggie disguise her condition. She'd let out her winter skirt, but it was already getting tight again. The morning sickness was as bad as ever and, with food still rationed, the poor girl worried that the baby wasn't being nourished. On top of that, she was making all sorts of excuses to keep away from her father's shop.

Early one evening as the two friends sat in the parlour reading, Edna appeared at the door with a pile of mending.

'Ah, I've got the two of you together at last. Have you anything to tell me, Margaret Gallienne? Or were you planning on keeping it a secret forever?'

Maggie jumped up, her face the colour of loganberries.

'I don't know what you mean, Ma.'

'You know perfectly well what I mean.' The older woman turned to Lydia. 'I suppose you're in on it, too? The pair of you must be stupid if you think you can hide it from me.'

Lydia put a protective arm round her friend.

'Don't be too hard on her, Mrs Gallienne—'

'Too hard?' The words shot out like bullets from a revolver. 'She's gone and got herself in the family way, with not a husband in sight. And there's a war on. What am I supposed to say?'

Maggie was sobbing now, tears trickling down her cheeks.

'I was scared to tell you, Ma, that's the truth of it. Scared you'd be angry – scared you'd throw me out.'

'How could you think you could hide it from me, you stupid girl? Who's the father? It'd better not be that Charlie Vaudin. Just wait till I get hold of him. I'll give him the back of my hand.'

'Of course it's not.' Maggie blushed. 'He's much too young for me.'

'Oh, you like them older, do you? So who is it – come on!'

'He's, well, he's—'

'He's a coward, that's what.'

'He's no one you know.'

'Don't be ridiculous – there's hardly any young men about any more and those who are—' Realisation flooded the older woman's face. 'Unless—' She slumped back on to the sofa, her face white. 'Please, please tell me it's not true.'

Maggie nodded miserably. 'I'm sorry, Ma.'

'Whatever will your Papa say? If he finds out it'll be the end of us all.' Edna wafted her face with her hand.

'And what makes you think he'll find out?' It was Maggie's turn to shout. 'He's too busy reading the paper most of the time to even notice.'

For a moment, nobody spoke.

'The baby's father will stand by her.' Lydia's voice sliced through the silence. 'She won't have to face it alone.'

'Oh well, that's all right, then!' Edna retorted. '*He* can bring up the German bastard.'

'I hate you – all of you.' Maggie ran crying from the room. 'I never want to see you again.'

Lydia laid her hand on Edna's shoulder. 'She'll calm down, Mrs Gallienne. I know it's a shock, but—'

'It's not just a shock – can't you see? It's the end of my family. I will never, ever, be able to hold up my head again.'

CHAPTER 33

'Have you heard the news, Mrs Gallienne?' Lydia burst into the room.

'Steady on there.' Edna looked up from her knitting. 'You nearly went flying. What's the fuss about?'

'It's Anne, Hilda's granddaughter. She's coming home.'

'She can't be. The war's not over yet, well not officially anyway.'

'They've given her special permission, from what I can gather, on compassionate grounds. She'll be travelling back on the same boat as our soldiers.'

'That *is* good news.' Edna tugged on the ball of wool. 'She deserves a hero's welcome, if anyone does, poor lamb. Where did you hear this?'

'At the police station. I came straight away to tell you.'

'The police station? Have you been asking about the rector again?'

Lydia nodded, annoyed with herself for letting it slip. 'And I'll carry on asking till I get a proper answer.'

'We all need answers, that's for sure.' The older woman's eyes filled with tears.

'What is it, Mrs Gallienne? What's wrong?'

'It's Reg. He's taken it badly about the baby. He wants to know who the father is. I've told him I don't know. I'm starting to wish it was Charlie Vaudin after all. At least he's one of our own.'

'Maybe Maggie should tell her pa the truth?' Lydia knelt down and warmed her hands on the hearth. 'He might take it better than you think.'

'If he knew his daughter was a Jerry Bag, heaven knows what he'd do. Kill them both, I shouldn't wonder. Anyway, in my day girls *in that condition* were locked away out of sight. Some of them never saw the light of day again.' The older woman's eyes misted over.

'What happened to the babies?' Lydia was curious now.

'They were sent to the mainland. Or to Jersey, where they were brought up in a good, God-loving family. No decent island girl was ever allowed to raise a bastard.'

'But it's different now, surely? What if Maggie married the father? Would that make it acceptable?'

'Acceptable?' Edna's voice rose to a screech. *'Acceptable to marry the enemy*? I'd rather die than let that happen.'

'Don't you think you should talk to Maggie about this?' Lydia persisted.

'What's the point? The girl's taken leave of her senses. I've no idea what's going on inside her head.'

'She's lonely, she's scared, and she's scorned by the people she loves. It can't be easy.'

'She should have thought about that before she—' Edna bristled. 'We could have thrown her out! What more does the stupid girl want?'

Just then Maggie appeared at the door, her burgeoning stomach on full display.

'Are you talking about me?'

'We're discussing what will happen when the baby's born,' Lydia said rather too quickly.

'I won't be a burden, if that's what you're thinking. I've already made plans of my own.'

Her mother's face blanched. 'What sort of plans?'

'You'll find out soon enough. I won't be here for much longer. And now, if you'll excuse me, I need to lie down.'

'You see what I mean?' Edna said, when Maggie had left the room. 'She doesn't have an ounce of sense any more.'

'Maybe not.' Lydia bit her lip. 'But at least you do still have your daughter.'

'I should be thankful. Is that what you're saying?'

'No, it's just that so many people have lost their loved ones.'

'Dear God, now you're trying to make me feel guilty. How could you, Lydia, after all we've done for you? You've had a home here and the love of a good family. What more could anyone want?'

'Nothing, Mrs Gallienne.' Lydia stood up wearily. 'There's nothing I need at all.'

Later that night Lydia lay in bed staring at the ceiling. It was time she found somewhere else to live – she'd relied on the Galliennes' kindness for far too long. The 'unborn bastard', as Reg Gallienne insisted on calling his imminent grandchild, was slowly destroying the family and she'd been too selfish to see it. She sat up and punched the old pillow, black and white ticking showing through the worn pillowcase. Tomorrow she would make a decision.

'Leaving us? Oh, Liddy, how could you?' Maggie's eyes filled with tears. 'Where will you go?'

'To Flo Brouard's, for now at least. Besides, the war will be over soon.'

'Don't say that, please. I'll lose Kurt when the war is over. You can't walk out on me, too.'

'I'm a nurse, don't forget. I can be with you at the birth.'

'Is it because Ma shouted at you?' Maggie's thumb hovered in front of her mouth.

'Of course not. But I've virtually ignored my own mother to save her from the Germans, or from abuse from islanders. I think it's time I made amends.'

'Have you told Ma about your plans?'

'No, I wanted to tell you first.'

'She won't want you to leave, I'm sure of it. Listen, Liddy … is it because you're unhappy?'

'What's that got to do with it?'

'Quite a lot. You think I don't know how you feel. You think I'm stupid, selfish and blind to the real world, but I'm not. Okay, I admit, I didn't believe it in the beginning. I thought you were sweet on that stupid Kommandant. But now – you're missing Martin, aren't you? I mean, really missing him.'

Lydia glanced at the clock. 'Can we talk about this tomorrow? My shift starts at noon.'

'That's right, push me away, why don't you? You're such a bloody martyr.' Maggie aimed a kick at the door. 'You're in love with Martin Martell.

'Okay, so I miss him. I miss his unkempt hair, his smiling eyes and his stupid childlike grin. I don't know where he is or why he hasn't written to me and it tortures me every moment of every day. Maybe he's forgotten me. Or maybe he's dead. Are you satisfied now?'

Maggie moved clumsily towards her friend and held out her arms.

'We're in this mess together. We can help each other, can't we? Friends forever, remember?'

Lydia felt a rush of guilt. What on earth was wrong with her these days? Pinning a smile on her face she returned the hug.

'Friends forever.'

CHAPTER 34

Liberation – 9 May 1945

The atmosphere crackled with anticipation as Lydia walked down the High Street where families milled around waiting for news. She could hear their voices rising and falling in the summer breeze, excitement tempered by disbelief. Rumour had passed from one to the other till it seemed the whole island was buzzing with talk of liberation. Hitler was dead! At long last, they were going to be free.

Reaching the town church, Lydia gazed at the home-made Union Jacks hanging from shop windows, her heart lifting. Ahead of her, crowds of people lined the Esplanade, waiting impatiently for the British troops to arrive. Someone with a sense of humour had suspended an old wireless set on the wall on Albion corner. Though silent, the message was loud and clear. Sets that had been buried or hidden from the Germans had appeared, like magic, overnight for Churchill's Victory in Europe speech.

'Our dear Channel Islands,' he'd told the nation earlier, 'are finally going to be free.'

It seemed as if every islander had come out to celebrate that day – faces scrubbed, hair brushed and shoes polished. Dressed in their Sunday best they hugged each other, tears flowing una-shamedly down their cheeks, all with expressions of intense joy.

Just then Sophie Romerill stepped out of the crowd, waving a flag in the air.

'My dear Lydia. How are you? I wouldn't be alive today if it wasn't for you. Isn't this wonderful?'

Lydia leaned forward and kissed her on the cheek.

'It's truly wonderful. Especially now I've seen you.'

'They're putting up flags along the Esplanade. It's all over, isn't it?'

'Yes, Sophie, it's all over.'

The old woman walked away, nodding happily to everyone in sight. Lydia gazed upwards as a cloud passed over the sun. It would all be perfect, she thought, if only Martin could see it too. She remembered the words he had written before he'd gone away. *Look at the moon tonight and, wherever I am, I promise I will see it too. Let it guide you through the dark until we can be together again.* Snapping out of her reverie, she made her way back down the Pollet. She had more pressing issues to worry about right now. Maggie's baby was almost due and the poor thing was terrified that Kurt would soon be sent back home. Meanwhile the Galliennes still refused to accept their daughter's plight. Other unwed mothers, Maggie reasoned, had survived the social disgrace, but Edna was having none of it. Maggie was guilty of sleeping with the enemy. That was a different matter altogether.

Crossing the road, Lydia saw two young men balancing on a bike, one pedalling, the other freewheeling down towards the White Rock. She recognised Freddie Le Saint in an instant, his head thrown back, long legs splayed out in front of him.

'Freddieeeee,' she shouted at the top of her voice, arms stretched out above her head.

Freddie waved back, a huge grin on his face. Did he recognise her? Did it matter? Everyone was happy. The news vendor's face was jubilant. '*WE ARE FREE!*' the *Star*'s headline proclaimed.

So much had happened in the five long years of Occupation. Children who were babies when the bombs came down had started school, their formative years spent in the shadow of the German flag. Some had lost their childhood, some their homes, their food, and ultimately their freedom. All that was about to change forever.

September 1945

The sun shone high in the sky as down the ship's gangway they came: husbands, mothers, sons, daughters, young and old alike, waving wide-eyed at the masses spilling over the White Rock in a frenzy of welcome.

Some, mere children when they left home, returned as young men and women, their cautious expressions giving way to sheer joy as they recognised their loved ones. One after the other they fell into the arms of their families, words superfluous as the long years of separation finally came to an end.

Lydia stood by the harbour wall shading her eyes from the early autumn sunshine. It was four months now since the Liberation with still no word from Martin. Just last week she had written to the offices of the Controlling Committee asking for help to find a missing prisoner of war. Martin had risked his life for his fellow islanders. Surely the States could do something in return?

All internees, she was told, had been freed on 23 April 1945, the elderly and sick repatriated by the Red Cross via Sweden. The States had no names as yet but would advise her as soon as they received any information. So many lives, she thought wryly, reduced to a piece of paper.

Lydia remembered her dream. Floundering in the sea at Vazon Bay she saw Martin's inert body floating on the surface, far out of reach. He looked peaceful, as if he were asleep. Calling his name till her strength ebbed away, she sank down inexorably under the waves.

'Look, it's Charlie,' someone shouted, jolting Lydia back to the present. Straining forward, she saw Hilda Le Quesne's nephew getting off the boat, waving his hands above his head. A cheer erupted from the crowd. One of the island's best loved policemen, Charlie Coutanchez had been interned in Germany since 1942. A Red Cross message had finally reached his aunt, helping to ease the pain of her granddaughter's tragic death.

Lydia waved until her arms ached, grateful for another life saved. Maybe it would be Martin next time.

The following day Lydia arrived at Hilda's home. Makeshift bunting stretched over the gables and a Welcome Home party was in full swing.

The door was opened by Hilda's granddaughter, Anne, who had left as a plump eleven-year-old and returned as a strikingly pretty young woman. Her dark hair was held on top of her head by a tortoiseshell barrette and her eyes, though sad, were a glorious shade of blue.

'Welcome back,' Lydia smiled, pulling the girl gently towards her. 'How old are you now? You look so grown up.'

'I'm almost sixteen, Miss Le Page, and Wendy would have been twelve on November the ninth.' She bit down on her lip.

'Call me Lydia, please. There was nothing you could have done to save your sister, you know. It was an accident. No one's fault.'

'I know that now. I just wish I could have been with her.'

'Well, you're here for your grandmama now, and that means a lot, believe me. She's waited so long for this day. Which reminds me: did I hear something about a newly baked cake?'

Just then Charlie appeared, his face gaunt, his eyes flitting nervously round the room. He walked forward to shake Lydia's hand.

'I owe you a big thank you for looking after Auntie Hilda. She'd not have got through it all without you.'

Lydia forced a smile, the pain of Hilda's loss hovering silently between them.

'Anyone would have done the same. Now tell me about Biberach. What was it like? How did they treat you?'

'Some were treated badly, some not so bad.' His eyes glazed over. 'But you don't want to know all that. It's in the past now.'

'You're wrong, Charlie, I do.'

'Put it this way, miss. It's a good job the truth never got out or the British would've killed Hitler with their bare hands. People were shot in cold blood in front of us, some for disobeying the rules. Others, women included, had to plead for their lives, crawl in the mud on their hands and knees and beg. They were killed anyway.'

Lydia winced. 'But why?'

'The officers were supposed to carry out the Führer's orders. Some were human, but most weren't. They didn't like us islanders, you see.'

'It's amazing any of you survived.'

'I don't reckon we would have, Miss, not without Mr Martell.'

'Mr Martell?' Her pulse quickened.

'Yes, you know, the rector. The one that got done for collecting the news. Took charge, he did, made us laugh when we wanted to cry. Kept us all in good spirits.'

'Martin was with you in Biberach?' She gave an involuntary shudder.

Charlie nodded. 'Came a while after me. Shame, it was, the way they treated him. Bastards, all of them, if you'll forgive my language.'

Lydia steadied herself on the back of a chair.

'Is he ... is he dead?'

'Probably, for all we know.' Charlie shook his head. 'They gave him a terrible beating on some trumped-up charge, till he was too weak to stand. The next thing we knew he'd disappeared. There was no body, no nothing. Some said he'd been spirited away by the nuns, God bless him. Let's hope it was true. Ah, here comes the tea.'

Charlie was still talking, but Lydia was no longer listening. The room seemed devoid of colour, like a silent movie playing over and over again. Martin had been in Biberach. Martin had disappeared. He'd been beaten badly, but maybe, just maybe, he could still be alive. The thoughts crashed round in her head.

'You sent a Red Cross message to your aunt, didn't you?' she asked as Charlie handed her cup of tea. 'Did anyone else send them?'

He nodded. 'A few. But the Jerries were fussy about what they allowed through. The rector told us to keep diaries to tell our families how we felt – you know, for when we made it back home. So we wrote things down every day and it kept us sane, it did.'

'Well, at least you're back.' Lydia struggled to keep her voice calm. 'It's the best thing that could have happened to your aunt – and to you.' She stood up and reached for her coat.

'Going so soon?' Hilda appeared at the parlour door. 'Is everything all right?'

'What? Oh, yes, fine, thanks. There's something I've forgotten to do. It's lovely to see you together again. Thanks so much for inviting me.'

Once out of the house, Lydia ran down the path and kept on running until she reached home.

CHAPTER 35

'I'm scared, Liddy.' Maggie clutched the side of the chair. 'I've never been so scared in all my life.'

Lydia's smile was reassuring. 'You'll be fine. Baby's on its way, but I'll stay with you till we get to hospital. The ambulance won't be long now.'

'I don't know what I'd do without you. My folks have put up with me so far, but Pa still doesn't know about—'

'Never mind that now. Remember what I told you. Just breathe through each contraction.'

'I do, I am – if only someone could take it all away.' Maggie stuck her thumb in her mouth till the pain subsided.

'That's it – now lie back and rest while you can.' Lydia wiped her friend's brow with a damp sponge. The Galliennes were playing in a bowling tournament that afternoon and Maggie had begged her not to disturb them. They'd agreed to stand by their daughter, but not without a great deal of resentment.

By the time the ambulance arrived Maggie was in a state of panic. Each contraction overwhelmed her and she shrieked louder than before. Lydia glanced at her watch. It was gone six p.m. and she was on duty again at seven thirty in the morning. She had promised to stay with Maggie and she would keep that promise. It was going to be a long night.

'There's something I want to tell you.' Maggie's voice cut into her thoughts.

'Yes, what is it?'

'Kurt and I – we were married weeks ago, before he was sent away.'

'Married?' Lydia's voice rose in shock. 'But how?'

'Well – not really married in the eyes of God. But we had a special ceremony and exchanged rings.' She opened the neck of her blouse to reveal a curtain ring on a chain. 'He's in England now, in a prisoner of war camp. When he gets to Germany he's going to send for me and the baby.'

'Oh, Maggie – why didn't you tell me he'd gone?'

'I was scared, I suppose. Scared and confused. I know he's still the enemy, as far as everyone else is concerned, but I really do love him. The rest doesn't matter to me.' She yelped as another contraction rolled over her.

'Just concentrate on your breathing. We've got the little one to think of now.'

Reg Gallienne paced up and down the hospital corridor while Lydia plied him with hot drinks and encouragement.

'How is it going?' he asked for what seemed like the hundredth time.

'It's slow progress,' she replied. 'The baby's in the breech position so it's taking longer than usual.'

'Breech position? What does that mean?'

'It's more complicated than a normal birth. The child will be born feet first.'

'All right, all right, I wish I hadn't asked. Just let me know, will you, when it's all over?'

Nodding swiftly, Lydia headed for the maternity ward. Maggie's life could be at risk as well as the baby's, but how could she tell that to her poor father? She'd read about the dangers of breech birth: mother haemorrhaging to death, baby stuck in the birth canal or strangled by its own umbilical cord; the list went on. Straightening her cap, she quickened her step; there was no point in fretting about that now.

Inside the delivery room, Edna was fussing over Maggie, their differences temporarily forgotten.

'Come on now, give it your best. That's my girl, I know you can do it—'

Maggie spotted her friend straight away.

'Liddy – thank goodness you're here. Stay with me, please? I can't bear this much longer.'

Lydia glanced at the senior midwife who nodded in assent.

'Matron's let me off early today, Maggie, and I wouldn't miss it for the world.'

Her friend's thin smile turned into a grimace.

'Good, because believe me, I'm never, ever, going to do this again.'

The midwife pulled Lydia to one side.

'The baby's showing signs of distress. We've called for the obstetrician and he's promised to be here as soon as possible. In the meantime, just do your best to keep her calm.'

Half an hour passed before the doctor finally arrived.

'We may have to do a Caesarean.' His voice was grave. 'The baby's lodged in the birth canal and the mother's getting weaker.'

'Too late,' the midwife yelled. 'I can see the baby's feet. We might need a blood transfusion. Nurse Le Page – stay right there. Now, come on, Maggie, push.'

One by one, two tiny feet appeared, followed by a mass of purple-tinged flesh. 'Careful, now, just breathe gently!' Precious seconds dragged by as the midwife slid the cord from the around the child's neck.

'What's happening to my baby?' Maggie's voice pierced the air.

'We're doing all we can, Mrs Gallienne.' As the head finally appeared, the obstetrician grabbed the child by the legs and slapped it sharply on the back.

The child let out a wail as, fearing the worst, Lydia jumped back in fright.

'It's a boy,' the midwife said at last. 'A beautiful baby boy.'

Lydia had gone twenty-four hours without sleep. Stumbling through the hospital grounds, she wept openly, her body shaking with irrepressible sobs. Was she crying for Maggie? Or was it for herself? Holding the baby for the first time, she'd been overcome with a yearning that gnawed through her chest and spread through to her very soul. This child could have been hers – a child born out of her love for Martin. And now it was too late. If only he had written, if only she had some proof that he was still alive. Ashamed of her thoughts she wiped her eyes, covered her head with a cotton scarf and set off down the road.

'The baby's a bastard!' Edna Gallienne spat the words from her mouth. 'Nothing but a German bastard.'

Maggie's eyes blazed. 'How could you? That's not what you said when he came into the world. He's my son, Ma.'

'Yesterday I thought I might lose you.' She glared at the tiny infant. 'And all because of *him*.' Edna was sitting by her daughter's hospital bed, the curtains drawn protectively around them.

'This is your grandson. Don't ever call him a bastard.'

'And why not? Give me one good reason why not?'

'Because Kurt has asked me to marry him.' Maggie lifted the child from his crib, softly stroking his head. 'And Heinz will make us a proper family.'

'Heinz? You've given him a German name? God help us all.' The older woman leapt to her feet. 'Damn you, Margaret Anne Gallienne, for bringing such shame on our family.'

'I'm proud of him, whatever you may say.' Maggie held her baby to her breast.

'You're proud of Hitler, too, no doubt?' Edna shouted. 'Is that what this is all about?'

'Heinz is my flesh and blood, Ma, *that's* what it's about. Love him as I do, or you'd better forget he exists. Whatever you say, we're going to live in Germany.'

'Germany?' Edna's face crumpled. 'But you can't leave Guernsey now. Don't go, please. Don't do this to me. I love you, don't you see?' She pulled the child from her daughter's arms. 'I can love him too, if I have to. Please stay, I beg you, please say you'll stay.'

Arching his back the baby cried out, a thin wail that hung in the air between them.

'You don't know what you're saying, do you, Ma?' Maggie's voice wavered. 'You don't know whether to love or hate us, that's the saddest part. I'm sorry I've caused you so much grief, but this is my life now and I'm old enough to do what I choose.'

'Are you really going away? To live in—' It was Edna's turn to whimper.

'Yes, but we'll come back to see you – if you want us to, that is. And you can always visit. Now give me back my baby.'

Edna blinked, placing the child back in his crib.

'You're tired, my girl, and I'm far too upset to know what I'm saying.' She rubbed her eyes with the sleeve of her blouse. 'Rest now, both of you, and I'll come again in the morning. Maybe then we can make sense of it all.'

CHAPTER 36

Lydia stirred her coffee so hard it spilled out on to the saucer and splashed her lap. Rubbing at the stain with her hankie, she glanced around, but no one in the cafe gave her a second look. Why on earth had she agreed to meet Charlie? She was regretting the decision already.

There was so much she needed to know about Biberach but this wasn't the right way to go about it. Besides, if Charlie guessed her feelings for Martin she'd be even more vulnerable. She glanced at her watch – five minutes to go – she could finish her drink now and leave before he arrived.

'Ah, there you are.' Charlie appeared at the door, his face creased into a huge grin. 'You beat me to it. Sorry to keep you waiting.'

'Don't worry, I caught the early bus. I usually walk, but what with the rain and everything—' She gestured to the chair in front of her, hoping he couldn't read her thoughts.

'You're looking well,' he said, removing his cap. 'A lot thinner than before I went away, but as pretty as ever.'

To her dismay, Lydia blushed.

'Can I get you something to drink, sir?' The waitress hovered opportunely in front of them.

'I'll have a cup of tea, please, and another for the lady?' He smiled at Lydia.

'That would be lovely,' she nodded. Charlie looked taller than she remembered in his uniform, his hair neatly cropped to within an inch of his head.

'You've done a grand job with Auntie Hilda, Miss Le Page. Perked up no end, she has, since our Anne came home. I wanted, you know, to say thanks.'

'No thanks are necessary, I can assure you.' Her smile was genuine. 'And please call me Lydia. So, how is Anne?'

'Between you and me she's gone and got herself a beau, an English soldier no less. Quite sweet on him, she is. Wouldn't be surprised if we heard wedding bells before long.'

'Wedding bells?' Lydia's jaw dropped. 'Surely she's much too young for marriage? Does Hilda know?'

'Not yet. But the girl's nigh on sixteen now and a proper young lady, too. There's many a young 'un wed since the war started.'

Lydia's mind was racing. Poor Hilda. One child dead, the other contemplating marriage. It didn't bear thinking about.

Out loud she said, 'Well, let's just hope your aunt understands. I grew quite fond of her while I was working at the church.'

A flicker of recognition crossed Charlie's face. 'Of course, I remember now, you helped at Torteval. That's how you knew the rector.'

'Yes, I knew him quite well.' She kept her voice steady. 'It must have been dreadful for all of you, stuck in that awful place.'

'I came out of it better than most. Kept my mouth shut when I really wanted to bawl. Martin, well, he knew the Jerries were bastards and he said so. Stuck up for us all, he did. Didn't do him much good though, did it?'

'Is that why they…?' She swallowed.

'Beat him? Yes. The war was coming to an end and the Nazis knew they were finished. Took it out on him, didn't they.'

'You said he was tortured? Do you think he could possibly

have survived?' She examined her hands. 'I have a church meeting tomorrow. I think I should, er, pass on what I know.'

'I watched them cart the poor fella away, and he didn't look long for this world. Covered in bruises he was and his face swelled up so much as you wouldn't recognise him. They threw him in the back of a truck and that was the last I saw of him. Best say he's missing, presumed dead.'

'Do *you* think he's dead?' Her voice trembled.

'Put it this way, it would be a miracle if he'd survived.' Charlie glanced over her shoulder. 'Ah, here comes the tea.'

Lydia blinked. A vast abyss had opened up in front of her and she longed to disappear into it.

'Is anything wrong? You've gone very pale. Can I get you a drink of water?'

She raised her eyes to see Charlie hovering nervously by her chair.

'I feel a bit faint, I'm sorry. It's very muggy in here. I think I need to go home.'

'Don't worry, I'll call the station and get a police car round right away.' He winked. 'We'll have you back home in no time, and that's a promise.'

Charlie stood at the parlour door, dressed in his Sunday best suit, clutching a bunch of flowers.

'Mrs Gallienne was kind enough to let me in. I brought these to cheer you up.'

'That's very kind of you,' Lydia nodded, 'but the doctor says it's only a chill. They've given me some time off work but it's really not necessary.'

'I'm sure you deserve a rest.' He shifted awkwardly from one foot to the other.

'It's a good job no one saw me arriving home in a police car the other day,' she managed a weak smile, 'or they'd think I'd been up to mischief.'

'There's worse ways of travelling. It was an emergency, and that's that.'

Lydia stifled an artificial yawn. 'Whatever it was, I'm fine now and you don't have to worry any more.'

'I'd best be going then. Look after yourself and maybe we can have that tea another time?'

'Why not? And, Charlie?'

'Yes?'

'Thanks for coming.'

Lydia took a deep breath as the door closed behind him. She hadn't spoken to anyone since she'd heard the news about Martin, refusing to accept that she would never see him again. Her nights were filled with strange dreams where the sea had taken control, the little land left was covered in cold white light and none but the dead could speak. Why did the dreams still haunt her? She knew she should go back to her studies, pick up her old life where she had left off, but that was impossible. Instead she'd been offered a permanent job at the hospital which had now become her home.

Desperate as Lydia was to confide in Maggie, her best friend had quite enough on her plate already. It was two months since the baby's birth with still no news from Germany. Could Kurt have changed his mind? Or, far worse, had it changed for him?

Lydia shivered as the sash windows rattled in the wind. Grabbing the patchwork blanket her mother had knitted, she pulled it over her shoulders. Christmas would soon be upon them, the first since the Occupation ended. Folks were busy planning their celebrations and who could blame them?

The door swung open again, interrupting her thoughts.

'Charlie gone already?' Edna raised her eyebrows. 'I hope you didn't send him away.'

'I was feeling a bit tired.' Lydia faked another yawn. 'Look, he brought me some flowers.'

'What a thoughtful young man he is. Now then, there's a letter here for you. Must be important – it's come from England.'

Fear gripped her stomach. 'Thanks, Mrs Gallienne.' She shrugged off the blanket. 'I'll take it up to my room.'

The envelope was thick blue vellum, the handwriting scripted in black ink. Her hands trembled as she tore it open.

24 Hartington Gardens
Failsworth
Manchester
January 26 1946

Dear Miss Le Page

I am sure you will be aware that my beloved husband, Arthur Le Moigne, died of dysentery in the Biberach Internment Camp, Germany in May 1944.

You may wonder how I came to have your address. Arthur left me a list of people to contact in the future, should he not come home, and your name was among them. Please forgive me for leaving the task for so long.

I loved my husband very much and believe he was a true hero. However you both came to meet, I know that he must have valued your friendship a great deal. It would mean so much to me to hear about his last days in Guernsey.

In the meantime, should you ever come to England, please be assured you will always be welcome in my home.

Very sincerely yours
Cynthia Le Moigne

Lydia folded the blue vellum sheet in two and placed it in her bag. The disappointment was crushing. It was not news of Martin after all. She stood up and smoothed down her skirt. When had she become so selfish? Cynthia Le Moigne was a widow. Nothing could be worse than that.

CHAPTER 37

January 1946

Christmas had come and gone. After five years of Occupation the islanders were still trying to get back to normal. Presents had been opened, homemade crackers pulled, the celebrations creating a mood of unashamed joy.

With Sea Breeze still in disrepair, Lydia lived in the nurses' home, working long days at the hospital to help her keep sane. Her sleep was still full of nightmares, Martin's waxen face vanishing under the waves, his dying words drowned by the sound of screeching seagulls. But with each new dawn she was more determined than ever to uncover the truth about what had happened to him.

The mood was still sombre in the Gallienne household. Edna and Reg allowed their daughter to bring her baby home, on condition the child be called Harry instead of Heinz, and Maggie mooched around wondering if she would ever be reunited with Kurt.

Meanwhile, Charlie had become a regular visitor at the Vrangue. Every week while on duty at the station, he would scour the official paperwork for news of Martin before reporting back to Maggie. The answer was always the same.

'But surely they must know *something* by now,' she'd snapped, finally losing her patience. 'I still don't believe he's just disappeared.'

'A lot of people have disappeared, I'm sorry to say.' Charlie's voice was gentle. 'The rector was left for dead. I can only tell you what I saw.'

'But he *could* still be alive, couldn't he?' Her voice grew louder. 'Maybe he's lost his memory? Maybe he doesn't know how to get home?'

Charlie shot her a tolerant look. 'His name is on the missing persons list. You're not next of kin, I'm afraid, so there's nothing more I can do.'

The minute he'd gone, Lydia swore under her breath. Charlie was doing his best and she hadn't so much as said thank you. She was acting like a spoilt child. She really didn't like the person she had become.

'Lydia, how are you?' Hilda Le Quesne's thin lips stretched into a beam.

'Still busy at the hospital. There's more responsibility now I'm qualified. How's Anne getting along?'

'Very well, thank you. She has a young beau on the mainland, would you believe. He's coming over to see her in a few weeks' time. Nothing too serious, mind, but at least it's made her smile again.'

'That *is* good news,' Lydia nodded politely, remembering Charlie's words.

'And that's not all.' Hilda glanced around the crowded market, her voice dropping to a whisper. 'I reckon our Charlie's got his eye on you. Proper struck, he is. You could do a lot worse, you know.'

Lydia swallowed her dismay.

'We're very good friends, your nephew and I, Mrs Le Quesne, but's that's all. I think you must be mistaken.'

'I was good friends with our Herbert, too, before we were wed.' Hilda tapped her nose. 'You mark my words; I can feel it in my water.'

257

Lydia thought back to the last time she'd seen Charlie. They had climbed the cliffs above Fermain Bay over winding paths covered with wet leaves, up and up till the winter sun shone through the trees and the wind took their breath away. She felt safe in his company, the brittle edges of loneliness temporarily smoothed. Charlie had made her feel close to Martin, helped to keep his memory alive. But anything more than friendship had never even crossed her mind.

'A penny for your thoughts.' Hilda's voice brought Lydia back to the present. She glanced at her watch.

'Goodness, is that the time? I'll be late for my shift. Bye for now and do give my regards to Anne.'

With that she was off down Market Street, past the town church and on to the Esplanade. She wasn't late at all really, but she needed some time to sort out her feelings. Walking briskly, she followed the road to the foot of the Val des Terres before starting the winding ascent. For some time now she'd been thinking of going to Germany to see for herself the camp where Martin had lived. If she took his photograph with her maybe someone, somewhere, would remember him? She would have to lie about where she was going, but she couldn't move on with her life until she knew what had really happened. Decision made, she quickened her pace. If Charlie had hopes for their future, it was time she faced up to the truth.

'Come in and sit down.' Matron Le Brun smiled warmly.

'Thank you for seeing me at such short notice.' Lydia dropped into the chair, clasping her hands together to stop them shaking.

'What is it, my dear? Is something troubling you?'

'The fact is, Matron, I wish to ask for unpaid leave. Now that the war is over I'm hoping you will consider my request. If that's not possible, I will, of course, hand in my notice immediately.'

Leaning forward, Matron folded her own hands in front of her on the desk. 'You're one of my best nurses. May I ask why you want to leave?'

'I wish to go to England.' Lydia lowered her eyes. 'To the college where I was studying. I never got a chance to say goodbye.'

'I see.' The silence hovered in the air between them. 'I know it's none of my business, but are you sure this is the right thing to do?'

'I've made up my mind. I'll always be grateful for the opportunity you gave me to train as a nurse and I owe you nothing but gratitude.'

'You have repaid me time and time again, Nurse Le Page. Come now, please don't talk as if you're never coming back. I sincerely hope you will continue in the profession. In the meantime, as you have clearly made up your mind, I will grant you three months' unpaid leave. You can request a further three months after that, if necessary.'

Lydia's face broke into a smile. 'Thank you, Matron. You won't regret this, I promise.'

'Good. Now run along, before I change my mind. Oh, and Lydia?'

'Yes, Matron?'

'Did you ever hear what happened to the rector – the one from Torteval Church?'

'The Reverend Martell?' Lydia held her gaze. 'No, I'm afraid not. It seems he never escaped from Germany.'

'There's something I've been meaning to ask you, Lydia.' Charlie fiddled nervously with his cap. He'd come to meet her out of work and they'd taken the coast road home. 'We've been friends for quite a while now and I wondered if you would consider walking out with me – you know – making it official.'

'Oh, Charlie – you're a warm and generous man, and I've grown very fond of you.' Her voice cracked. 'But—'

'You don't think you could ever love me?'

'It's much more complicated than that.' She stared at a lump of hewn rock, its surface covered with frost, like tiny frozen tears. 'Before I can think about the future, there's something important I have to do.'

It was Charlie's turn to look away now.

'I think I understand.'

'Do you? I'm not even sure I do myself.'

'You're still in love with him, aren't you, Lydia? Martin Martell?'

She stood quite still, the chill air numbing her senses.

'I have to know, for certain, if Martin is dead. I have made up my mind to go to Germany to find out what happened to him and, if necessary, to bring his … his body back home.'

'You must do whatever is right.' The hurt in his voice was palpable. 'I will do everything I can to help. Only, Lydia, please don't shut me out.'

She took hold of his hand.

'I would never, ever, shut you out. If you can find it in your heart to understand, then—'

'Just say what you want me to do.'

'It won't be easy. I want everyone, especially Mama, to think I'm going back to England to visit my old college. In other words, I need you to lie for me.'

Charlie bowed his head. 'I would lie for you till the end of my days if it would make you happy.'

'Thank you, Charlie.' Impulsively, she pressed her face against his. 'Thank you for everything.'

*

Lydia hugged her mother. Six months of good food had brought colour back to the old woman's cheeks and her chest cough had disappeared, despite the cold weather.

'You look very well, Mama. Better than I've seen you for a long time.'

'Is that why you're leaving me again, my girl?' Her mother's eyes filled with tears. 'You're a trained nurse now. You needn't go back to England. I thought you wanted to give up your studies.'

'And I will, of course I will, but I have to go back to Leicester first to tie up a few loose ends and explain the reason for my decision. I owe them that at least.'

'Can't you just write?'

'I've done that already, but the professor still wants me to finish my diploma.' She hated lying but she had no choice. 'Anyway, you'll have plenty to keep you occupied when you move back to Sea Breeze.'

'What a wonderful day that will be.' Emily's eyes misted over. 'I never ever thought it would happen.'

The old house on the cliff had suffered considerable damage under the Nazis. Towards the end of the Occupation they had kept it as officers' quarters, knocking down walls and destroying the decaying greenhouses. Recently it had been bought by the States of Guernsey who intended to convert it into a rest home. Under the agreement drawn up by the family solicitor, Emily Le Page would earn the right to live there free of charge for the rest of her life.

'I walked past Sea Breeze yesterday,' Lydia said, glad of the opportunity to change the subject. 'It was getting a new coat of paint and there were all kinds of workmen inside.'

Emily nodded. 'Do you think your Papa would have approved?'

'Of course he would. I can picture him now up in heaven, smiling to himself and smoking his pipe.'

'You're a good girl, Lydia, and I'm very lucky to have you. If it wasn't for you I never would have survived. Have you thought what you'll do with the money from the house? My needs are few now.'

'Not yet, Mama, no. Money's not important to me at the moment, though I'll always be grateful to—' she struggled to find the right words, 'to my family for making it possible.'

Emily held out her arms. 'Go on with you. Have a safe journey, and let me know as soon as you arrive.'

'I'll write the moment I get there, I promise.'

'Oh, and Lydia?'

'Yes, Mama?'

'Don't forget about Charlie. I'm sure he'll be waiting for you when you get back home.'

CHAPTER 38

The old train trundled through the streets of St Malo, gathering speed as it steamed out into the countryside. Lydia leaned back in her seat allowing the air to seep from her lungs. The previous night she had posted a letter to Mama to say she'd arrived safely in England. She'd used an English stamp in the hope it would be delivered anyway.

On the opposite side of the carriage a balding man in his late forties shot her a hesitant smile. Beside him a girl of about eight with a pale face and dark blonde curls observed her with curious eyes. Lydia turned towards the window. The rain had stopped, leaving the landscape bathed in a wintry sheen. As far as she could see, an abundance of apple trees stood in neat rows, like headstones on nameless military graves. How many lives had been lost, she wondered, in years of futile war? A sudden draught made her shiver. Pulling her coat round her shoulders, she leaned back and closed her eyes.

An hour or so later Lydia woke to the sounds of the brakes screeching on the tracks. She peered through the window. All around them the grassland was sparse and pitted with craters, a legacy of the Allied bombs, but there was no sign of a station. The carriage door opened and a military policeman entered, his face inert. The stranger opposite folded his copy of *Le Monde*, showing his papers while talking in rapid French. Lydia reached into her bag and held out her passport. After a few seconds the policeman nodded wordlessly and disappeared.

'*Mademoiselle, vous êtes très jolie.*' The little girl who had spoken smiled shyly and Lydia smiled back, grateful that her newly grown hair was visible under her hat. Her French might be passable, but the last thing she needed right now was to engage in conversation, however innocent, with a stranger. Years of Resistance work had left their mark.

The child untied a brown paper parcel and pulled out a chunk of bread along with a pat of creamy white cheese. Lydia's mouth watered. She'd been too nervous to eat on the Channel crossing, something she now regretted. To everyone's disappointment, food at home was still rationed, the flurry of longed-for delicacies having failed to arrive. She would have to wait till Luxembourg to buy something now. Searching the bottom of her bag for a boiled sweet she glanced at her watch. Nine more hours and they'd be in Biberach.

Lydia woke as the train braked, jolting her out of her seat. She peered through the window, covered now with mud and dust, blinking at the desolation around them. Scores of buildings were reduced to rubble while those still standing were damaged irretrievably, their roofs blown off, their insides open to the sky. Among the rubble were dozens of refugees, carrying what few belongings they possessed, their eyes staring bleakly at a world they no longer recognised. A child in rags played with a burnt-out bicycle while an old woman stumbled, her face grey and pitted, one arm bound in a makeshift sling. Spying a scrap of food, the woman stretched out and jammed the morsel into her mouth, like a wild animal.

Lydia recalled Otto's face, a rare flash of tenderness in his eyes as he spoke of his home country.

'*Our young men are dying too, Lydia. There is no fairness in war, no right and wrong.*'

Further along, women of all ages dressed in makeshift uniforms were clearing rubble from the streets. So this was Hitler's army now.

As the train approached Biberach, Lydia clutched her head in her hands. How naïve she had been! How removed from the cruel reality of war! Germany had been devastated by bombs, their people terrorised, just as they were in Britain. This was a battle nobody had won.

After walking for more than an hour it appeared on the horizon like an unwanted mirage: Oflag V-B, the internment camp where Martin had spent his final years. Set on a hill on the north side of Biberach town, bordered by high barbed wire fences, the camp was unrelenting in its misery. Rows of single-storey concrete huts stared back at Lydia, while more barbed wire covered the windows. In the distance the remains of what looked like a garden was now choked with dead weeds. Behind the camp the Alps rose majestically, watching over the earth. Lydia felt a sudden desire to climb the nearest mountain, to claw with her hands till she reached the clear fresh air of the summit.

Slowly she followed the perimeter wall, moving tentatively from post to concrete post, her eyes adjusting to the impending gloom. She reached out and grasped the barbed wire fence, oblivious to the rusty spikes cutting deep into her flesh. Falling to her knees she gulped in the cold air, her sobs drowned by the wind.

They had beaten Martin in this terrible place, beaten him as punishment for his strength of mind, beaten him for his beliefs. She could picture him now standing in the summer sunshine, his face solemn as he watched the children play. He had given those children hope, something to live for. At least nothing could change that now.

'Please don't leave,' she whispered as the crimson blood congealed on her skin. 'No God, wherever He might be, could love you more than me.'

She had no idea how long she stayed on the ground. Opening her eyes at last, she saw that the light had begun to fade. The two-day journey from Guernsey had left her exhausted, the bitter wind cutting through her clothes as it began to snow. Wearily, she stood up and headed back towards the town.

'Can I help you, ma'am?' The American military policeman stopped in front of her.

Lydia raised her eyes, a flicker of hope igniting inside her.

'Maybe you can.' She searched through her bag and pulled out a photo of Martin wearing his clerical collar. 'Have you seen this man?'

The officer shook his head. 'Sorry, ma'am. So many civilians are missing these days. Have you tried the convent? I've heard they sometimes take people in.'

'Convent?' She was listening intently now.

'St Dominikus. It's a few miles down the road from here.'

'Then I'll go, right now. Can you show me the way?'

He pointed to a jeep parked across the road. 'Better still, I can give you a lift.'

'You can? Thank you *so* much.'

'A pleasure, ma'am. Hop in.'

The Convent of St Dominikus stood on the edge of a forest, like a vast crumbling castle. Lydia gazed in awe as they passed the iron gateposts and made their way down the neglected path surrounded by wide banks of frozen grass.

The officer jumped out of the jeep and opened the passenger door.

'I'll leave you here, ma'am. I hope you find what you're looking for.'

Thanking him for his kindness, Lydia climbed the worn stone steps, taking care not to slip on the ice. The silence clung to her skin. Lifting the heavy brass knocker, she heard a distant groan, like someone waking from a very long sleep. Seconds later a bell clanged gloomily in the distance. Muffled voices were followed by the sound of footsteps approaching. Could Martin really be here in this dark and hostile place?

The ancient door creaked open.

'*Ja?*' Peering through the crack, the nun's face seemed as old as the building itself.

'*Guten Tag.* My name is Lydia Le Page.' She broke into fluent German honed by her months at the Kommandantur. 'I have come to enquire about a missing person. His name is Martell – the Reverend Martin Martell.'

Heaving the door open, the old woman gestured her guest through the stone-clad vestibule and into what looked like a massive dining hall.

'Have you seen him?' Lydia persisted, pulling out the photograph. 'I have travelled here from the Channel Islands. He was here at the camp in Biberach.'

The nun shook her head. Silent tears crept down through the creases of her skin, now almost translucent with age.

'The man you speak of, he was here with us, but—'

'But, what?' Lydia swallowed the rising fear. 'Is he dead?'

'No, not dead.'

'Then what?'

'We rescued him. He had a high fever and nothing brought his temperature down. For a long time he didn't speak. He got better, but one day, the fever, it came back. He said he must go back home. We told him no, he wouldn't survive the journey, but he wouldn't listen. Then he disappeared.'

'When exactly did he leave?'

'One week ago, maybe two. He left in the night — no food, no clothes, no money. We've asked God to bless him. There's no more we can do.'

'Did he say why he wanted to go?' Lydia's voice wavered.

'Only that he had something important to do.' The old woman shrugged. 'As I say, he was very ill.'

Lydia dropped to her knees, oblivious to the cold marble floor beneath her.

'Please God, don't let him die.' Yet how could he survive this desolate land in such a fragile state? She had long since carried the pain of loss, like a heavy weight lodged under her breastbone. Now it seemed the weight was too heavy to bear. She lay at the nun's feet, drained of strength, breathing in the damp that permeated her skin.

'Martin is dead. Martin is dead.' She repeated the words like a mantra but still they made no sense. Sight and sound merged into an empty chasm as the truth hit her with such force, squeezing the breath from her lungs. She felt light-headed and peculiarly free from pain. 'I'm coming to join you,' she whispered.

Lydia's eyes flickered open. Through the darkness she could see the distant light of candles and hear the sound of organ music coming from high above.

'Am I in heaven?' she whispered. 'Please let me be in heaven.'

'Ssshhh… You're at the Convent of St Dominikus. You're exhausted. We've brought you to the bedchamber to sleep.' The nun's face swayed in the shadowy light, her eyes incongruously bright.

'You stay here till you're better. We'll give you hot drinks and food to make you strong. And we'll pray for you.'

Lydia lifted her head, rubbing her eyes with the back of her hand.

'You are so full of kindness, but I cannot stay. I must carry on with my search.'

'For the Reverend Martell?'

She nodded. 'I've been to the old camp, to Oflag V-B.'

'Ah yes. The place is empty now. The soldiers, they pack up and go.'

Lydia fell back against the pillow. 'I needed to see the place where... I just had to go there.'

'You are the lady the Reverend spoke of?'

'He spoke of me? Are you sure? How? When? Tell me, please.'

The nun replied hurriedly in German. Before he left, Martin had put in her safekeeping several letters he'd written while in the camp. If he didn't return within a year, he had made the nun promise to send them on to the Channel Islands. The old woman reached under her habit and drew out a piece of paper scribbled with an address in black ink.

Miss Lydia Le Page, Sea Breeze, St Martins, Guernsey, CI.

'That is you, is it not?'

Lydia was hysterical now, tears running down her face.

'That is me, yes. Can I see the letters? Do you have them here?'

The old woman nodded. 'Wait here and I will get them for you.' Bowing her head, she shuffled out of the room.

CHAPTER 39

Biberach, Germany

March 1943

My Dearest Lydia

I look into the sky at night and hope that the same stars are watching over you... There is so much I want to ask. Are you safe, my darling girl? Do you ever think of me as I think of you? I often wish we'd had more time to talk before I was arrested and I pray every night that you have not suffered at the hands of the enemy.

Here at Biberach, I have had many hours alone to think. I know now that I loved you on the day we first met, though I would not admit it, even to myself. I only wish that I had told you sooner. How different our lives could have been.

What can I tell you about our journey here? On leaving Guernsey, we were transported to France trussed up in the hold of a ship, treated no better than cargo. We spent three months at the Camp de Royallin, north-east of Paris before being moved on to Germany. We were loaded into cattle trucks without food or water: men, women and children awaiting our fate. When we finally arrived here at Biberach everyone cheered – yes cheered! We were still alive – truly the most amazing feeling! Though the camp is freezing cold and very Spartan it is not as bad as I expected: on a clear day you can see the Alps rising up majestically from behind the barbed wire.

Here I have found myself a new role. The Channel Islanders – and there are many – have formed into a group, if not of resistance, then certainly of defiance, and I lead them as best I can. Sometimes it feels like the prayer group all over again. We sing loudly to drown the sound of beatings, we steal food from the kitchens for our children and, though we have no safe means of sending letters, each day we write a diary for our loved ones back home. In this way we keep you alive in our hearts.

Our rooms were filthy and crawling with vermin when we arrived, but now we have hand-made pictures on the walls and mats for the 'tables' where we eat our watery soup. Sometimes there is German sausage and hard, black bread which we make into savoury pudding. Always before supper we sing 'God save the King'.

It is strange, but the young children here really believe they are on holiday. Paradoxically, they have a 'freedom' not unlike that at home. Lessons are perfunctory, play is encouraged, and they roam around the camp and gardens without fear of straying from the fold.

Some of the women have been separated from their husbands and the shock of not knowing their loved ones' fate has been very hard to bear. Last week a six-month-old baby died of malnutrition and the poor mother, wretched with grief, rejected my offer of prayers. 'What sort of God would take away my child?' she asked, and who could blame her? I long to make a difference in this pointless war but sometimes, like that mother, I too question my faith.

The thought of you sustains me through each new day. I know that I will love you always.

Yours,

Martin

May 2 1943

My Dearest Lydia

I miss you and think of you throughout each day. With your soulful eyes and defiant smile, you live in my heart like a flame in the dark. I desperately hope that you have not been punished for the sins that I committed and that you remain unharmed. Wherever you are I know you will be brave.

We are allowed to send Red Cross messages now but they are heavily censored and do not always reach their destination. I have decided not to make contact this way for fear of incriminating you or, indeed, anyone else in the prayer group. Instead I put my feelings down on paper and I promise to deliver them to you in person one day.

What can I tell you about our life here? The first Red Cross parcels arrived this week and have been our saviour. Food is still sparse, but we have enough to live on and are grateful for that. To be fair to the soldiers, they do not touch our food parcels, handing them over within a few hours of arrival. We have learnt how to use every piece of packaging from the parcels; string, paper and straw. Even the tins reappear as badges, rings, coins and a myriad of other toys for the children who, mercifully, are oblivious to the cruelty that is meted out by our captors. One man was severely beaten yesterday for scratching a 'V for Victory' sign on the door of the lavatory. Others are threatened with guns and made to work without food as punishment for their 'crimes'.

You will be surprised to know that there is a flower garden here at the camp. As the temperature rises we can see the buds begin to appear, heralding the onset of spring.

Let us hope this time next year we will be back on our own dear island with the world finally at peace.

The new 'prayer group' we have formed for the Guernsey people of Biberach has proved to be a great success, though it won't surprise you to know that we are usually too preoccupied to pray.

We meet every week to try to help those who are most in need. We keep the memories of home alive and make constant plans for the journey back home. Fortunately, religion is generally respected by our captors, so our meetings are more or less undisturbed. This is not the case, however, for those of the Jewish faith who have a tendeny to disappear suddenly from our midst. Why should they be persecuted? Do they know their ultimate fate? I hope not, for these are strong-minded people with a deep respect for their own kith and kin.

Right now we are planning a concert in which everyone will take part. You'd be amazed at the 'instruments' we have managed to acquire. Someone even smuggled in a mouth organ – we've no idea how – but it has given us much pleasure. Two of the men are building a drum kit, and the children have learned how to make music with paper and wooden combs. I had no idea that some of our fellow islanders could sing so sweetly; I've even threatened to round them all up for the Torteval Church Choir when we get home.

My love is yours, until we meet again.
Martin

September 1943

Dearest Lydia

The summer is almost over and every single one of us longs for home. We held a painting competition for the children last week (papers and crayons were provided by our captors – maybe they have a conscience after all?) There was no theme – we just told everyone to paint what they could see – whether it be real or *imaginary. Would you believe, my darling girl, that every single one painted a picture of home? I confess my eyes were wet as I gazed at the beaches, bursting with crabs and sandcastles, the Hanois lighthouse surrounded by seagulls, and the boats leaving the harbour with boxes of tomatoes bound for the mainland.*

I told you in my last letter that the little ones think they are on holiday, but for some of them now the holiday has lasted too long; they just want to go home.

I have been truly heartened by the strength that our people have shown. Time and time again I have seen the men save their own meagre rations for their families, sometimes at enormous cost, as it is the men who take on the most onerous duties. Illness is another big problem. We have little or no medication so a cold can quickly turn to pneumonia in these harsh conditions. The women make medicines using wild herbs collected from the gardens and these work wonders, if only for morale.

How are you, my darling girl? Do you still attend the prayer group? I hope so. These people are your friends and I know they will protect you, whatever happens. It is this, and only this, that helps me to bear our separation. One day you will read these words and all of your suffering will be at an end.

Until then I remain

Yours,

Martin

December 1943

My dearest love

Winter has finally set in and the camp is covered in ice, but memories of home still keep us warm. Men, women and children return each night to separate dormitories, but when the day breaks we come together again to face the beginning of another day. Women are generally respected here (though I'm not sure respect is the right word). Shall I just say that, thankfully, they are left alone. The children have invented a game of 'touch' where they run from one end of the hut to the other to ward off the cold. Last one to finish has to help with the chores.

I have been amazed by the multitude of talent there is here; many people have created sketches and paintings of our beloved island or written poems using the German Prisoner of War stationery issued by the camp. These days, the military have handed the running of the camp over to the civil police and they allow us to send mail. I am suspicious of their motives and will do nothing to incriminate you, dearest Lydia, so I continue to write in secrecy as before, and store my thoughts and feelings until we meet again. When time stands still, I think of you as a ray of sunshine filtering through the bleak reality of life here.

Do remember the night you slapped me across the face? I had followed you, fearing for your safety in the blackout, but believe me, Lydia, I had never in my life experienced jealousy until that moment. I had preached against what I saw as a selfish emotion, denouncing such feelings from the pulpit, and yet this was something that had played no part in my life.

When I knew you were spending time with that man (even now I cannot bear to write his name) my jealousy took on a life of its own. Anger, mixed with crushing despair, pushed me to desperation. I was cruel to you, I know that now, and I had to face the guilt of knowing that I had sent you into his arms. Can you forgive me for what I have done? I hope so, for I can never forgive myself.

It is getting dark now and I must not waste the candlelight.

Yours, as ever

Martin

Lydia stood once again on the platform at Biberach Station, her battered suitcase containing the precious letters clutched in her hand. She had devoured each word, each thought, each phrase; this was her way of bringing Martin back home.

Over the last few days she had trailed round doctors, hospitals, police stations, churches and endless public places taking with her the photograph of Martin, hoping for even a spark of recognition. She'd been dismissed with barely a look or sometimes a simple shake of the head. It was hopeless; so many people were displaced, so many missing, so many dead. Her request, it seemed, was commonplace. Endless questions filled her mind – every one of them unanswered. Why hadn't he written from the convent to tell her he was still alive? Why had he left secretly without the strength or the means to travel? Could he still be alive? She recalled their first meeting when she'd offered to help with the Sunday school. How arrogant he had seemed then. She could still picture his face as he came into the classroom to apologise for his rudeness. (Had he been rude? She could hardly remember now.) And then there was the day he told her about his parents disowning him, the memory still so vivid in her mind.

'Why did you join the Church?' she'd asked. 'You seem so out of place somehow.'

'They made me do it.' His laugh was full of irony.

'Who did?'

'My parents.'

'I don't understand. Why would you do something against your will?'

'My will?' He threw his head back again. 'Against *their* will more like. They're agnostics. I did it to make them angry.'

'I see,' she said, not seeing at all. 'And did it?'

'You bet it did.'

Lydia turned her face towards the oncoming train. *Could*

Martin have survived against all the odds? A single tear squeezed from her eyelid and slithered towards her mouth. Maybe she would never know.

CHAPTER 40

The tall man with the lean limbs and lopsided grin hauled himself out of the taxi. Leaning awkwardly on a walking stick, he gazed up at the rambling house in front of him.

'No need to pay, sir.' The driver shook his head. 'It's a pleasure to have you back home.'

'Thank you, Cyril.' The man's eyes glistened. 'I can't quite believe I'm here myself.'

'Need any help?'

'No thanks. I have no luggage to speak of.' Limping, he made his way up the rectory steps.

A middle-aged woman opened the door.

'Good morning. Can I help?'

'Good morning, madam. I'm Martin Martell, formerly Rector of Torteval Church. May I come in?'

The woman's jaw dropped as she stepped backwards.

'Oh, my word, that is… Yes, sir, do, please do come in.'

'Who is it, Mrs Mauger?' A voice rang through from the hall. 'It's someone to—'

The owner of the voice appeared. 'My God – Martin?'

'Hello, William, how are you?' Martin stepped forward and held out his hand to his fellow clergyman.

'How am *I*? Good God, man, we thought you were *dead!* Come in, for goodness sake.'

'So did I, at one stage, but I'm mending well now.' He leant on the wall and waved his walking stick. 'Once I get rid of this, I'll be good as new.'

'You need a bit of meat on those bones, by the look of things, my good man. Come into the drawing room and Mrs M will get you something to eat.'

Martin put down his knife and fork with a sigh.

'You've eaten barely half your meal, sir,' Mrs Mauger chided. 'That's my best shepherd's pie, I'll have you know.'

'And I'm very grateful, but that's just the trouble. It's *too* good, I'm afraid. My stomach is more used to rations and watery cabbage soup. This lot would have kept me going for a week .'

The housekeeper laughed. 'Go on with you, sir. I'll take your tea into the drawing room and you can sup it with the reverend. Well, I'll be blowed. You're both the reverend now, aren't you?' Shaking her head, she ushered him out of the door.

'Ah, Martin.' Stephen Le Riche shook his hand yet again. 'Sit yourself down and tell me all about it.'

'Thank you.' He pushed his walking stick to one side and sank down into the chair. 'There's not a lot to tell, really. I spent two and a half years in Biberach on the Swiss border. It was mostly full of islanders like me. They elected me as their leader and we managed to keep up morale, but if we had a death the mood changed and some of us vented our anger on the enemy.'

'Go on.'

'The Channel Islanders were treated differently from the other internees. The Jerries watched us carefully because they knew we'd been sent there specifically on Hitler's orders.'

'Ah yes, of course, the reprisal for the Germans in Iran. What about you, personally?'

'I think they saw me as a troublemaker. They accused me of rabble-rousing and discouraging the internees from helping the

Germans. Our Guernsey friends didn't need much discouragement, believe me.' He laughed, a strange hollow laugh that echoed around the room. 'So when I stood up to the soldiers one night I was beaten senseless. It annoyed them even more when I didn't resist the blows. That's all I remember. When I woke up I was in a convent. I found out later that I'd been left for dead. The nuns, it seems, rescued me from outside the perimeter fence. I still don't know how they managed to carry me back.'

The older man nodded. 'Truly a miracle.'

Martin stood up and leaned against the mantel.

'The trouble is, I don't recall anything after that. After I woke up I had no idea where I was or how long I'd been there. That feeling was far worse than any injuries I'd sustained. It was as if I had lost part of my life. So, though the nuns were my saviour, I had no recourse but to leave. I had to get home. I left without a word and I am not proud of that.' He bit down on his lip. 'I even stole money from the poor box for my journey.'

'How did you manage without papers?'

'I smuggled my way on to the train and became a master at avoiding the military police. The nuns had made me a new clerical collar and it turned out to be my passport to freedom. When I am fully recovered I intend to go back and repay them in full.'

'Yes, yes, my boy, I'm sure you will. In the meantime, you must stay here — after all, this is your home. My tenancy is only temporary until you are ready to resume your duties. What do you say?'

'That's extremely kind and I will gladly take up your offer. But firstly there is someone I must find. Someone who—' He stopped. 'Someone who was the sole purpose of my journey.'

'Will you not wait till the morning?'

'No, thank you. I must go now.'

*

Martin approached the house in the Vrangue and rang the doorbell. 'Hold on,' someone shouted over the sound of a baby crying.

Maggie lifted the latch and stared, open-mouthed.

'Reverend Martell – Martin. I can't believe it. I thought you were—' she hesitated, 'er, still in Germany. Please come in.'

He stepped into the vestibule, leaning heavily on his stick, and smiled down at the pram.

'Aren't you going to introduce me to the little one?'

'Yes, I'm sorry – it's just that, well, it's such a surprise to see you. Please meet Heinz, or should I say Harry, my son.'

Martin cupped the baby's chin in his hand.

'Hello, Harry. What a lovely little chappie.'

'Can I get you something? A cup of tea perhaps?'

He coughed nervously.

'No, thank you. I'm sorry to be so blunt, Maggie, but I've just been past Sea Breeze and it looks empty. They've got scaffolding up and workmen there. What happened to the Le Pages?'

'Mrs Le Page sold up to the States. They're turning it into a nursing home.'

'And Lydia?'

Maggie blushed. 'She's not here, I'm afraid.'

'Not here? But where is she? I have come a long way to see her.'

'Do sit down, Reverend Martell,' Maggie said in a kindly voice, 'and I'll put the kettle on.'

'Is she at work?' he persisted, his eyes darting around the room.

'I'm afraid she's gone away.'

Martin's face twisted with pain. 'Where to?

Just then the back door opened, bringing with it an icy blast of wind.

'Ma, Mrs Le Page,' Maggie shouted, clearly glad of the respite. 'Look who's here!'

'Well, well,' Emily's thin lips broke into a smile. 'The Reverend Martell. This really is a miracle. What a pity Lydia can't be here to see it.'

Martin leaned on his stick and shook each woman's hand in turn. 'It's a pity indeed. Maggie was just about to tell me where she's gone.'

'She's gone to England.' Emily removed her hat. 'To see the professor about her studies. She said she would come straight back, but now—'

'I see,' Martin interrupted. 'You think she might stay?'

'I'm not sure.' The woman's eyes misted over. 'She never got over losing her papa, poor girl. I haven't seen her smile, really smile, since he died. And these last few weeks she's been so sad, I hardly recognised her at all. Perhaps she needed to get away from the memories. That Kruger man – she thinks I don't know – he was almost the end of her.' A worried look crossed her face. 'Are you all right, Reverend? You're looking very pale.'

'I'm fine, really. Tell me what happened to the Kommandant.'

'They sacked him.' Emily sounded matter of fact. 'Sent him packing. That's when Lydia got a real job. She trained as a nurse. We're all so proud of her.'

'I'm sure you are.'

'You look tired, Reverend,' Edna interrupted. 'Can we offer you a bed for the night?'

'That's very kind, but I understand there's a place for me at the rectory. There is so much I still have to do.'

'I understand. *N arestae daute*!' Emily smiled sadly. 'You'll want to go back home.'

Martin nodded. 'There is one thing you could do for me, Mrs Le Page. Do you have an address for your daughter?'

'Address? No, I'm afraid not, though she dropped me a line when she arrived in England. I'm sure you could contact her at the technical college, if it's urgent.'

'Thank you. But that won't be necessary. Good day to you all.'

CHAPTER 41

Flo's eyes widened as she threw open the front door.
'Lydia – you're back – thank God for that! Come in, my girl,
come in.'

'What's wrong?' Lydia dropped her bag on to the polished
wood floor. 'Is it Mama?'

The old woman nodded. 'She's run up a bit of a temperature
and I can't get it down. Gave me a bit of a fright, she did, what
with moaning and thrashing around.'

'Have you called Doctor Wren?'

'He's on his way. He's sure to be here soon. Run along to her
room now, will you?'

Emily was lying on her back, mumbling under her breath.
Lydia took hold of her mother's hand. It felt warm and clammy.

'Mama, wake up, it's me.'

The old woman's eyes flickered open. 'You've come at last.
There's something I need to tell you.'

'Shush, Mama, everything's going to be fine. Please don't
worry about a thing.'

Just then the doorbell clanged in the hall below.

'That'll be Doctor Wren. He'll look after you now.'

Lydia paced the floor outside the room while the doctor examined her mother.

'Please, oh please,' she whispered, 'make her well again.'

Dr Wren's eyes were troubled when he finally emerged. 'I think the fever's burning itself out, but I'm worried about your mother's mental state. Have you any idea what's made her so confused?'

'No, I'm sorry. I've been away in England. She seemed fine when I left.'

'I'm not blaming you, my dear,' the doctor's voice was kindly now. 'But there's something really troubling her. I think the two of you need to talk.'

'You mean now?'

In an hour or two, maybe. I've given her a light sedative so she should sleep for a while.'

'Thanks. I'll sit with her till she wakes.'

'Of course, my dear.' He patted her shoulder. 'I'll come again tomorrow, and then we can decide what to do.'

'What is it, Mama? Tell me what's wrong.'

'It's the boat.' Emily's voice was barely a whisper.

'What boat?'

'The one that killed my poor sister—'

'Don't upset yourself about it now.' Lydia squeezed the sponge and wiped her mother's brow. 'A car caused the accident, not a boat, remember? It was all such a long time ago.'

The old woman turned to face her daughter.

'What's happening to me, Lydia?'

'Nothing. You've had a fever, that's all.'

'I promised to say nothing, I promised not to frighten you, but—'

'Don't worry, Mama, I know who my real parents were. You told me everything.'

'I lied to you about the accident. They were in a boat. You were there with them, don't you see? You were with them in the boat when it sank.'

'Me? That's impossible.' Lydia swallowed hard.

'You were there, I tell you—' The old woman's voice rose to a scream. 'You went over the side, poor little mite.'

'No, Mama! It can't be true. Why didn't you tell me this before?'

'Because of the dreams, the nightmares. They started after you lost your parents and you've had them ever since.'

The dreams, the nightmares – drowning in the sea. Lydia's heart dropped.

Emily raised her hand from the pillow and touched her brow. 'The doctors said you might be damaged, you know, up here if you knew what had happened. You were floating on the water when they found you, your eyes closed, a heavenly smile on your face.' She began to sob. 'They pulled you out of the water lifeless; they thought they had lost you too. Your ma and pa, bless their souls, lay dead on the ocean bed.'

Lydia held her mother's hand, her mind whirling. So many things were starting to fall into place: the dreams that haunted her at night and the terrifying sensation of water creeping over her face had been a part of her life for as long as she could remember. But now she knew that these were not dreams, they were memories. *The fear was real.*

'I'm not angry, Mama,' Lydia eased herself on to the bed beside her mother. 'I'm glad you've told me. It's such a relief to know at last. Shush now. Close your eyes and sleep.'

Lydia stood on the rectory steps, her dark curls swept back, her eyes covered by a thin veil.

'Can I help you, miss?' The housekeeper peered through the gloom.

'I would like to see the Reverend Le Riche. I have bad news, I'm afraid.'

She opened the door. 'You'd better come in. Wait a minute! I know you, you're Jack Le Page's daughter! Whatever's the matter?'

Ignoring the question, Lydia stepped into the vestibule, her face pale with grief. 'Is the Reverend available, or not?'

'He's with someone at the moment, my love, but don't worry, I'll tell him you're here.' She led Lydia into the cheerless drawing room stripped of clutter, the dark curtains drawn against the night. In the far corner stood Martin's desk, the leather tooling covered with a white cotton cloth, like a shroud.

'You look worn out.' The older woman clasped her shoulder. 'Let me make you some tea.'

Lydia flinched. 'I don't need tea, thank you all the same.'

'Well, sit down please, and at least take the weight off your feet.

'I'm so sorry, that was very rude of me … it's just that—' She stopped as the sobs shook her body.

'There, there, don't take on so, my love, it can't be as bad as it won't be mended.'

'I know you are trying to be kind, but I don't need your tea or your sympathy. *I'm fed up with people telling me lies—*'

Just then the Reverend Le Riche appeared at the drawing room door, his spectacles perched on the end of his nose.

'What on earth is this terrible commotion?'

'Thank goodness it's you.' Lydia ran towards him. 'I've come about Martin – the Reverend Martell. I've just returned from Germany and I have to tell you—' her voice broke, 'everything points to the fact that he is dead.'

'No, no, my dear. You are wrong.' The old man observed her black attire. 'Whatever your reasons, you should not be in mourning. You see—'

'Why not? What else is there for me to do? I've had enough of false hope.' She clenched her fists till the nails dug into the palms of her hands. 'Why won't anyone believe me?'

'Because, my dear—'

The door swung open.

'Oh, I'm sorry, I didn't realise you had—' Martin's voice rose to a shriek. 'God in heaven, *Lydia? Is it really you?*'

Lydia jumped at the sound of his voice, her eyes transfixed. Her mind was playing tricks on her – cruel, merciless tricks. If only Martin *was* here now, standing right in front of her, but she no longer knew what was real any more. She was tired of the dreams, tired of the voices in her head, tired, so tired of it all. She was sinking now, down where no one could reach her ever again. She slumped to the floor as the blackness welcomed her in.

She opened her mouth to cry but no sound escaped from her lips. The water seeped in, insidious at first, creeping between the crevices of her teeth, flowing through the soft flesh of her cheeks and underneath her flailing tongue. Down through her throat it streamed, gathering momentum now, reckless with freedom, sure of its destiny. A haunting wail filled the air, leaving only silence in its wake.

Then she was floating, inanimate, the sun shining on her skin, tender and warm... The voice called out, gently at first, then soaring, high into the cloudless sky. 'It's all right, my darling, Mama's with you—' Now she knew she was safe.

Lydia opened her eyes. Through the mist she could see him, his eyes bright with longing, a tender smile stretched across his face. Wearily she turned her head to the wall, cursing the demons that had haunted her for so long.

'Lydia, it's me, Martin.' The words floated over her. 'I've come back to you. I've come home.' She lifted her hands and covered her ears with her elbows, just as she did as a small child. He was dead and she knew it.

His arms came round her now, thin, bony limbs she hardly recognised. Reaching out she touched his hair, now tinged grey at the temples, her fingers moving slowly across the scarred face.

'Can it really be you?' Down she trailed, down towards his lips.

He watched her with hollow eyes, slowly taking her fingers into his mouth.

'Martin.' She grasped him, her hands digging into his flesh, her hair breaking free and spreading across her face.

'Darling girl, my beautiful, darling girl.' He was crying now as their bodies crushed together.

She could hear his heart beating, an eerie echo of her own.

'I love you, Martin. I should never have given up hope—'

'Believe me.' His lips silenced hers. 'You never did.'

CHAPTER 42

Lydia gazed at the scene in front of her, absorbing every detail. Martin was sitting at his desk, sifting through a mountain of papers, concentration etched on his face. She had come to the rectory this morning to help sort through his belongings, but she felt powerless to move. So many thoughts were still crowding round in her head.

'A penny for them.' Martin interrupted her thoughts.

'I was just wondering. Why didn't you write to me before you left the convent? If I had known you were alive, I could have—'

'It wasn't that simple, I'm afraid. You might have forgotten me by then, written me off. Good God, you could even have married someone else. I had so much time to think. Besides, what right had I to expect anything from you? The only way I could know for sure was to come home.' He stood up. 'And now it's my turn to ask a question.'

'Anything. What is it?'

'Why did you let me think you were in love with Kruger?'

Lydia's face flushed crimson. 'I wanted to explain. I just—'

'Please tell me. I need to know. You must have had a very good reason to lie.'

Slowly she got up and stood by his side. 'When I couldn't find Hitler's plans in the safe, I made up my mind to break into Sea Breeze. The Kommandant was away and—'

'You did *what*?' His eyes flashed with anger.

'Well, not break in exactly. I still had the key to the back porch so I, well, I let myself in.'

'You must have been crazy – why in heaven's name didn't you tell me what you were planning to do?'

'Because I knew you'd stop me. And I was right, wasn't I?'

Martin lowered his eyes. 'Go on.'

Lydia recounted the story as quickly as she could.

'It was then I found a letter from my Papa.'

'A letter? What did it say?'

'That my real mother and father died when I was eighteen months old. I am the daughter of Emily Le Page's sister, May, and her husband, an Austrian-born Jew.'

Realisation swamped his face. *'My God – you're Jewish.'*

'I am, along with my father and his parents before him.'

'And you thought this would put me in danger, too?'

She nodded miserably. 'You were risking enough already. The last thing you needed was to be associated with me.'

'My poor girl.' He fingered her hair. 'So your papa was not—?'

'My real father, no… I still haven't taken it in. I'm not sure I ever will. I love Mama, of course I do, but Papa—' Her bottom lip wavered. 'He meant the whole world to me.'

'What I don't understand is your parents – your adoptive parents, that is – why did they keep it a secret for so long?'

'At first Mama begged Papa not to tell me. She said I was too young to understand. Then as I got older she thought they might lose me if I knew the truth.'

Martin let out a low whistle. 'But the Jerries – how would they have found out about your past, if it was such a well-kept secret?'

'That's just it. One day I opened a letter that should have been addressed to the Kommandant. It said something like "Your precious assistant is a Jew". It was a terrible shock, but at the time I thought it was a sick joke. She bit her lip. 'I managed to destroy the letter but I never felt safe again.'

Martin pulled her to him and rested his head on her shoulder. 'Oh God, what have I done to you?'

'Given me love? Given me hope?'

'No. I almost destroyed you. I have to live with that.'

'There is something I have to do,' she said after a long pause. 'Something that won't wait.'

He frowned. 'What is it? What's wrong?'

'It's Charlie – Charlie Coutanchez – remember him from Biberach?'

'Of course I do. Everyone knows Charlie.'

'I've been seeing him, while you were away.'

'Seeing him?' Martin pulled away and walked across to his desk.

'Yes, you know, going out for walks and having tea now and then. It was Charlie who told me that you were in Biberach, that you'd been beaten by the guards. When I was with him, I felt closer to you somehow. It seemed possible that you could still be alive—' She was babbling now, trying to justify her actions.

Martin sank into his chair. 'I see.'

'No you don't.' She moved towards him. 'Please understand. It was friendship, that's all.'

'Is that how Charlie Coutanchez views it?' He held her gaze. 'Is it, Lydia?'

'I believe he may have wanted it to develop into something more.'

'Then I agree you must go and see him. You must tell him of the feelings that once existed between us and then, only then, can you decide what to do.'

'The feelings that *once* existed between us? How could you say that, Martin?' Her voice cracked with fear. 'I've never stopped loving you – you must know that. I had every intention of talking to Charlie but that's the end of it. There's nothing else to discuss.'

'Do as I ask, Lydia.' He turned and walked through the door. 'Just do as I ask, please.'

There was no point in arguing. Biberach had robbed him of his sense of reality. She was losing him all over again.

Lydia could see from Charlie's face that he already knew.

'Good morning, Miss Le Page,' he greeted her formally as she approached the station counter. 'It seems congratulations are in order. I gather the prodigal son has returned.'

'Indeed he has, sergeant. But how did you know?'

'I saw him yesterday with my own eyes, getting out of a taxi. It's nothing short of a miracle.'

Lydia held her breath. 'I'd no idea you'd seen him. I was hoping to tell you myself. Is it possible, I mean, could we have a word in private?'

'There's no need for that.' Charlie's face was set. 'I think we've said all we have to say, don't you?'

'But there's something I want to explain.'

'Believe me, you don't have to. I understand perfectly. Please send my best wishes to the Reverend Martell. I hope you'll both be very happy.'

'We can't just leave it like this.' Lydia lowered her voice, glancing nervously around her.

'As far as I'm concerned, the matter is closed. And now, if you will excuse me? I have work to do.'

Lydia stood at the edge of the Fairy Ring, its grey stones darkened by the rain. Here she could find solace in long-forgotten childhood memories that surfaced through the pain. Across the grassy ridges the ocean met the horizon, like one vast leaden sky.

Since the last time they'd spoken, Martin had avoided her,

ignoring her phone calls and refusing to answer the door. So she'd gone to the church very early that morning and caught him coming out of the vestry.

'Why won't you speak to me?' she'd shouted, all pride abandoned.

'I'm leaving the Church for good.' He avoided her eyes.

'Leaving? But why?'

'I achieved all I set out to do, but not in the way I intended. I learned more in Biberach then I ever did from my holy orders. There's no longer a place for me here, Lydia.'

She stepped back, fielding the words like a physical blow.

'Isn't this all a bit sudden?'

'I had plenty of time to think about it while I was away.'

'But what will you do?'

His forehead fell into a familiar frown. 'I don't know yet, but in the meantime I intend to travel. The Church has paid me in my absence, so I've plenty of time to make up my mind about the future.'

'How far will you go?' She was beginning to sound like a child.

'Far enough away to allow me to think.'

'I see.' She wanted to ask if he would return, but the words lodged in the back of her throat. What did it matter? He'd already made up his mind.

Now, standing by the Fairy Ring, her dark eyelashes drenched with rain, Lydia looked up at the clouds searching for an answer. But no answer came.

'I'm losing him, Maggie.' Lydia flopped on the sofa beside her friend. 'I can't believe it but it's true.'

'What do you mean?'

'He's leaving the ministry for good. He says he no longer belongs.'

'I'm not surprised, really.' Maggie pulled a face. 'He always was made for better things.'

'This is serious, can't you see?' Lydia swallowed her anger. 'He's leaving Guernsey. He's leaving me.'

'I'm sorry, Liddy.' Maggie tucked a blanket round the baby's shoulders. 'But I don't believe he'll do it. What brought this on?'

'I told him I'd been seeing Charlie Coutanchez, just as a friend. But you know Martin, he wouldn't listen. He seems to think he'd be *doing the honourable thing* by letting me go.'

'That's ridiculous. When was this?'

'Does it matter? He doesn't want to see me again.'

'Look, Liddy. I may not always be bright as a button but one thing's obvious. You two are meant to be together. Have you quarrelled?'

'No, nothing like that. He's always been so principled. He thinks Charlie has more right to be with me than he does.'

'And what does Charlie think?'

'I really don't know. He's not talking to me, either.'

'Oh, Liddy!' Maggie hugged her friend. 'What on earth are you going to do?'

The following day at sunrise Maggie pushed her son in the pram to Torteval until she arrived at the rectory. After knocking on the door she rang the bell for good measure.

'Maggie! What are you doing here?' Martin rubbed his eyes.

'This is the rectory, isn't it? And you are the rector?'

'For now, yes.'

'Then can I come in?'

'Of course. I'm sorry.' Glancing at the sleeping child he ushered Maggie into the vestibule. 'Can I offer you a cup of tea?

'Never mind the tea.' She marched past him into the drawing room. 'I want you to christen my son.'

'I see. Is that why you've come?'

'What other reason could there be? He's a bastard, Heinz; don't forget. A German bastard at that. Will you christen him or not?'

'God does not judge little children, Miss Gallienne. I will do whatever you wish.'

'Well, that's a relief, I must say.' She stretched to her full height. 'The mighty God doesn't frown on bastards. But what about cowards? What does he think of those?'

'I don't know what you're talking about.'

'Don't you, *Mister* Martell? Now there's a surprise. You see, I have a friend who's fallen in love with a coward. A principled coward, but a coward, nonetheless. And that makes him lower in my eyes than any child born out of wedlock could ever be.'

Martin loosened his collar.

'If you're talking about Lydia, this is nothing to do with—'

'I always admired you, Martin,' she interrupted. 'You brought a bit of life into the place. I thought you were strong. But how wrong could I be? You're just like all the other men left on the island – weak and full of hot air. Lydia loves you, you stupid man, and you're too proud to see it.'

Just then the baby cried, a stark, hungry wail that filled the air.

'And who are you to call me stupid?'

'At least I'm honest with myself, which is more than you've ever been.'

Silence hung in the air like smog, until Martin finally spoke. 'I'll do what I can for the child, I promise.'

'Why thank you.' Maggie reached for door. 'Don't worry, I'll let myself out.'

A letter was waiting for Lydia when she arrived back at the Vrangue. She recognised Martin's handwriting instantly. Picking it up, she saw that her hand was trembling. It could only be bad news.

Dear Lydia

There is something I have to tell you, something I should have told you right from the start. My fiancée, the one you saw in the photograph, did not leave me as I told you.

I had made her a promise and I broke my word. This would have been shocking enough for a lay person but I was at theological college studying to be a man of the cloth. My fiancée's parents were horrified. They accused me of dragging her name into the mud and leaving her with no future.

There was worse to come. As I mentioned, Janet decided to sue me for breach of promise. My shame was compounded, but still I could not change my mind. I knew I didn't love her, Lydia, and that a marriage without love could destroy us both. What I didn't know then was that she had suffered a nervous breakdown, and that this was not the first time she had been treated for the same illness.

Soon she had withdrawn from the world and wouldn't speak to anyone. In desperation I asked her again to marry me, but this time she refused. A day later she took her own life.

I am not asking for forgiveness, only for your understanding.
Martin

They stood side by side overlooking St Sampson's harbour.

'Thank you for coming.' Martin gave a nervous cough. 'I just wanted you to know that the Church has accepted my resignation. I leave Guernsey for London a week tomorrow.'

Lydia stared at the fronds of seaweed swaying back and forth in the water beneath them. 'And you won't change your mind?'

'No, I'm afraid that's impossible.' He followed her gaze. 'I hear they've finished Sea Breeze at last?'

Lydia nodded. 'Mama's moving in next week. She's so excited, she just won't talk about anything else.'

'I'm happy for her,' he nodded. 'Your mother has waited a long time for this.'

'She'll have company, too. It'll be just like the old times.'

'And what about you, Lydia? What are you going to do?'

'I'm going to keep on nursing, for now. Matron seems to think it's my vocation. And they're talking about building a nurses' home with a training wing attached. I think it's a wonderful idea.'

'I'm sure it is. You'll probably end up running the place, given half a chance.'

Lydia couldn't stand it any longer.

'Listen to me, please. It wasn't your fault Janet died, yet you've carried the blame all these years. I can't imagine what you've been through, but at least you didn't ask for my forgiveness because there's nothing to forgive.'

She watched as a frown appeared on his forehead, fighting the urge to reach up and smooth his brow.

'What are you saying, Lydia?'

She swallowed the lump in her throat, afraid of losing the moment.

'I'm saying this doesn't have to be the end. There is another option.'

'And that is?'

'I could always come with you.'

'As my assistant? Is that what you mean?'

'I'd settle for that, of course. Anything, as long as we're together.'

With one swift movement he dropped his stick, pinning her against the sea wall.

'Lydia Le Page, are you asking me to—?'

'Well, I *do* have leave of absence from the hospital. And there *is* a place I'd really like to visit.' She wrapped her arms round his neck.

'And where might that be?'

'The house where I was born.'

Martin was smiling now, just as he did on the day they first met.

'A honeymoon in London – what a good idea.'

Lydia smiled back. 'I take it your answer is yes?'

EPILOGUE

A warm wind rustled through the grass as the sun slipped down over Pleinmont Point. They stood side by side lost in their own thoughts, staring out into the ocean.

'This time tomorrow you'll be there,' Martin whispered, 'back in London, the place where you were born.'

Lydia nodded, brushing a stray lock of hair from her eyes. 'I'm so excited, but if I'm honest, a little scared, too.'

'Why? You've no need to be.'

'This will change so many things. I don't suppose I'll ever be the same person again.'

'That's true, but then neither will I.' He caught her hand, the cluster of rubies on her left hand reflecting the horizon.

'Isn't it an extraordinary sight?' She followed his gaze. 'Like pink candyfloss in the sky.'

'It's perfect. There's just one thing that worries me. Is three months long enough for a honeymoon?'

She nodded, oblivious to the gentle teasing in his voice. 'There are so many things I want to see – Buckingham Palace, the Houses of Parliament, the Victoria and Albert Museum and my real parents' home.'

'We'll make up for the time we've lost, and then maybe we'll settle down. It's time you had a home of your own.'

'Guernsey's my home.' Lydia closed her eyes. 'But I'd rather be with you.'

BIBLIOGRAPHY

The Silent War, Frank Falla

The German Occupation of the Channel Islands, Charles Cruikshank

A Child's War, Molly Bihet

Channel Islands at War, George Forty

Occupation Nurse, Peter & Mary Birchenall

Guernsey Under German Rule, Ralph Durand

The Model Occupation, Madeleine Bunting

Guernsey Green, William M Bell

Living with the Enemy, Roy McLoughlin

Guernsey Under Occupation: The Second World War Diaries of Violet Carey, Edited by Alice Evans

ACKNOWLEDGEMENTS

This book would not have been possible without the support of my husband, Les, who, despite being an Englishman, loves Guernsey almost as much as I do. I owe a great debt to my paternal grandparents, the late James and Edith Brown who, as I grew up, recounted their experiences of living through the Occupation of Guernsey.

I am also indebted to the authors mentioned in the bibliography whose knowledge of the island's history is greater than mine can ever be.

Special thanks go to Ed Christiano who, as well as designing the excellent cover, gave me encouragement throughout the writing process.

Finally, thanks, Elaine – you know what I mean.

Lightning Source UK Ltd.
Milton Keynes UK
UKHW011154130622
404347UK00002B/134